Ares' Story

Grove of the Gods

Book 1

First Published in Great Britain 2020 by Mirador Publishing

First edition: 2020

Any reference to real names and places are purely fictional and are constructs of the author. Any offence the references produce is unintentional and in no way reflects the reality of any locations or people involved.

A copy of this work is available through the British Library.

ISBN: 978-1-913833-45-9

Mirador Publishing
10 Greenbrook Terrace
Taunton
Somerset
UK
TA1 1UT

Ares' Story

Grove of the Gods

Book 1

Sarah Luddington

Chapter 1

DRAKE YORK WALKED THROUGH THE open gates. Tall, solid metal and coloured a steely blue with the name – *Annwn University* – super embossed in artistic rust on the front. The main building stood at the head of a wide concrete drive, hugged by verdant grass and old horse chestnut trees, basking in the brief warmth of an Indian summer. Four turrets rose from the corners of an imposing grey stone three storey structure. The weight of learning at the old university leaked outwards, flicking at the unwary and unprepared student. Drake brushed at the sensation, removing the tendrils from his thick canvas jacket.

"You'll not stop me, old girl." His words were soft and delivered to the thick wooden doors he approached. He walked up the wide, shallow steps in the same grey stone. He paused at the top for a moment, the bubble of the past pushing against him, until the moment he forced a step over the threshold. The building's sense of self, quivered for a moment, readjusting to his invasion. Drake allowed a small smile to ghost over his lips. Old places always found his kind unsettling.

Signs pointed the way to the reception and Drake found the modern sweep of a pale wood and chrome reception desk jarring against the huge stone doorways and low fan vaulted ceiling. This would once have been a grand entrance to a hallowed hall of learning. Full of black gowned students moving around like adolescent crows. Now it resembled a clash of timelines – the modern and the ancient attempting to blend but never quite well enough to be comfortable. Much like Drake.

"Good morning, how can I help?" asked a woman in her thirties with the makeup of someone in their twenties.

Drake smiled. The woman's pupils dilated and her cheeks flushed red. "I'm a transfer student from the US. Drake York. You should have my details on file?" He gave her the best of British accents, the knack of manipulating people with his voice practiced and easy.

She tore her eyes from his face and very red nails clicked over the keyboard. "Yes, here you are, you've come in from Harvard – very impressive."

He shrugged, giving it just enough of a dismissive air to make her believe it didn't matter. It didn't matter to Drake to be honest, but nonchalance aided his disguise.

Turning in her chair the woman rose and picked up a bundle of papers. "Welcome to Annwn Uni. I'll call someone and have them collect you so you can start your orientation. We aren't a large campus but we do have lots going on. Are you staying on campus?"

"I have rooms in the town," Drake said before he caught himself. "I mean I have an apartment." The aged reference would jar the woman's memory of him, it would make him stand out and Drake didn't want to stand out. Not here. Not anywhere. Not any more.

With a nod to the woman Drake moved away and took a soft chair nearby while she located someone to help him. The original plan, the one he had devised some weeks before, was to present as an American. However, since returning to England, to this part of the ancient land, it was clear the masquerade would slip. Perhaps a stronger regional accent would be wise, though that brought inherent dangers of its own if he struggled to remain in the 21st century.

His musings were cut short by the rapid descent of steps from one of the sweeping staircases either side of the modern reception desk. A young man, slim with a tangle of dark hair, pale skin, in a tatty sweatshirt hoodie and jeans, approached with a tight smile fixed in place. His eyes were crystal blue and his lashes long.

"Are you Drake York?" He held out his hand.

Drake rose in a fluid movement making the young man step back and drop his hand. "I am." Drake couldn't stop looking into those fragile bright eyes. "Who are you?" UK non-regional English again. An inward sigh, the decision had been made.

"Finbarr Wiseman, Fin if it's easier." The hand returned and Drake took it, trying to keep his touch gentle. Fin smiled. "Your hands are cold."

"My heart is warm." He spoke without thinking, never a wise decision. Fin's colour heightened and the handshake stilled but held. Drake did not want to let go, this young man stirred long dormant ashes in the darkness of Drake's burned out, exhausted, soul.

Fin drew his hand back and the flash of regret over his sharp features warmed Drake. "I'm an orientation guide so even though you missed Fresher's Week I can help you with anything you need."

"Anything?" Drake hadn't meant the word to be filled with quite so much innuendo but he didn't regret it when Fin's pale cheeks warmed even more.

He shifted, uncomfortable under Drake's scrutiny. Drake softened his voice and his body language. Someone had hurt this gentle soul.

"Sorry, I'm nervous," Drake lied, "and that usually makes me a buffoon. I apologise if I've made you uncomfortable."

"No, it's fine, I'm sorry as well." Fin gave Drake a more genuine smile. It gentled his sharp features and Drake noticed the very slight imperfections in Fin's face for the first time. His two front teeth were just a little crooked, an attack of acne had left slight scars over his soft cheeks where he'd only need to shave every few days. The thing Drake noticed most though were Fin's eyes, he had dark circles under them and a wariness in the depths that tugged at Drake's instincts.

"Shall we go and look around campus?" Drake asked. Whispers of something familiar tickled his neck and long dormant memory of olive groves and warm sun rose to wash against the present. Drake hadn't thought about that time in so long and he wondered why the presence of this Finbarr Wiseman made him remember a past turned to ruins.

Fin drew in a sharp breath as if lost in his thoughts as well, yanking himself back to his current duties. "Looking around the campus," he chuckled and shook his head, "of course, let's start here."

Drake followed Fin through the old building and into the central courtyard with its square of grass and a stone fountain in the centre. Drake almost laughed, the fountain looked like it was supposed to be Hermes, water coming out of a cock the god would find insulting.

The old building, with its dozens of mullioned windows, watched the two strolling men. Drake caught the scent of incense from an open window and music from others. Fin chatted about the history of one of Britain's oldest universities and the supposed ghosts walking the old halls of residence. Most of the rooms here were student accommodation.

Fin showed Drake the original library, with its leather-bound books and older parchments. Students were not permitted to remove the volumes and many of the old vellum manuscripts and scrolls had to be used with soft white gloves. Heavy wooden beams, dark bookcases and long heavy wooden desks gave the rooms an antiquated feel Drake enjoyed and recognised.

"It's never very busy in this library. The newer one is the other side of the campus near the modern lecture theatres. I like it here though. The dusty peace gives the whirling mind a chance to calm." Fin blushed the moment he stopped talking, as if embarrassed by his genteel confession.

Drake found it utterly charming and couldn't hide his smile. "I think dusty peace is a sanctuary in this modern time, more people could find beneficial. We forget how calming books can be to the whirling mind. How grounding research and academic rigour are. There's an ebb and flow to study that one can find comfort in."

Fin's face turned from youthful beauty into angelic splendour when he smiled, with no artifice and true passion in his bright blue eyes. Drake gazed into the skies seen through a sleeping wave tickling a magical shoreline.

Drake shook himself, disturbed by the pull this young man had on his old heart. When was the last time a smile made him paraphrase a long dead poet? *I'm going soft in my dotage.*

When they left the old building Fin took them to the main house block for first year students who had just left home and the large cafeteria. A hideous addition to the area from the sixties.

"I hope someone was hung for creating that monstrosity," Drake said.

"Not quite but you're not the first to make that suggestion." Fin waved a hand around, the slim wrists poking out from his jumper. Drake noticed the darker and damaged skin, his jaw clenched. "This uni is so beautiful, especially on a day like today. It's an amazing place to study and we have some great lecturers who work here."

"What are you reading?" Drake asked, realising it should be the first question out of a student's mouth. The equivalent of – what do you do for a living?

"Ancient Greek Studies, which means we look at society and the literature. It's fascinating."

Drake almost swallowed his tongue in shock. "Greece?"

"Yes, have you been? I was so lucky, my father worked for the British Embassy in Athens for ten years while I was growing up, so we were all there. It gives me a bit of a head start over most of the others with the language. This is my final year, of course, so come the summer I'll be free to return. I want to explore the islands properly."

"You want to go back to Greece?" Drake asked. His eyes burned with the repressed emotions caused by Fin's words.

"I'd love to. I love Greece and the entire mythology. I love stories – all stories but especially those. Homer, Euripides… I could talk about them all day."

Drake managed a weak smile. His mind tumbling through possibilities and finding them all equally terrifying. He pushed the crazy back, focusing on Fin. "I'm sure. I'd be happy to share your thoughts."

Fin's eyes brightened again and melted more of Drake's resolve to stand strong against the tug of his cock. "Really? Most people want me to shut up."

Falling at Fin's feet and begging him to talk about Greece and her stories would not be heroic, so Drake merely nodded. "Really."

"What about you? If you don't mind me saying so, you don't look like a first-year student."

Drake fell back on well-rehearsed words. "I'm a PhD student. I've been studying at Harvard for a few years. I'm here to do some different work on my thesis."

"Wow, you're streaks ahead of the rest of us."

Drake smiled. "I finished traditional schooling very early and I'm lucky enough not to have to worry about work for the moment. A small inheritance means I can focus on my studies. My area of interest for my paper is how the modern world recreates and uses the ancient stories, those that go back to the original written languages. The archetypes used and how they influence the societies in which they are told, then how those stories are used now in our current saturated society."

Fin's eyes widened. "So you really are interested in Greek culture."

A small nod was all Drake allowed himself. The hysterical laughter building in his belly needed controlling. All of Drake's stronger emotions needed controlling.

From the hideous housing block, they explored the main learning centre, wandered over a small bridge that spanned a stream running through the middle of the campus and onto the student bar, gym, Students' Union and other recreation areas. Behind this were newer living areas for older students who needed peace and quiet. They talked easily, the level of comfort between them forming and solidifying in ways only instinct could govern.

"Where are you living?" asked Fin.

Drake glanced at him, sunlight stuck to Fin even when a cloud obscured the warmth of the day. "I have a small set of rooms in the town. I like my privacy too much to share a kitchen or worse a bathroom."

"I know what you mean. It's not easy. Fortunately, I have a room with a private bathroom but a shared kitchen. I live in that block on the top floor. It has amazing views I spend too long watching." Fin pointed to a building at the back of campus. His joyful innocence bounced around Drake in such a puppy-like way Drake found himself enchanted by more than the young man's fragile masculine beauty.

Drake had chosen this university because he'd been drawn here and the surroundings helped. Rolling wooded hills enclosed the verdant valley and the town was small. The university was one of the town's main sources of income. Old farming cottages rubbed against Victorian terraces and small modern housing estates, but the fields and woodlands tumbled away. The only blight in the area came from a factory near the mine works which couldn't be seen from the campus.

He watched a murder of crows rise from the nearest clutch of trees. The sound of their rough voices in harmony with the kiss of the sun and caress of the wind. The blaze of colour from the copper beech against the blue and white of the sky formed the perfect backdrop for the aerial dance. Croaking screams and wheeling flight, the sleek and precious black feathers. Memory… So many memories… Drake rubbed his fingertips together sensing the feel of the bird, the first on any battlefield after the killing.

"I love all the corvid birds," Fin whispered.

Drake's eyes sharped on his face, but Fin didn't seem to notice, too caught up in the dance that moved away towards more suitable accommodation in a distant copse of trees.

"They are harbingers of many a story," Drake murmured. "Loved by gods, feared by men."

"Men fear all they cannot understand. It's why we tell each other stories, in an effort to explain the world." Fin shook himself and laughed. "Sorry, you know all this of course."

"Never apologise to me for speaking your mind," Drake said.

"Finbarr, where the hell have you been?"

Drake, caught up in Fin's sweet face, hadn't noticed the other man approach. It startled him to realise he'd been so lost in such innocence.

Fin, a moment ago expanding his awareness into the crows, retreated with such a sudden snap it made Drake's stomach clench in real pain. A young man, strong, blond, confident in his stride and his handsome face, walked towards them.

"Ajax, I thought you were in lectures until two?"

Ajax didn't look at Finbarr. He only had eyes for Drake and they weren't friendly. "It is two thirty, we were supposed to be meeting for lunch."

Drake watched Fin open his mouth, then snap it shut.

"Sorry."

Drake just knew that hadn't been what Fin wanted to say.

Ajax smiled. A caustic flash of teeth. "It's fine. I know how you get when you're writing. Who is this?" Only now did he glance at Fin before returning his attention to Drake.

"A new PhD student, Drake York. I'm a liaison student this year, remember? They called me down to help him with orientation. I was going to go to the bar if you'd like to join us?" The last was offered as a sop.

Drake heard Fin's desperation and hope that Ajax would turn him down.

Hard brown eyes focused on Fin. "No, I have things to do at home. Perhaps you could make yourself available later if you aren't too busy?"

The sarcasm made Fin shrink into himself even further. "I'll call you when I'm done."

"These duties don't help with your work, Fin, you are struggling enough as it is, perhaps you should consider giving up your extracurricular activities?"

"Maybe," Fin said with a faint smile meant to appease the bigger man.

The entire exchange horrified and amused Drake. Horrified that anyone would treat Fin so badly, amused because he looked forward to doing battle with Ajax at some point. He watched the arrogant shit stride away. "Interesting friend you have there."

Fin whispered, "He's my boyfriend."

Drake didn't miss the embarrassment in Fin's voice. He smiled. "I'm sure he is, for the moment."

Chapter 2

Finbarr Wiseman cringed at Drake's words. The implications of missing his lunch date with Ajax and being found in Drake's company were not lost on him. Walking down the stairs from the old library in the main university building and seeing Drake York sitting in the chair had been a world shifting moment for Fin, robbing him of the memory of Ajax, never mind the date.

Tall, slim, dark hair and darker eyes with an almost swarthy complexion, Drake York made Fin weak at the knees just by standing up and allowing his hard features to soften with a smile. When they had shaken hands Fin almost fainted at the speed his heartrate kicked up. After discovering Drake had interest in Fin's beloved subject, ancient Greek mythology, he almost melted on the spot.

The sexual interest Drake demonstrated from the moment their eyes met left Fin confused and flustered. Two states he spent most of his short adult life trying to control and navigate.

He knew he didn't want to discuss his relationship with Ajax. He didn't talk to anyone about his relationship with Ajax, including his far away family.

Fin wanted desperately to push back the feeling of being drained by Ajax. Sometimes being around the more dominant man just left him empty of energy to the point he could barely think. "Still want to go to the bar for a bite to eat? The food isn't bad if you like chips and it's taco day."

"I would like that very much," Drake said. "If it isn't too much trouble for you?"

Pulling a smile up from his boots Fin said, "We all need to eat, right?"

"We do, but just look at that for a moment." Drake reached out and touched Fin's arm, pointing to the woodland again. A buzzard had come to join the crows in the sky. The acrobatics were breath taking and as Drake crooked his index finger a few times it appeared as if the battle of the skies were coming closer. "Watch them," Drake said. Fin leaned in closer to hear his gentle, hushed voice. "Feel their connection to their world and revel in their grace. It will help."

The warmth rushing through Fin's blood at this shared experience did help banish the exhaustion of moments ago. Though he thought it was probably Drake's hand on his arm, not the crows, which made him feel better. He caught the scent of Drake's aftershave, woody and a heavy musk, it mingled with the fresh air to give an exotic mix reminding him of Greek woodlands in the heat of the summer.

Drake's handsome face turned, his eyes a dark embrace of forbidden promises. They were so close Fin only needed to shift a little to steal a kiss. The thought shocked him back to sanity.

"Feel better?" Drake asked.

Fin smiled at him and managed to step back a little. "Very much, thank you." How could he endure this sweet torture? Drake smelt and looked like the human version of catnip.

Together they walked down the path to the student bar and entered its dark interior. A scattering of students were either sat at the bar, grouped around the low tables or playing pool in the corner. The large TVs at either end were showing football from teams no one seemed interested in and the place smelt of hormones, beer and stale food. Fin didn't like it very much, but they did cheap food that was better than the stuff in the canteen.

The local eco-warriors were huddled in the corner by the window. Tatty jumpers pulled over their hands, piercings, and coloured dreadlocks or shaved heads the theme.

Drake stopped and cocked his head to one side watching them. "What's that all about? They seem earnest."

"They are the local protesters."

He shivered as Drake's dark eyes fixed their considerable attention on him. "What are they fighting against?"

"The mining. Lithium as it is now, rather than the tin and clay, I guess." He wanted to change the subject. It reminded him of Ajax. "What would you like to drink?"

"My treat," Drake said. "Perhaps they have a nice bottle of red wine?"

Fin laughed. "Cheap plonk more like. Beer or spirits are your best bet and it's a bit early for spirits."

"Let's hope I can get a decent bottle of wine from somewhere." Drake had to raise his voice over the music. "A fine dark ale will do, what will you have?"

"Beer is good. I suggest the Goblin's Ale."

"Goblins." Drake shook his head. "And for food?"

"Chips is okay."

Drake frowned for the first time. "Finbarr, you need to eat well to stay strong. Allow me to order for us if you find a table away from the noise so we can talk in peace. Do you eat meat?"

"Only when I can afford it," he answered.

"Glad to hear it. Well, I can afford to spring us some real food, so this is my treat after you have given me so much of your valuable time." Drake turned to the bar and Finbarr took their drinks outside.

The winters here were long and wet, so making the most of the weather was always at the top of Fin's agenda. He counted the joy in the little things, especially when the big things were too difficult to handle.

He sat on the hard stone surface and winced. Ajax had not been kind the night before. Fin closed his eyes and focused on things other than the previous night, it didn't do to dwell, he'd learned that long ago. He thought about Drake's smile, rather than Ajax's and allowed the accompanying warmth to thread through his blood.

A large gentle hand pressed with care onto his shoulder. A flood of comfort and tenderness shocked sudden tears to spring into Fin's eyes. Drake moved around him and sat, the heat of the man close enough to further give the sense of safety Fin craved.

"Alright, Finbarr?"

"Fine." He closed his eyes and took a deep breath. "It's just nice to have the warmth, you know?" He didn't mean the sun.

"I do, the country is as dark as her ancient gods used to be and that's pretty dark."

Fin opened his eyes and Drake trapped him, the snare closing too fast to escape, not that he wanted to on this occasion. "I think the Greek Pantheon is just as bloodthirsty as anything the ancient Britons used to believe."

Drake took a sip of his pint and licked his lips, surprisingly good and flowery. "More so in many cases."

Fin mirrored the gesture and stared into his drink to avoid doing anything even more foolish. "Do you think it's strange that all these stories from a distant land, a religion that only found a home here because of the Romans, are so important?" Fin asked.

He watched Drake think about his question with a seriousness rare in students. "No, I don't think so. I think the English are a peculiar race, they horde shiny things like magpies and that includes knowledge. It didn't take much to convert the island to Christianity and they nurtured the religion before returning it to Europe during the rise of Charlemagne. They loved the advent of the Protestant revolt and helped spread it all over the world in various forms. They tried their damnedest to destroy the old gods in all their forms. Yet they now embrace atheism."

"Don't forget the New Age stuff," Fin said.

Drake chuckled. "Indeed, the New Age… what do we call them? Cults?"

"Seems a bit harsh." Fin laughed, knowing the university was full of such enthusiasts.

"Perhaps, though they can be dangerous. Summoning old gods to an old land can have some unforeseen consequences… I should imagine."

"They can also be helpful. My parents are great believers in alternative faiths these days."

"Are they close by?" Drake asked, changing the subject.

The pang in Fin's chest never dulled with time. "No, they live in Australia now. I haven't seen them much over the last few years. We video chat and stuff but it's not the same. Sometimes you just need a hug from your family but they are happy and that's what's important. My dad had a health scare from stress so they deserve every minute they have together. I hope I'm as happy in love as they are one day."

He hadn't meant to say the last part aloud. Glancing up from his drink to apologise for being too soft he saw Drake reach over the table for his hand. The connection sent a shock jabbing through him.

Drake said in the softest voice, "Perhaps you will be soon."

The waitress, a local woman, arrived with their food and burst the bubble, or spell, Drake cast over everything. Never before had he met someone so intense. It scared and exhilarated him. Ajax, when he turned his attention to seducing rather than bullying, felt the same but the level of dominance had a harder edge that always made Fin feel like 'no' might be a bad idea. The few occasions he'd tried it had proved it the unwise option.

Fin looked at their lunch and discovered two plates of the bar's best steak and salad.

With skill Drake shifted the conversation onto safer grounds and they discussed the many adventures written by Homer and the role of women in the stories, how they were often disregarded by later translators all of whom were men. Fin found the subject fascinating but Drake could have recited a shopping list and he'd have been enchanted. He just loved listening to Drake's dark voice rise and fall as they batted ideas about. The quick intelligence and the breadth of his reading left Fin in awe as an undergraduate. It wasn't until they finished their lunch that Fin realised he still knew almost nothing about Drake's past.

"So how did you end up at Harvard? Are you even British?" Fin asked over their second pint.

"I am not British by birth, more by accident. As we said at the beginning, the British are very good at welcoming new and old side by side, that appeals to me."

Fin frowned. "That's a wonderful non-answer."

Drake chuckled, his dark eyes dancing with mischief just as Fin's phone went. "Shit." The screen showed a picture of Ajax with his arm slung over Fin's slim shoulders. Ajax dominated the image. "I have to get this." With the phone in his hand he rose from the table. Guilt clawed at his guts turning the steak meal to dust in his stomach.

"Where are you?" Ajax barked.

"Um, working in the library."

"I need you here, the parents are home tonight for dinner."

The sawdust turned to acid. "Oh, um, are you sure you want me there? I mean, don't you need to discuss business? And you know how much they don't enjoy me being around at family events." Understatement. They didn't seem to care their eldest son dated men, but they really cared that those he dated were kept at a distance from their family. They always gave Fin the impression they considered him nothing more than a chew toy. Mind you, Ajax often made him feel that way as well.

"I want you here." The order left little wiggle room.

Fin's eyes blurred with tears for a moment as his shoulders tensed. "Sure, what time?"

"Seven thirty should be fine. We eat at eight."

Which meant Fin would need to be there before seven if possible. "Sure. I'll be there soon." He'd need to shower, change, dress for the occasion and button down his time with Drake so it didn't show.

Ajax ended the call without a goodbye. Fin sighed and turned. Drake watched him with an expression Fin couldn't interpret. Unless the man had a superhuman ability to hear he couldn't be angered by Fin's pathetic passive submission to Ajax's demands. Even if Fin made himself sick.

He walked back to the table. "Sorry, I have to go."

"What about helping me find my way around?"

Fin managed a laugh. "This is it, I'm afraid. You'll need to find your way around the lecturers tomorrow, we can meet early if you like and I'll introduce you. Who is your tutor?"

"Dr Janet Moran."

Fin's smile became stronger. "She's lovely. I'll take you up to meet her tomorrow. She's my year group tutor as well. Shall we say nine at the main reception?"

"I could collect you from your room," Drake said.

Fin squirmed. He needed to keep Ajax and Drake away from each other. "Um, no, not a good idea. I'm not sure where I'm staying tonight. We'll meet up in the main reception."

Drake studied him for a moment. "Alright, if you think that's best."

Best? No it wasn't for the best, but Fin didn't have much choice in the matter it seemed so he nodded, thanked Drake again for lunch and left half his pint on the table.

Chapter 3

THE NIGHT CLOSED IN AROUND Drake. The streets quiet everywhere but the university campus; heaving with the young souls it protected in its hallowed halls. Drake sensed the old land resisting his tainted heart and trying to keep him away from all that innocence. Amused by the land's efforts to shove him away, he ignored the old building. Places like this, raised on the ancient temples and natural areas of worship, tried to protect the souls attached to their presence. This one had the temerity to push back against his probing mind. He dismissed its noise. He only wanted the location of one soul, one fragile heart and he couldn't find it on the grounds.

"Where are you, Finbarr? You should be in bed at this hour." Drake's musing had his long legs chew up the miles to an older property at the head of the valley. The house drew his attention from the moment he'd driven into the area. It dominated the skyline, forcing the eye down from the hilltops and distant moorlands behind it. The vast house rose from a rocky outcrop with sweeping gables and flying buttresses of dressed dark stone. A cross between a castle and a rich man's folly, a place designed for vampires to seduce virgins, or werewolves to take their last stand against rampaging villagers. Ghosts and monsters should walk its grounds and as Drake made it to the high walls and impressive gates he sensed just that behind the imposing façade.

The wall he looked at stood at least three metres high. There were no trees close to it, almost as if the occupants didn't want to give their enemies the advantage of cover if the walls were to be breached. Drake, long familiar with the tactics of sieges on walled towns and cities, found it impressive.

He also knew Finbarr's heart beat inside the house behind the walls. If he attempted to scale the three-metre obstacle whatever lay on the other side would sense his presence and move in to fight or at the very least, uncover his secrets. Drake was in no shape to let that happen. It took most of his strength to maintain his daily routines, so betraying his existence to whatever lay behind that wall didn't seem wise.

Ajax. A name he knew all too well and one he'd never liked. The tall blond would find a fitting adversary in Drake for Finbarr's fair attentions and Drake never lost. The young man, whether he knew it or not, needed a champion. Fin might not want Drake in his bed, and that boundary would be accepted, but Drake couldn't walk away from the soul yearning for help. Nothing had touched Drake the way Fin did in so long he had almost forgotten what it meant to care for something real and present in this world. He turned away from the house and walked back through the night to his lodgings.

THE FOLLOWING DAY DRAKE ROSE early, ran for fifteen kilometres using the footpaths over the nearby hills, and arrived in plenty of time for his meeting with Fin.

He smiled the moment he walked through the doorway, Fin sat in the soft chair he'd used the day before, checking his phone.

"Good morning."

Finbarr looked up. A discolouration and slight swelling marred his lower jaw and cheek. "Drake, you're early."

Covering the distance between them with too much purpose made Fin push back into the chair and his eyes widened in alarm. It brought Drake up short. Fin's breathing hitched in shock.

"Sorry." Drake held his hands up. "I am sorry. I didn't mean to startle you, Finbarr. Forgive me, please. I just…" He waved a hand over his own cheek rather than raise a hand towards Finbarr's face. It had taken Drake a long time to learn, but apparently violence didn't solve problems the way his natural personality always wanted it to, he had learned temperance – eventually. When he saw it inflicted on those under his protection it fed the baser instincts he fought to control.

"This?" Fin tried to smile but he winced. "I got turned around at Ajax's place during the night, too much to drink, and stumbled into a wall. Stupid of me." The delicate skin over his cheek would darken further as the day went on.

Drake suppressed a growl. "It's strange how walls like to jump out at people."

Fin looked away and Drake realised his mistake. The young man's pride would not want him to intervene, not yet. They were professional friends only, and this was their place of work. Drake could hunt down Ajax later and pull his wings off, which is probably what Ajax did to flies as a child.

"Dr Moran is expecting us in ten minutes. We can go up now. She's usually early as well." Fin led the way up the stairs.

Drake allowed his eyes to wander down the slim back to the swell of Finbarr's pert backside and long, slim legs. The jeans weren't overly tight, but they didn't hide much either and the shirt Fin wore allowed glimpses of pale skin when he moved his arm up the banister. Drake's mouth watered.

Dragging his mind away from his carnal desires took a lot of effort. He tried to concentrate on the dark hallway, portraits of past alumni and chancellors that decorated the wood panelled walls. There were concessions to the modern world such as fire extinguishers and exit signs, but the old building resisted modernity.

The doorway to Dr Moran's office stood open and Fin knocked for a moment before entering with a smile. "Hi, Dr Moran. I have Drake York with me. Is it okay if we come in?"

Drake entered and stopped short. Dr Janet Moran rose from behind the desk. A woman in her middle years, small, slim, hair cut short in a pixie style a mixture of white and the mousey brown common in England. Her eyes were hazel and her skin clear of blemishes except the lines around her mouth and eyes.

An amused smile greeted him as she held out her hand. "I'm glad to meet you at last, Mr York."

"Drake, please," he said, taking her hand with caution, this just made her smile widen further. She appeared to be an average woman but Drake *felt* so much more at their brief contact. He just couldn't place exactly what he was feeling and it made him uneasy.

"It's rare to have a student of your pedigree in the university."

He frowned for a moment, before pushing back the strange flash of recognition and took back possession of his hand from her firm grip. This often happened, he caught a sense of something in the odd person who crossed his path, like he had with Finbarr, but it didn't mean anything – not always. The times it did mean something were often moments of great change in his existence. It put him on edge to have it happen twice in this tiny town that whispered in his bones.

The weight of her gaze and Fin's curiosity forced him back into the present. He smiled, pushing it outwards a little, which just seemed to make Dr Moran chuckle. He didn't affect her the way he could affect most women. They began talking about Drake's PhD and the work Fin did to help Dr Moran. It seemed Drake could work with Fin as well and Drake took up the offer to help the department with some of the undergraduate workload. If it meant spending time with Finbarr, that was more than enough reason to help. It also kept him close when it came time to deal with Ajax.

After they had spoken with Dr Moran about his thesis and set up a regular time to go over his work in detail, they left the office. It wasn't until they were back in the hallway Drake realised he had paid no attention to his surroundings while around the good doctor, a mistake and something he needed to rectify. Understanding the world someone immersed themselves in helped him learn how to manipulate them if necessary.

When they reached the bottom of the stairs Fin said he had lectures and raced off before Drake could arrange another opportunity to spend time with him. Drake followed at a more leisurely pace. Leaving the building and deciding to explore the campus alone this time, despite the drizzle, Drake wandered towards the Students' Union building. Outside were a group of the eco-warriors, some of whom he remembered from the day before, handing out leaflets.

"Do you know what they are doing to our water system?" asked a young woman thrusting a leaflet into his hand.

"Um…" Drake took the rough piece of paper without looking. The young woman had the softest brown eyes he'd seen in years. With her warm skin tones, wide open face and stream of brown dreadlocks decorated with silver and wood, she resembled a woodland creature.

"They are poisoning the water, destroying the water table and stripping the very land under our feet. They repeatedly flout the laws and code violations are happening all the time. People in the town are sick and it is getting worse. We need leaders to stop them, to bring about change and the only way to do that is to make the leaders listen to us – all of us – who are at the bottom of their capitalist system."

She spoke with such venom and passion Drake found he couldn't move away. Her vital energy and earnest words reminded him of philosophers and academics from history who had died for their beliefs.

"Can you prove your arguments?" Entranced by her zeal he didn't notice the group of men coming over the small bridge towards the Union until they were among the protesters.

The first Drake knew of their incursion was a shout of alarm and a scattering of leaflets.

"Shit, fuckers," the young woman cursed. She thrust all the leaflets into Drake's hands and turned to face the men.

Drake watched her push between Ajax and another young man with more metal in his face than the average Sumerian priest used to use. Ajax towered over the woman but she showed no fear. An Amazonian indeed. He watched the interaction with interest.

"Get out of my way, girl," Ajax snarled.

The woman stepped into his space as the bigger man tried to move past her. "No. You will not bully us, we are legitimate protestors and we have the right to be heard. You and your family might be able to stop us protesting in the town but you cannot stop us here at the Union. This is our place and you are not welcome." She pushed out her small chest, eyes blazing with righteous fury.

Ajax lifted his hand, rage flashing through his eyes.

Drake had seen enough. "I don't think so." He stepped forwards and placed a hand on Ajax's shoulder.

A spark powerful enough to jar both men separated them in an instant.

"Get your hands off me," Ajax snarled.

"Leave her alone," Drake snapped in return, closing his fist. The spark hurt and shocked him in more ways than one. He fought to remain focused.

Ajax stepped back, his pack paused – waiting for blood in the water. "Or what? Finbarr told me all about you last night before I made sure he had something else to think about. My boy worships me – you should remember that – before you try to take up his time."

The anger that flashed hot and bright in Drake threatened to overwhelm his common sense. "I suggest you find somewhere else to be right now." Low words, not aimed to travel, meant only for the recipient and laced with a power Drake held tight in his soul. He knew more about violence than any child of the soil in this damned place and he fought to keep it leashed in a body built for an academic not a warrior.

Ajax's sneer turned into something more calculating. Not fear, unlike his companions, but something close to assessment. It made Drake aware of how close to the edge he'd stepped.

A smile crossed Ajax's pretty mouth. "Well, aren't you going to be interesting?" He turned to his people. "Leave them. They aren't worth the recycled paper they use to print their rubbish on." He pushed past the woman and strode into the Union building with half a dozen lackeys behind him.

"Fuckers," muttered the girl, taking the crushed leaflets out of Drake's unresisting hands.

"You should be careful, he is dangerous."

She began straightening the leaflets he'd crushed. "Only to poor Fin."

Drake focused on her. "You know Finbarr?"

She smiled with a wistful expression. "He was my boyfriend when we first arrived here. Went to the same sixth form. Needless to say I lost him to that walking cock. I didn't have a problem with him being gay but his taste in men is terrible."

"What's your name?"

"Saskia."

"Drake."

"Guess you're gay as well if you've annoyed the walking cock."

Drake laughed. "If you mean Ajax by that description, I like it." She grinned. "And I am neither gay nor straight nor any of the other descriptives that are currently popular. I find interest in the heart and soul of a person, the mind comes next, then their physical form." He allowed his eyes to rove over Saskia.

Her cheeks pinked as if compliments were new to her. "Oh, right, well, if you really want to annoy the walking cock then we have a meeting tonight to discuss ways we can prevent an expansion of the tin and lithium extraction at the mine. The walking cock will be so pleased. If you know Fin, maybe you can retrieve him from the dark side and bring him along."

"I will give it some thought." He looked at Ajax through the windows to the bar. "Annoying the walking cock might become my new hobby."

Saskia looked through the window as well. "You should know his family controls the entire university, the town council, the police, everything here. He can make your life very difficult."

"I can handle difficult. They own the mine you are so unhappy about?"

She nodded. "Yep, Aegis Corporation. Every business in town is tied to them one way or another. If the businesses in town help our protests their leases are cancelled or refused renewal. It's why we don't have any shops even vaguely New Age here. If you have any kind of a conscience, don't live here." Rage and glum acceptance marred her pretty face.

"Thank you. You've been most informative." Drake left the protesters at the Union and returned to his rooms in town.

THAT EVENING, AFTER SPENDING THE day in the library and on the internet doing research for his PhD, Drake returned to the Union. The protestors filled the back half of the bar and Saskia stood on a small platform with several other students and someone who didn't look like a student. He wore a corporate casual look and after making enquiries, Drake discovered he came from a large environmental organisation who wanted to help the local protest groups. He was talking about lobbying governments. In Drake's considerable experience of such things, he knew money would win in the end – it always did – but he loved watching Saskia's rapt attention on the speaker.

Her level of intensity and dedication impressed him.

"She's mesmerising, isn't she?"

Drake turned and smiled. A tingling warmth filling his cold belly for the first time all day. "Fin, what a welcome surprise. I wasn't expecting you to be here."

Fin shrugged. "Ajax has gone to some football game so I'm off the hook. He's fine with being gay here, but not out in the real world."

"You don't sound bitter about it." Drake saw the dark circles under Finbarr's pretty eyes were worse.

"Bitter? No. I'm not bitter. Relieved perhaps." He rubbed his eyes. "Sorry, long day. You don't need to hear my maudlin issues."

Drake didn't think the evening's entertainment in the bar would help lift Finbarr's dark mood. He wore a cloak of heavy sadness and it made Drake ache to feel it. "Would you like to go for a walk? It's a lovely evening and I believe there will enough of a moon if we wait for full dark."

Fin stared at Saskia for a moment. "Sometimes I forget how beautiful she is when she's roused by a mission."

"She mentioned you were... involved."

Finbarr blinked. "You talked to Saskia? She doesn't normally share anything with anyone she considers *vanilla*."

Drake laughed. "Many things I've been called over the years. Vanilla has never been one of them."

Even in the low light of the bar Drake could see Fin's blush. He chuckled, threw his arm over the smaller man's shoulders and guided them out of the bar. The night had just turned to dominate the sky with a thin strip of dark blue behind the hills in the west. Venus sat high in the sky and the moon, in her full grace, rose behind the hills to the east.

"Selene," Finbarr said.

Drake looked at him in surprise. "Most people don't know her by that name."

"I love the moon and her light. Always have. I guess a lot of people connect with the moon rather than the sun."

Drake thought of how pleased Apollo would be to hear that. "It's not always been so. People were scared of the night in times past. These days we have street lighting, people to call for help, we do not believe in the monsters of the night. Perhaps if we knew more about the darkness we would fear it as well and the moon would seem less friendly."

They walked over the bridge and Fin guided them down a path Drake hadn't explored yet, it seemed to lead to a playing field then a stile in the thick hedge bordering the university.

"Or," Fin said, "the moon gives us light for those nights and by doing so, when her face is full, chases the creatures back into the shadows."

"Those shadows are thick on a night like tonight." Drake had used them often enough to hide in when necessary. Though this conversation didn't seem to be lightening Finbarr's mood and Drake longed to hear him laugh.

Gradually, as they walked, Drake teased Finbarr into relaxing and just a hint of laughter followed. When they reached the stile and Drake helped Fin climb over it, he made sure to stand a little too close, and their chests brushed.

Fin gasped, his hands on Drake's broad shoulders. "You shouldn't do that," he said, smacking Drake on the arm but not moving away.

Drake looked down into Fin's blue eyes and watched how they shifted to be almost grey in the silver light of the moon. "I will not play fair, Fin. I plan to win you from the walking cock by any means at my disposal."

Finbarr licked his lips, drawing Drake's attention. A hawk watching a mouse. "You really did bond with Saskia – walking cock is her favourite phrase when talking about Ajax."

"She's not wrong."

Finbarr placed a shaking hand on Drake's chest and pushed him back. Drake could have resisted but instinct told him to allow Fin control. "I need a friend, Drake. Not another headache."

Drake turned away without replying. "Where are we going?"

Finbarr's sigh hurt but Drake wasn't about to promise away his chances of pursing the young man.

"There's a place I want to show you. I wanted to show you at the weekend but Ajax has made plans…" The mood darkened again. If every mention of a lover turned a mood sour, it meant the lover was no good. Drake needed to break whatever ties Fin had to this walking cock.

They strode along a hedgerow and Drake could see the thick red berries of the hawthorn. He broke off a small branch and handed it to Fin. "Hawthorn frees the heart and eases pain. It allows the bearer, or drinker of its tea, the chance to find the heart's true desire. On a more practical note, it's also good for blood pressure."

Fin chuckled. "So, if you can't convince me with words you'll resort to herbs and witchcraft?"

"Whatever works, in my experience." Drake paused at the sound of an owl. "Wisdom is keeping her eye on us tonight. I'll have to prove I'm the better man."

"You really do talk in riddles an awful lot. It's disquieting. I'm never quite sure what you mean." Fin sounded amused and annoyed all at once.

They were approaching a copse of ancient trees that were combined with young coppiced hazel and alder. Drake paused and made Fin stop. He placed a finger under Fin's chin, coaxing the younger man to look up. "Trust I mean you no harm, Finbarr. Trust I will always protect you. Riddles or not."

Chapter 4

FIN TOOK HOLD OF DRAKE'S wrist and pulled his hand away. Eye contact with Drake left him breathless and confused. No one looked at him the way Drake did, as if peeling away sections of his soul with tender affection.

"You don't know me, Drake. You shouldn't say such things." Fin needed to put a stop to Drake playing these games. Coming to this lonely spot at night was a mistake. It gave Drake a chance to take liberties and Fin's ability to cope with men *taking liberties* left him humiliated and broken more often than not.

When Fin had arrived at the university with Saskia he knew he was gay but he didn't have the courage to tell her until he met Ajax. For most of the first year Ajax had been charming, funny, confident and loving. Things had changed though over the months of the second year. Ajax began chipping away at Fin's confidence, stealing his joy in the simple things in life. No longer finding Fin's love of the scent of a rose adorable when Fin stopped in the street to sniff a flower in someone's overhanging garden. These days, Ajax found it pathetic and weak. He tore apart Fin's academic skills and what little confidence remained in his physical appearance. Fin just couldn't seem to walk away. He knew Ajax was destroying him but his will didn't match his heart, it had no strength and he didn't know why. He needed help – badly.

Now, this older, handsome, strong man had walked into Fin's life but also wanted to dominate it in the same ways as Ajax, or that's how it made Fin feel in his vulnerable state. Fin needed to untangle himself from one controlling man, he didn't want another.

Unfortunately, however much Fin needed to be free he couldn't deny how Drake occupied his thoughts. Where Ajax bullied, Drake seemed to offer options and accept decisions. Being attracted to strong men couldn't always lead to abuse could it? Surely a man could be strong and gentle at the same time? Or was it all some elaborate charade so Drake could get a quick fuck and leave Fin to pick up the damaged and scarce pieces of himself?

The hole, in what remained of his confidence, grew larger every day. It exhausted him to keep going with his studies, attending lectures, talking to people and dealing with day to day chores. Over the summer he'd tried to go home but his family were a long way from the UK. In truth he had nothing else in his life but Ajax and the university.

Fin needed a friend. He wished he could turn to Saskia but he knew how much she hated Ajax and he didn't blame her one bit. Fuck! When had he become such a victim? Or had he always been a victim?

"Oh, Fin, thank you," Drake whispered beside him, drawing him from his dark thoughts.

They were in the woodland. The moonlight, filtered by autumn leaves and branches, dappled the ground and plants. In the spring there would be bluebells, wild garlic and wood anemones, a riot of colour and smells. Now the woodland smelt of the coming winter, rich loam, the scent of changing leaves, and gathering damp. Drake's steps slowed and Fin watched him run his fingers over the smooth bark of young alder, or the rough bark of old willow.

A crow of delight startled Fin.

"Ha! Chestnuts."

Despite his sad thoughts, Fin smiled as Drake stripped off his jacket, knotted the sleeves and began picking up the prickly gifts.

"We'll roast these over the weekend and eat them with good beer to hand. Maybe Saskia could join us? I like her, she's a bright spark like you."

Fin didn't reply and Drake didn't seem to need one. He was supposed to be spending the weekend with Ajax doing something with the local pheasant shoot. Fin couldn't imagine anything worse than spending his time around dead animals and the deader souls who killed for sport.

"Oh, mushrooms!"

At this, Fin laughed at last. "You know if you pick them and put them in your jacket it'll be ruined."

"I can wash it. We'll have mushrooms and chestnuts for Sunday lunch." Drake grinned and his dark eyes were bright in the moon's pale light. He was truly beautiful.

"How do you know which mushrooms are safe?" Fin asked, crouching beside the mushroom hunter and beginning to look under leaves.

"Lots of practice, lots of patience, a few good books and years of experience." He smacked Fin's hand. "Not that one. You won't like that one. Besides you have to leave enough to give the woodland folk something to eat. We'll come back with libations to say thank you."

"You sound like Saskia."

"She's very sensible. You shouldn't take from these places without offering something in return. It's not polite."

"What could I possibly give a woodland it might want?"

"Not the woodland, those that live here, that give it life. A little bread, honey or wine and an honest thank you will be enough." Drake rose and walked further into the wood. He stopped. Shock and awe written large on his face. "Oh, shit, I didn't realise…"

Fin stopped beside him and smiled. "I know, it's beautiful right?"

Drake took a step back and placed his jacket, now full of food, on the ground. Fin watched in amused silence as the man took off his boots, socks and stood on the muddy path in bare feet. He began muttering under his breath and seemed to have forgotten he had company as he dropped to his knees and bowed his head to the ground. Considering how rude he'd been about New Age 'cults' Drake's behaviour seemed odd.

When he sat back on his heels those dark eyes were closed and he appeared lost in meditation. Fin took the opportunity to study the delicate chiselled features. The curve of the firm mouth and the tangle of black curls.

He could be a statue of classical beauty brought to life by Pygmalion magic.

When Drake opened his eyes the moonlight reflected off them in colours of rose gold and bronze. A trick of the light but an odd one considering it was night. The man rose and walked, still bare footed, into the grove, heedless of his muddy knees. A small spring erupted from the ground at the bottom of a shallow rocky cliff covered in thick moss and lichen. Beside the spring rose a massive oak whose branches encompassed the entire area and dominated all the other trees. Coloured strips of fabric hung from the lower branches, ensuring even in the darkest part of the winter the vast tree would never be naked. Fin knew of the superstitions about wishes tied to the branches but he'd never left an offering himself. Maybe he should and the tree could rid him of Ajax without him having to fight for his freedom.

Fin didn't follow, he just watched as Drake picked his way through the mossy stones and freezing water to the place the earth opened. Heedless of the cold Drake once more dropped to his knees and cupped his hands to collect the spring water. He brought it to his face and sniffed.

From nowhere, fear swept through Fin with the speed of a hurricane. Every human instinct screamed at him to run. He drew in a sharp breath, limbs trembling. Mind confused by the onslaught. Nothing threatened him that he could see but Drake. Why the panic?

"You never have to fear me." A voice of sunshine coated in dark honey came from the man on his knees. "Come, Finbarr, named for the warriors of this land, come and meet a woodland properly."

The light of the moon played tricks on Fin. Drake shone with a golden glow, which shouldn't be possible in the silver of the moon. His black hair looked longer and his body thicker with muscles under a shirt now masquerading as leather and bronze amour, intricately made from a design gone to dust millennia ago. Those eyes, usually so brown as to be black, were the rich but delicate colour of rose gold.

"What the fuck —"

Drake dropped the water in his hands and offered one to Fin. "Come, Fin, there is no harm in this place for you. Others perhaps, but not you."

Compelled by his instincts to run, Fin's heart told him he looked into the face of a wolf. You knew it was dangerous but the human in charge says it is safe and you want to touch that majesty so very badly.

"Your heart speaks true, dear one," Drake murmured. "I am not always such a tamed creature, but for you…"

The instinct to run released its hold on his legs, the fear slithering away so abruptly it made him dizzy, and Fin stepped into the clearing. Where Drake seemed to know the most graceful way to navigate the mossy stones and water, Fin found his boots slipping and sliding on everything. Drake, jeans soaked, rose and took his hand. The spark of some unnameable energy raced through Fin at the contact. His eyes widened in shock. Painlessly, it ripped the seams of his defences open and Fin felt the grove surround him in warmth and colour.

Everything shone. Dead branches were deep brown. Leaves, despite the autumn, vivid in their colours of deep green or rust. The rocks, inert and useless, were now a soft grey or warm yellow depending on their form. The trees, they shone with silver and a thousand shades of the rainbow. Blue and silver danced through the trickling water around their feet and as Fin turned his gaze to Drake he drew in a sharp breath.

"What are you?" he whispered.

Drake cupped Fin's face and traced his eyebrows with his thumbs. Every moment of contact between them brought forth such trembling and quivering. Fin could scarcely breathe. The air, such a normal thing, had motes of light dancing on the breeze as if they were tiny fairies.

"You ate mushrooms you should not have done and in the morning all this will be a dream, dear one." Drake gazed into Fin's eyes with utter devotion.

Fin shook his head, trying to clear the weird psychedelic sensation. "I didn't eat any mushrooms."

A fine dark eyebrow rose. "Didn't you?"

Fin wasn't sure to be honest. Maybe he did? Maybe he was tripping and Drake didn't look like something from a painting by a grand Renaissance master?

He turned his eyes to the spring and the place from which it poured. Rather than something beautiful to match its surroundings the entire area looked black.

"No." The sound of protest came from his heart and he clutched the small branch of hawthorn.

Drake turned to look as well. "The water is polluted. Where Mother would give her bounty she can only give poison. Look deeper, Fin and you'll see what I do."

Fin, now holding one of Drake's hands crouched in the water and touched it. Tiny threads of black curled around his fingers. Small motes of more black travelled in the silver-blue water swirling around their feet.

"What is it?" he asked, tears coursing down his cheeks. He must be really stoned.

"Pollution. Look at the old man." Drake pointed to the big oak.

Fin raised his eyes to the tree and sobbed. Despite his majesty and age Fin could see death stealing through the thick roots, the trunk and up into the dark autumn leaves. "He's dying."

"Yes," Drake murmured, and his sadness hurt Fin. "All of this place will be lost soon."

"How can it be stopped?" Fin asked, wide-eyed as he looked at Drake. Terrified of the future like never before.

"I don't know. But Mother is asking for help. The old man is suffering. I have been called to this place and I have but one duty now I know why I have been called."

"What is that?" Fin's heart raced at the thought of standing beside Drake as he performed this mighty duty.

"War. I am war." Drake stood and a terrible sadness now cloaked the golden man. "I bring war to those who defy me. I am here to protect what remains of Mother's sacred places. Without them the world we walk cannot heal."

"Ares?" Fin whispered as the grove tilted sideways and his head splashed into the water of the river.

Chapter 5

"DAMN IT," DRAKE SNAPPED. HE forced the rippling tide of energy down and away, closing himself off to the joy and grief flooding the clearing. Bending, he lifted Fin's head out of the water before the boy drowned.

"You shouldn't have done that," said a deep, slow voice from behind Drake.

Drake ground his teeth together. He knew perfectly well what he should and should not be doing. He'd just been alone so long and he ached for the sweet soul in his arms. Every moment in Fin's company drove the ache back, and in its place bloomed hope. "Don't moan at me, old man. He's impossible to hide from. When he wakes he'll think it all dreams." At least that was the hope.

Drake turned to face the new speaker. A small, wizened man with large eyes and tangled hair of deepest green sat against the trunk of the oak tree. He had a twisted staff in one hand and a sprig of mistletoe in the other.

The old man shook the mistletoe at Drake. "Dreams change men's minds and that boy has been through enough in his short life. I'm surprised you cannot see such a thing. Or perhaps you are just as foolish as you were lifetimes ago and you do not care."

Drake lifted Fin from the stream without any obvious effort. "I care, old man. I've learned much, especially this last hundred years."

"Then why are you talking of war? Your games led to this." The old man waved his stick about, encompassing everything from the state of world politics to the plastic bag snagged on the nearby bramble bush.

Drake shook his head. "I don't think you can blame me for all the world's ills." Though he blamed himself often enough for the thought to wear holes in his mental carpet as he paced back and forth.

"I blame the Romans. That's you." The stick now pointed at Drake.

He huffed and turned his back on the tree for a moment. "I walked these lands before you, old man. Mind your tongue." Drake began to pick his way through the stones, reaching the bank and placing Fin on the soft ground. When he turned back to the tree, the old man continued to watch him with the patience only a tree can exude.

Drake sobered and stared at the spring's birthplace. "How bad is it?" he asked, nodding to the spring.

"As bad as it can be. I am dying, which is the way of things even for me. We don't fade as your kind do. We children of the wild don't need worship to exist. We are a part of the whole, part of Mother, and as such remain without the devotion from the children of the soil." He sighed, it took an age. "This place was once so powerful the children of the soil came from everywhere to sup the waters and take shelter under my boughs. Now though, I listen to their chatter and there are no prayers, no kindness, so few wishes. Mother's milk is tainted deep inside her. It is a cancer to her, and to us, but the children of the soil do not understand. Alas, I fear they never shall and we are on such a cusp. Such a cusp..." the old man's voice faded.

Drake sat, crossing his long legs and lifting Fin's head onto his thigh so he could stroke the soft dark hair. "It's why I'm here isn't it?"

The old man nodded. "I should think so, though we of the Grove do not have the power to summon the likes of you. Mother, however, she can still call to the children of the heavens when necessary."

A bark of bitter laughter came from deep inside Drake. "I don't have the power to summon the likes of me these days. The only reason I could show Fin any of this," he waved a hand about the wood, "is because of you, Mother, and Fin's talents. Whatever they are."

"The child is strong but feeds another. You need to take care you don't kill him, Belatucadros."

Drake's head shot up and he snapped out, "Don't call me that. I haven't been that in forever."

"Perhaps you prefer Mars? Ares? Camulus? Or the thousand other names given to you?" the old man provoked.

"I don't care for any of them. I am none of those things, not any longer. I haven't been for a very long time. Two thousand years more or less. So stop being a petty pig poker and help me help you." Drake didn't have the time or patience to explain the march of history to a tree.

The old man snorted. "You are too impetuous to help us."

"I was. Even I can change," Drake snapped. The past crawled over his skin, making it writhe. He buried his fingers in Fin's hair to help keep him in the present.

The old man watched the internal battle with patience. When Drake won, the old man said, "You'll need to change. This place, outside the Grove, has darkness pushing at our boundaries. Such darkness that makes the children of the soil sick in mind and body, so sick we can never hope to help them. They are stuffed with poison."

Drake sighed. "I know. I see it."

The old man cocked his head and narrowed his eyes, the skin on his face folding just as the bark on his tree grew. "You have changed."

"I am weak, tired and old." Drake gazed at the stars shining through the branches above them. "I am a shadow at midday. I am a waft of incense within a hurricane. I am the memory of a ghost. The sickness out there is far stronger than I will ever be again." Drake's heart ached at the thought. He'd once walked this world without fear or censor. Worshipped by every hearth in the oldest and mightiest of empires. He'd ridden beside Alexander, Julius Caesar, Boudicca, and so many more he'd forgotten their names and times.

"You need to be more than you have ever been if you are to save the children of the soil. To save us," the old man said. No begging, no rage, just acceptance of his fate being in the hands of another.

"I don't know how…" Drake whispered and he watched Finbarr sleep as he felt the old man return to the oak tree.

Drake bowed his head. Whatever he'd been for those few moments with Finbarr watching him the power had fled, and in its place sat a lump of coal rather than the crystalline perfection of a diamond reflecting the light of his brother Apollo. Ten thousand shards of brilliance were nothing but blackened dust and had been for more years than he could count.

Fin began to stir in his lap. Drake should carry him home but that required the strength of a god and right now, Drake didn't have the strength he needed to walk home either. If he hadn't felt the need to summon the deep magic of the old site to show off to Finbarr he wouldn't feel like he'd been drinking with Vikings for a winter.

"Those were the days," Drake mumbled before shaking Fin. "Come on, beautiful, time to wake." The young man stirred and opened his vivid blue eyes. Drake stroked his soft cheek.

"What happened?" Fin lifted his head before he slumped back into Drake's lap.

"A little woodland mischief. I made a mistake with a mushroom. You'll be fine. Come on, let's get you home, imp."

"Not an imp. I'm a woodland god," Fin said, rolling onto his back to gaze up at Drake. "You are so handsome, why on earth do you waste your time with me?"

Drake realised his young companion had hangover troubles from the magic. "Because something inside you calls to something inside me and I haven't felt anything stir in the ashes of my heart for a very long time."

A long slow blink as Finbarr untangled the sentence. "How long?"

"Years and years."

Tears sprang into Fin's eyes turning them into jewels. "Who broke your heart? I'll kill them for it."

Drake chuckled. "It's a long list. Come on, let's get you home before I do something *you'll* regret in the morning." He tapped Fin on the nose making him snort.

Fin didn't move to Drake's prodding though. "Like what?" Fin licked his soft lips.

Drake stilled, his hunger roaring forth almost overwhelming his self-control. "Fin, my loyalty to your sober wishes regarding us remaining friends can only be stretched so far. Don't push me. I am not a gentleman."

He watched as Fin worked himself upright and moved away. "Sorry. Of course. You're right."

Drake rose, his movements fluid and sure. He buried the hunger under a tonne of old bones that were left in his memories. "When you do surrender to me, Finbarr, it will be perfect and you'll be sober, but right now I need to see you safely back home."

Saskia left the Students' Union after the rest of her crowd. She helped with the clean-up but loitered on the small bridge over the stream and looked towards the playing fields enjoying the peace of the night. Two figures were making their back from the far side. A triste in the woodland? Half of her was amused, half of her angry that her safe place had been violated. Logically she knew most of the university wandered down there at some time or another, but Saskia always felt like it belonged to her and she dreaded leaving the place and the town at the end of the year to pursue her career out in the wide world. That is of course if she managed to pass her final exams and turned in her dissertation. Neither seemed likely at the moment.

A few minutes passed, in which she watched the full moon begin to set and the wandering lovers draw closer. When the couple turned into Drake half carrying Finbarr fear shot through her.

"Damn it," she muttered, a shard of possessiveness for her old boyfriend muddled her thoughts. If it were Ajax holding him up she'd be really worried but for some reason she didn't understand in the least, she trusted Drake. At least a little.

Deciding she should check on Fin, she left the bridge and strode towards the pair of miscreants. "What on earth are you doing to him?" Her opening salvo might as well be aggressive, she had nothing to lose.

Drake stopped, looking exhausted. He carried his coat rather than wearing it, the night wasn't that warm. Fin leaned against him and didn't seem to be aware of her presence.

"Saskia, good. Can you help? I'm not sure I'll manage him up the stairs to his room."

Already moving to take Fin's other side, she slipped under his arm. "What's wrong? He never drinks too much."

"Bad mushroom. My fault. I wasn't paying attention to what he was doing. If he starts talking about glowing gods just ignore him, I think he's been reading too much for his degree."

As lies went, it was pretty smooth in its delivery but Saskia's family specialised in lying, her parents were adept at it and she could smell bullshit from a thousand paces. It made her love life really difficult.

"Fin ate wild food at night in the woodland with you?" she asked, giving Drake her best – *yeah right* – eyebrow.

"I never mentioned the woodland."

"You're soaking wet and covered in mud."

Drake managed to look down at himself while helping Fin over the small bridge. "Oh."

"Hmm."

"I didn't hurt him." Drake sounded so defensive she almost laughed.

"Never thought you did. What is he doing with you and why is he in this state?" she asked.

"He wanted to show me the spring and the grove. Things became a bit intense and there were mushrooms involved."

"Jesus, Drake, have you any idea what the walking cock will do to him if Fin decides to confess all? I warn you now, Fin is a really bad liar – even worse than you."

Drake snorted. "I'm a very good liar. I've had years of practice."

"Yeah, well, you aren't good enough if you can't fool me. If you want to seduce Fin fine, go right ahead, but don't endanger him by playing games with Ajax." Saskia helped guide Fin through the door to his student block, the silence telling. Only third year students who worked hard lived in this building.

They wrestled the semi-conscious and uncoordinated Fin up the stairs and through more heavy fire doors. When they reached his small room they paused, both panting, while they leaned Fin against the wall.

"Fin? Keys?" Drake demanded.

"Pocket," Fin slurred. He focused on Saskia. "Hey, my favourite girl. Do you know how pretty he is?" Fin pointed at Drake – sort of.

"Must have been one hell of a mushroom," she muttered, ignoring Fin. "You want to search his pockets?"

Drake looked at Fin's tight jeans and Saskia watched him swallow hard. She stifled the urge to giggle at the older man who looked so uncomfortable. "I'll do it." She began going through Fin's pockets. "Sorry, big man, not exactly what you planned I'm sure."

"Loves ya, Sassy."

"Love you too, Fin." She found his keys and handed them over to Drake.

He paused and stared at the door. "Maybe you should help him. It's not appropriate for me to manhandle him in his room."

She watched the dark eyes; they were torn between concern for Fin and something else – something she couldn't quite grasp…

"What happened out there?" she asked Drake, making certain he heard her seriousness.

He sighed. "I may have become a little moon struck. I just don't want Fin to pay any kind of price for it. Please, just help him. I'm not very good with too much temptation and if Fin – well – he wants us to remain friends but in his current condition he might change his mind and I cannot suffer hurting him when he sobers up."

Saskia nodded. "Okay, I can live with that as a sort of truth. I'll help him. It's a strange place that grove and can affect the mind if you go there with an open heart."

Drake unlocked the door and held it open for her. "You know the place?"

She smiled back at him. "What do you think I'm fighting for? Even I can feel it's dying because of the pollution that must be in the water. I've taken test samples and I'm waiting on lab results, but it takes forever unless you've a lot of money or power. The only money and power in this town makes sure I'm silenced more often than not."

"I'm going to be sick," Fin announced.

"Oh good," Saskia said. "Run off now, pretty boy and I'll keep an eye on him."

Drake backed away as Fin lunged for his bathroom. Saskia watched the door swing shut, then went into the bathroom and rubbed circles on Fin's back while he puked. In the eighteen months or so they'd been apart they'd hardly spoken, both moving in separate social circles, but her fondness for Fin had never left her and if she could help him untangle his life from Ajax by moving him towards Drake then she'd accept that mission.

She thought about Drake. Undeniably handsome, he stirred strange ideas and dreams in her hot blood, but none of them were focused on sex. In strange ways she had feelings of family towards him and Fin, it made her want to trust them and Saskia didn't trust anyone.

"Who the hell are you, Drake York?" she muttered as she rubbed Fin's back.

"He's a god. He's Ares," Fin mumbled before puking again.

"Of course he is," she said with a heavy sigh.

Ajax

AJAX STOOD ON THE BALCONY of his room, the cool autumn night alive in the large garden. His sharp eyes tracked the hedgehogs seeking shelter for their hibernation and the owls in the trees. He couldn't quite see the voles they watched in the formal gardens, but he did catch the flash of a fox's tail. His lips parted in a low growl and he considered hunting rather than dinning with his parents.

The door to his room clicked open and closed. His sister's scent came to him before she leaned against his back and placed her head on his shoulder. "You're gloomy. Your toy not entertaining enough?" she asked.

He looked down at her. Tonight she wore her rich blonde hair up in elaborate braids and curls. Her elfin features were enhanced in an understated way with a little makeup and she wore a short loose knit dress in russet red with kitten heels in the same colour. Gold decorated her throat, wrist and slim fingers. She did beauty almost as well as their mother.

"He's not my toy, Electra." Ajax had no idea where Fin was tonight. He could usually sense him, out there, on the campus or in the town with friends, but tonight the young man remained hidden. It made Ajax nervous, twitchy, and angry.

"That's how you treat him. Like I used to treat my dolls." Electra rubbed Ajax's arm. "Come inside, Father will be annoyed if you miss the first course. You know what he's like. Besides, if you're feeling lonely for your toy perhaps you'd like to play with someone else? It's been a while, brother." The manicured nails traced up Ajax's forearm and he couldn't deny the pleasure it brought to his body.

"I thought you liked your men submissive," he said, turning to study her fine features.

"Maybe I'd like something a little rougher tonight." She gazed up at him and flashed her big blue eyes.

They looked alike, something Ajax always enjoyed and were close enough to be twins. They shared the same family name, but they weren't blood – not really. Not that it would have mattered. They'd been fucking each other for years and he always enjoyed it.

He grabbed her chin, tipped it up and plundered her mouth. Her small breasts pushed against his chest and she whimpered. Ajax shoved her away. "I want Fin."

"Well, it seems you can't have him tonight." Electra's eyes glittered bright in the moonlight.

"I know, I wish I knew why..." Ajax's attention returned to the night. "It's the damned PhD student I know it."

"Oh, the older dishy one. Yes, I've seen him. Quite the catch. I'm tempted myself. Perhaps you should seduce him as well and we can have a foursome?"

Ajax shook his head in mock horror. "Electra, you really are a deviant bitch."

"That's why you love me even after all these years," she purred and returned to his arms. "You do seem pensive though, brother. What's wrong? It's not like you to care about toys."

He considered her question. She was right, he didn't care about the boys he fucked, but Fin had been under his skin since they'd met and Ajax drew so much power from the boy. Now though, that power kept turning to dust every time Ajax tried to pull it in – even when he fucked Fin it didn't feel the same. He didn't really need Fin's strength but it tasted like the finest claret when he drank it down.

"Oh," Electra said, leaning away from his body a little so she could look into his face, "you're addicted again."

"Am not," he snapped stepping away.

"Father and Mother will be cross." She turned away.

Ajax reached for her arm and pulled her close, tightening his grip. "You will not mention this. I will deal with it."

Her eyes turned sympathetic. "You always get too close, Ajax. It's why I don't keep my lovers for long, it never ends well. You must let him go."

"I'm not addicted. He's just good at sucking cock."

"Better than me?" she asked all teasing sweetness again.

Ajax laughed. "No one is better at sucking my cock than you, sister dear. Go downstairs and I'll join you in a minute. I look a mess." He didn't but he wasn't ready to face their parents just yet. It always took a measure of courage.

Electra drifted away and he returned to watching the university, just visible from his room. An unaccustomed weight sat in his chest. That man Drake would take Fin, Ajax could feel it in his bones and he didn't lose out to men like Drake. He needed a plan. One that would destroy Fin's desire for the stranger.

Chapter 6

THE SOFT AND REPEATING *RAP, rap, rap* on a hard surface brought Fin groaning and moaning to the surface of consciousness. He cracked open his eyes and winced at the intrusion of sunlight, then realised rain beat the windows and the sunlight was more of a hazy event at best.

"Fin?" asked the door.

"Not the door, dickhead," Fin mumbled, rolling off the narrow dorm bed in his room. He still wore his jeans and shirt from the night before. Both were muddy but now dry, they were heavily creased and smelt of river water. He didn't smell too clean either and neither did his bed. What the hell had happened last night? He never drank enough to be sick. He smacked his lips together, his mouth tasting of rat's fur and cow dung. He groaned.

It couldn't be Ajax at the door he didn't knock with any kind of care so Fin didn't have to worry about his appearance. If he didn't look his best, Ajax would be furious.

Thankful for small mercies, he cracked the door. "Drake."

"I have coffee, I have pastries, I have flowers." Drake smiled that smile of his and Fin's knees weakened.

"Flowers?" Fin felt his cheeks heat and his heart do a strange little dance in his chest. "I'm a mess. No one wants to see me like this."

"I'll take you any way I can have you and there's a shower just there. I'll cook you bacon for breakfast?" Drake's dark eyes were soft and full of something Fin didn't recognise. It was an emotion he'd never seen in Ajax's face. A mixture of desire and... fondness perhaps?

Shaking his head in mock horror Fin opened the door to his room and let Drake in. "Pastries yes, bacon for breakfast? Not yet. Give me a minute to clean up though."

Fin yanked off his shirt and wandered into his small wet room. He heard Drake moving around and some music playing. Drake had found Fin's stash of actual CDs, many of which he'd stolen off his parents. An album called Misplaced Childhood had Drake singing along – rather badly as it happened. It was good to know the man wasn't perfect.

He stripped, showered, brushed his teeth and ran a brush through his hair. At which point he realised he hadn't brought any clean clothes into the shower. "Shit." Going out in a towel was provocative. Going out in manky jeans was disgusting. Thinking about Drake seeing his skinny body also didn't feel like fun.

"Which shouldn't matter at all because you have a boyfriend," Fin told the mirror. Just the thought of Ajax brought a weight to his soul he didn't like. His attraction to Drake ran deep, really deep and the more he stared into the tired blue eyes looking at him in the mirror the more Fin realised how different life could be with a lover singing like a crow in the next room.

Drake began making up lyrics in the next room and Fin smiled. With a sudden clarity he'd been missing for months, if not years, he knew what he needed to do. End things with Ajax. Take the consequences, which would be traumatic for a bit, and spend more time with Drake. "Without instantly falling into bed with the man," Fin told himself.

Just for a moment it looked like the mirror image raised a sarcastic eyebrow, where Fin knew he frowned. *No way*. Hangover and shower steam created the illusion.

He tucked the towel more tightly around his hips, maybe just a little lower than necessary, and left the bathroom. Drake stood in the middle of the room, singing along and dancing. Fin just watched him and as he did more of the previous evening came back. Including the odd image of Drake as a Greek warrior in golden armour even larger than he was in Fin's bedroom. He also remembered Saskia helping him to bed. What the hell had he taken to trip out like that? Had Drake spiked him?

Maybe trusting Drake wouldn't be wise.

Drake chose that moment to twirl around. He stumbled as he caught sight of Fin and colour swept over his swarthy skin. "Oh, hey, coffee." Drake stepped aside and Fin saw a range of pastries, enough for an army, and several coffees. "I didn't know which kind you liked so I bought a variety. Sorry about last night – you ate a bad mushroom."

"I don't remember eating any mushrooms."

Drake shrugged. "You must have done because things got a bit weird and I thought Saskia should put you to bed."

Fin noticed Drake worked hard to keep his eyes high, rather than stare at all the naked flesh. Was it out of decency or maybe Drake didn't think he was that interesting to look at? It deflated his ego and confidence. "I better get dressed."

"Yes, no... Um..." Drake turned his back. "It would be the proper thing to do, as you wish to remain friends."

Warmth filled Fin's heart. Drake wanted to be a decent man but didn't seem to be immune to his charms. Fin decided Drake deserved a little payback. "Are we in a Victorian melodrama now?"

Drake's grin made a cage of butterflies in his stomach launch into flight. He said, "I don't think they have half naked gay men in melodramas."

"Shame, it might make people read them."

Drake laughed. The door to Fin's room swung open. Ajax walked in. His eyes took in the scene. Half-naked Fin, happy Drake, breakfast pastries and coffee on the desk beside the computer and pile of books.

Fin's world imploded with a soundless explosion. All the emotion in the room was sucked into a vacuum. "Ajax, it's not —"

"Don't you knock?" Drake snarled. He stood in the middle of the small room and glared at Ajax.

Fin, caught standing between the two men, grabbed the nearest item of clothing he could find. The canvas jacket Drake wore but had slung over the chair before beginning his private party.

Ajax's expression grew bored, never a good sign in Fin's experience. "I have no need to knock, the room belongs to *my* boyfriend." The possessive emphasis on the word 'my' made Fin's stomach twist from butterflies to worms.

Fin watched Drake's eyes darken and his body language change; shoulders rolling forwards, weight shifting to be balanced, his hands relaxed at his side but poised, coiled, ready.

The threat of violence expanded as Ajax shifted to match Drake. Fin wanted to retreat. He wasn't ready for this, for this decision, this confrontation. The moment Drake sent that smile in his direction he knew there would be a decision to be made, stay with Ajax or throw the dice and hope the promise in Drake's smile would come true.

The promise in Drake's eyes.

The warmth and safety Fin felt whenever they were close. That's how a lover should make you feel. That's how *he* wanted to feel, safe.

The last thing Fin wanted was more drama and the potential for violence in the room ramped up with every breath and heartbeat. Christ, he really needed to take control of his life.

"Drake? I need you to please leave me alone with Ajax. Perhaps we can meet later and talk about things." Fin sent the other man what he hoped would be a confident and steady gaze.

With visible effort Drake rolled his shoulders back and reeled in the intensity. "As you wish, Fin. You can return my coat when you come to dinner tonight with Saskia." His gaze flayed Fin's heart.

"That sounds lovely, thank you. It would be great to catch up with *friends*." Fin could use heavy emphasis on key words as well.

Ajax growled. "That fucking dyke is no friend of Fin's."

Drake ignored the provocation, stepping between Ajax and Fin in the small room. Fin felt Drake's fingers brush his. "Remember, if you need anything just call."

"Thank you for bringing breakfast over it was very thoughtful." Fin managed to give him a smile despite the rising fear of being in the room with Ajax without Drake's comforting presence.

Ajax snorted in derision. "Not staying to fight for him? Typical."

Fin sucked in a breath as Drake rounded on Ajax. "Oh, I'd love to fight for him, but I respect Finbarr too much to do something so crass. There is a time for war, for battles to be fought, but this isn't it and if you had an ounce of integrity you would recognise that as well. Fin's more than capable of making his own decisions and I will abide by whatever fate he decrees over our future."

The sudden movement, of Ajax meaning to poke Drake in the chest, caught Fin by surprise but not Drake, who twisted away to avoid contact. Ajax sneered. "He will never choose you."

"He might not, he might choose freedom from us both, but I will give him that chance, can you?" Drake asked. He nodded once at Fin and left the room.

Rather than easing the heavy atmosphere the tension grew worse. Fin struggled to meet Ajax's blue eyes – had he really thought they were beautiful? Now they looked like chips of old medicine bottles, dark blue with warnings of arsenic on them.

"Where the hell were you last night? With him?" Ajax barked. He towered over Fin, so close he could barely breathe.

All Fin had to do was cry out and others in the hall would come and help. Ajax couldn't do too much damage here and Drake had left the door open. Fin placed a hand on Ajax's heaving chest and pushed him back, straightening his spine in the process. "Yes. I was with him last night. We went for a walk after Saskia's rally. We are friends. We have a great deal in common."

Ajax did not move and his glare tightened. "He wants to fuck you."

Sadness fired through Fin at Ajax's use of language. Drake had a way of talking that wove time together, one moment a man of modernity, the next a gentleman only found in books of ancient loves long buried. "He wants to know me. All of me. Mind and body. Can you even remember when I was more than just a convenient hole for you to use?" His voice cracked.

"Don't be ridiculous. That's not how I feel about you." Ajax turned on his heel making Fin flinch.

"That's how you behave." Fin stepped closer to the door, just in case. "Listen, Ajax. I know I'll never make you understand but things between us have been unhealthy for a long time. It's over. I don't want you here and I don't think you should be in my life any longer."

Ajax laughed, a sound of glass breaking. "Don't be ridiculous. You're a passing fancy to a man like that. You won't leave me."

Fear dissolved in a vat of sudden loathing, so deep and integral to Fin's being he didn't understand why he'd not unleashed it before. He stepped into Ajax's space and balled his fists at his sides. Gritting his teeth, he snarled, "I don't give a shit if I am a 'passing fancy', leaving you has nothing to do with Drake, other than showing me there are better men out there than you. Get out of my room, get out of my life and leave me the fuck alone."

Fin's chest heaved with the anger and effort it took to stand up to Ajax. He'd only ever done it once before and it hadn't ended well.

"Hey, Fin, you okay?" came a call from outside his room. One of the others who shared the hall of residence must be in the kitchen.

"Fine, Ajax was just leaving, for good," Fin called out. He stared at Ajax until the bigger man moved.

"You'll come snivelling back," Ajax snapped.

He stormed out, grabbing the door and slamming it hard enough to make the plasterboard walls shudder and someone to shout in one of the adjoining rooms. The door bounced and slammed back. Fin realised Drake had clicked the lock off to help make sure Ajax didn't shut him in the room. That one gesture of care broke Fin's self-control. The stress of the last few minutes combined with the weird handover crashed over him and he collapsed on the bed in tears of grief, shame and relief combined. He just needed to wash it out of his soul.

Chapter 7

DRAKE STOOD IN THE KITCHEN of Fin's halls and waited. He might be able to give the illusion of respecting Fin's desire to deal with Ajax like an adult, but the instinct to protect the younger and smaller man also needed to be satisfied. He heard everything and coaxed one of the other's in the room to call out so Fin knew he wasn't alone. When Ajax slammed out of the halls Drake wanted to return to Fin but as he neared the still open door he heard Fin's tears.

For a moment Drake hesitated, his heart needing to help. He leaned against the wall and closed his eyes, listening to Fin's heart break from exhaustion and stress. Drake ached to move, to rescue, to protect. Hard won experience taught him to leave well enough alone for the moment. Fin needed respect and time. If Drake wanted more than a tussle in a hay barn – or the modern equivalent – he needed to wait for Fin to come to him rather than keep pursuing.

Sliding his fingers over the door before pulling it gently closed to give Fin some privacy, he muttered, "See, even I can learn eventually."

He followed Ajax outside and watched the big blond storm off. It would take little for Drake to race after the fool and pull him into small pieces – literally if necessary – but it wouldn't help anything in the long run. Something about Ajax bothered Drake more than watching a bully hurt his boyfriend. Ajax whispered darkness in Drake's blood, just as Finbarr whispered light. People rarely touched him as much as these two and the girl, Saskia did, also Dr Moran, his academic supervisor. He knew Annwn spoke of power and had called him across the water, but perhaps the town had called others.

Not all the things called to the place would be friendly, something else he knew from experience. Drake sighed as he watched Ajax storm off. He didn't want to fight, didn't want war, didn't want conflict – not really. Not anymore. It seemed even he was capable of change and it might have taken a long time for his base nature to learn the gift of peace, but he'd learned and ironically, he wouldn't give it up without a fight.

"Hey, big man."

He turned and saw Saskia approach. "I was just coming to find you."

Her glance flicked up to Fin's window. "Oh? What's he done now? Consumed some more mushrooms?" The sarcastic raising of her pierced eyebrow made Drake grin.

"No, but I did bring breakfast over as a peace offering. Unfortunately, Ajax put pay to my cunning plan to lure Fin away. I think he could do with a friend – a real friend – not another headache and I think I'm more of a headache right now."

She smiled at him and tilted her head to one side. "You're alright, big man."

"I'm not that big."

"You're bigger than me and you're not all walking cock. Besides I have the feeling you're bigger on the inside than the out – like the TARDIS."

"Thank you? I think?"

She patted his arm. "Trust me, it's a good thing. I'll go check on the delicate flower and steal his breakfast, so thanks for that."

"Dinner tonight? At mine? Make him come with you? If he has an escort he might be willing to cross my threshold."

Saskia nodded, dreadlocks bouncing. "Damn straight we'll be there – free food!"

Drake returned to his studies, determined to spend the day on his PhD.

He'd forgotten more than he remembered these days and found his academic efforts rewarding. Learning how to think, how to interpret information for other people, how to investigate the world through language and rigorous principles of study, appealed to him. There were those in his old life that would mock or scold his efforts but Drake had learned to ignore those thoughts. Sometimes, being humble won him more than any battle ever had.

THAT EVENING A NEST OF small birds fluttered inside Drake's chest while he prepared a simple meal including the chestnuts and mushrooms from the previous night. He'd opened a bottle of red wine and even bought cake so they could spend the evening discussing philosophy or politics or something else that interested students these days. The curiosity of the young mind never bored him and he often regretted not studying with the great masters like Alexander did or Augustus and Julius. He should have spent more time listening in the agora and forums of the ancient world rather than striding around fighting to build more empires that worshipped his primary form.

The doorbell chimed sending a quiver of anticipation through him. Wiping his hands on a dishcloth stuck into the waistband of his black jeans, he went to the door. Saskia stood there with a grin and holding bottles of cheap wine. Fin stood behind her, finding the iron railings much more interesting than Drake. He held the canvas coat though, draped over his arm.

Drake stepped aside giving Saskia a peck on her cheek. "You're just in time. The risotto is almost finished. The wine is open and the table laid."

Fin stopped in front of him and looked up. "Your coat."

"Thank you, Fin. How are you?"

The deep blue eyes were puffy and sore but no bruises coloured the pale skin. Ajax had not returned to do battle. A knot in Drake's chest relaxed. He'd been fretting all day at having to stay away from Fin but knew he couldn't interfere any more than he'd done already.

"I'm here as a friend, Drake. Nothing more."

Drake smiled at the focused concentration in Fin's expression. "Understood. I'm just glad to see you. May I offer a hug?"

Fin's eyes welled and he nodded. "I could do with a hug."

Drake took his coat and dropped it on the floor before wrapping his arms around Fin. He held the younger man as if holding the blossom of a wild red poppy. Fin leaned into his chest and tucked his head under Drake's chin. Damn it felt good, really good. Drake shifted just enough to bury his nose in Fin's untidy mass of warm brown hair, a delicate musk mixed with an orange scented shampoo. The refined scent made him giddy for more. He smelled of books and knowledge, not sword oil and horses, and Drake loved it.

"I think dinner needs stirring," Saskia called from the kitchen. "I'm not sure either of you want me in charge of this."

Fin pulled away and stared up at Drake. "Thank you," he murmured.

"For what?"

"For your kindness, Drake." Fin rose on his toes and his soft lips ghosted over Drake's five o'clock shadow. Drake wanted to whimper with the need to claim more but he loosened his hold on Fin and stepped back with a smile and a nod.

Dinner turned into a noisy affair with Saskia on fine form. Until the conversation turned to the grove Drake and Fin found themselves in the previous night.

"Every time I take samples and send them off for analysis the damned samples go missing," she complained, twirling the stem of her wine glass.

They sat in Drake's lounge, an airy room with a view over the surrounding hills during the day. Now the heavy curtains were closed and a fire flickered in the grate. The furnishings belonged to the landlady but were tasteful and in the case of the large sofa, expensive. Drake had no intention of slumming it like most students. Saskia sat curled up in an armchair by the fire, while Fin sat too far away on the sofa.

"What do you mean they go missing?" Drake asked.

She shrugged and frowned. "I don't have a car and the bus goes once a day from the centre of town, so I use the local post office to send samples of the water from the grove, and soil, but the labs says they never arrive. I find it hard to believe the labs lose the samples and the postal system isn't so bad they lose everything I post, so I think the walking cock's family have the post woman in thrall."

Drake's eyes widened. "Thrall? That's a term I've not heard for a while. What do you know about thralls?"

She grinned. "I read."

"Don't call him that," Fin said so quietly they both focused on him.

"Sorry, Fin." Saskia didn't look sorry.

Fin seemed lost in the colours of the firelight reflecting through his wine. "He was kind to me once."

Drake and Saskia exchanged looks. "I'm sure he was."

Fin's gaze snapped up to Saskia. "Why do you always think he's the bad guy? I told you I was gay before I got involved with him. It's not like I cheated on you."

"Hey, Fin, I don't think —" Drake shifted on the sofa, wanting to maintain the peace of the evening.

Saskia sat forwards. "No, it's okay, Drake. I know you didn't cheat on me, Fin. But you betrayed me by staying with a man who hurt you. By not coming to me for help when we've been friends for years – long before our disastrous sex life began. Also, you stayed with him knowing his family is responsible for destroying the ecology of the area. That's what hurt me."

Drake watched Fin. Tears stood proud in his eyes and he nodded. "I am sorry, Sassy. You are right on all counts. Just... try not to mention his cock around me. I'd rather not think about it."

Saskia glanced at Drake with wide eyes. Totally unqualified to help Fin with some constructive advice, Drake opted to reach out and squeeze his shoulder. Rather than pull away, Fin closed the distance and to Drake's surprise curled up against his chest.

Drake drew in a sharp breath and with great care he placed his arm around Fin to hold him just a little more tightly, a little more safely. The core of him relaxed, sighing in relief as did Fin. Drake didn't really understand the pull this young man had but the two of them echoed each other and drew warmth from that soft sound.

Drake fought to focus on the conversation. "I'll take the samples to a lab. You can come with me if you collect them." Drake couldn't help but rub his cheek against Fin's hair. "Science is still a little out of my wheelhouse." Understatement. He could forge a sword, but that had more to do with magic than science.

"We need photos of the kaolin mine works and the waste produced as well. The way Aegis Corporation mines their properties here is not consistent with European or even British law. Their cheap systems are polluting the underground water structures. I'm slowly collecting data but that family seem to have the entire town on their payroll."

"That's because they have," Fin said, sounding like a sleepy puppy under Drake's arm.

He pulled away a bit to be able to look down at Fin. "What?"

Fin blinked, trying to bring his mind into focus, he looked exhausted. "They have the university and the town council, some of the police and others on the payroll. Ajax thinks it's great. He can park where he likes, drive at whatever speed he likes, providing he doesn't hurt anyone, and pretty much do as he pleases. So can his friends. It's like they are immune."

"You have proof of this?" Saskia asked.

Fin shook his head. "I never managed to get any, though I did try when things started going wrong. I wanted to be able to report him for some... stuff... but when I said I would go to the police Ajax laughed. I'm going to be lucky if the university doesn't send me down for leaving him."

Drake closed a hand over Fin's where it rested on his chest. "I won't let that happen and neither will Dr Moran. She'll protect you."

"Ajax hates her almost as much as he hates you two."

I wonder why? Drake's thoughts flitted about faster than a humming bird's wings. "If you're serious about stopping the mine from continuing its work without better oversight, I'm willing to help. The grove is in trouble and needs protecting."

"Can I bring over some paperwork, get you to look through it?" Saskia asked. Her excitement at having help made Drake smile.

Paperwork? Drake had swords and charging castle walls in mind, but okay, they could start with paperwork if they must.

"Eco warriors," Fin mumbled. "I'm so tired."

"Eco warriors?" Drake asked.

Fin sat up in one movement and turned to look at Drake.

Drake's heart beat harder as he took in Fin's eyes. They weren't just blue, they shone like jewels cut from the finest of precious stone, lit from the inside.

"Are you ready for a different kind of war?" Fin asked.

Drake glanced at Saskia who sat back in the chair, slumped and unconscious, wine glass balanced on a knife's edge over the pale carpet. He rose and rescued the glass, checking her pulse as he did so, it beat slow but strong.

"Who are you?" Drake whispered at Finbarr.

"Don't you recognise me, Ares? Has it been so long?" Fin's face, all sharp angles and fine bones, took on another cast for a moment. A shade of a face long lost in Ares' past.

Drake drew in a sharp breath and his knees weakened. "Phemonoe?"

"Oracle of Delphi might be more accurate in this case, Ares."

Too much too fast. Drake shook his head trying to concentrate on one thing at a time. "Don't call me that name. I'm not that, not any more. I'm a drift of memory, surfing what remains, until I vanish forever. What are you doing in Finbarr?"

He backed off towards the fireplace, genuine fear making his body and mind crave the violence he wanted to leave behind. War was his drug, his food, his ambrosia and he fought against its call every damned day. His ancient past returning with a suddenness of a screaming bullet shocked him with an explosion of memories.

"Come, sit, Drake. You have nothing to fear from me."

"Is Apollo here?" he asked, afraid to look away.

Fin's eyes softened. "No, love."

Of all his brethren Apollo was the most dangerous to Drake. "You

shouldn't call me that, Phemonoe. You know how he feels about our..."
Drake lost the words necessary to finish. Inside, memories crashed through
him, drowning his present in a past of dust and blood.

Fin, graceful where he should be slightly awkward, moved to stand in
front of Drake, placing two hands on his large chest. "You are still beautiful,
my love."

Drake cupped Fin's jaw and tears stung his eyes. "I'm talking to the
Oracle not Phemonoe, right?"

"You loved us both, just as you do my new vessel," Fin, or rather, the
Oracle said.

"Yes, I loved you both. I lost you both when Apollo declared you sacred
and took you from me forever." The pain of that parting made the tears fall.
He'd been so angry with his brother he'd started another war with the
Spartans just to keep himself from going mad with rage.

"You never came back for me, Ares."

Drake closed his eyes. "Please, Oracle, don't call me that and give me
Finbarr back."

Fin's eyes grew sombre. "I can't give you Fin back. Or at least I can't
leave him. I'm sorry, Drake. He's my vessel. I've been quiet inside him for a
long time, trying to hide from that hideous soul-eater Ajax and his clan."

Drake shook his head, confused and ripped raw to the bone. "What are
you talking about?"

"One thing at a time. I need you," a sharp finger poked his chest, "to listen
and pay attention. You know I can't always keep myself coherent, though now
Fin's found you it should help. The grove *has* to be saved. As do so many
other places. Mother needs you, Ares, she has no one else to call on. No one
other than you, her warrior child of the heavens, to help save her from the
children of the soil. They will destroy her and you can join the fight —"

"I am not that creature, Oracle. I cannot help Mother. I cannot save her
from the children of the soil. They make their own way as they have always
done. I stopped having power among them almost two thousand years ago
and after the last century..."

Oracle held Ares still with a piercing frown. "Since when have you run from a fight?"

"Since I saw the world melt the sun. I stood and watched death find a new toy more deadly than anything I could ever have imagined or created even at my most powerful. The children of the soil are more lethal now than they have ever been. Have you seen what that new weapon of theirs can do? It splits the very heart of matter, the stuff they are made from, and undoes it in such a way as to destroy every drop of rain, mote of dust and breath of air. So much death, Oracle, all under the control of so few. That is not war, that is not noble men or women killing a few thousand innocents in a blood frenzy, that is annihilation on a scale even I cannot comprehend. I vowed never to go to war again."

Drake found himself shaking. He returned to the sofa and sat, head in hands. The day he watched the first atomic explosion, after witnessing the first and second world wars kill so many, he'd broken his sword over his knee and turned away from battle forever. He would never be a warrior god again. Never encourage violence. He would study peace. Learning the teachings of the great thinkers. Wait until the last of his energy drained away, as it did for so many of their kind, so he could return to the heavens and rest forever. Thanks to mankind's need for war, he'd already survived many of his siblings.

"You have changed."

Drake threw his hands up in the air in exasperation. "I know. I've been trying to explain that to everyone. I am different. I am a man of peace, of knowledge. I cannot help you. War is wrong."

"War is necessary to bring change. You must tear down the tower before building a new one, stronger and better and fairer."

"Since when does that ever work? Can't you get Pestilence involved from the new era and have him ravish mankind so the children of the soil can't destroy Mother's bounty?"

"No. Well, Pestilence will do what he does but I have no authority over him. I do have it over you however, and Mother has called on that power she granted me long ago." Oracle sat on the low table in front of the fire facing Ares.

"And now I have to give Fin up as well? For pity's sake Oracle can I not be left in peace until my time in this world is done at last? I could care about Fin, deeply, and make a life with him free of the machinations of my damned and cursed family." Drake almost wailed at the injustice and pain in his heart.

Oracle shook Fin's head in obvious confusion. "What? No, why would you give up Fin to do Mother's bidding? Don't be stupid."

"Because Phemonoe had to remain a damned virgin? Or had you forgotten that Oracle?" Drake snapped.

Oracle laughed. "You're funny. Fin's not a virgin."

Drake rose, unable to trust himself so close to Oracle in Fin's taut and beautiful body. They had loved each other, Ares and Oracle – Phemonoe had also loved him and he loved her in return. A complicated triangle but they made it work, until Apollo stepped in and ruined everything. "That's hardly the point. The point is you're a scared gift and therefore you have to remain impartial, kept sacred and free from the likes of me."

"Impartial?" they asked, sounding amused.

He rounded on the sitting figure. "Yes. Impartial. Able to give your gift of prophecy wherever it is needed and requested. Not be governed or controlled by the likes of me."

Oracle huffed in dismissal. "No."

"What?"

"No, you were wrong then, you're wrong now. Especially now. I am choosing a side. Your side. Our side. Her side." Oracle pointed at Saskia. "This war we are about to start with Ajax and his family is the only thing that matters. It's why Mother called you here. It's why I am here inside Fin and have been since his birth. I needed him to break his ties to the soul-eater before I could show myself to you, Ares —"

"I'm not him!" Drake shouted, pulling at his hair. "Do you know how much it cost me to give you up? Then I had everything stripped from me. Century after century more of me has been eroded. I am a shadow, a puff of smoke, I just wanted to fall in love for the last time and hold Finbarr in my arms for the few short years he has in this world before I am alone again. I am not going to war." A part of Drake realised it was too soon to have these thoughts about Fin – especially as Fin hadn't been consulted on his plan – but the more Drake thought about his future the more real his vague dreams solidified.

Oracle's arms crossed. "Mother has called. I have chosen a side. You will have your mortal boy and me. You will make this right. You will destroy the soul-eaters, who will become new gods if we aren't careful. You will become what the children of the soil need."

Drake opened his mouth to continue his protest just as Fin's body jerked hard. Drake leapt forwards and caught him before he hit the ground. "Shit." He brushed hair off Fin's face. "What the hell am I supposed to do now?"

Chapter 8

FIN STIRRED, A SHAFT OF light hitting his face. His bed was a lot more comfortable than usual and he felt a great deal more relaxed than he ever did waking up at Ajax's home on the hill. He opened his eyes and blinked hard a few times. Drake sat on the floor by the embers of the fire. Fin lay on the sofa under a thick blanket and Saskia slept curled up like a cat on the chair under another large blanket.

He watched Drake for a while, an unexpected luxury. Dark curls perfectly framed angular features and dark stubble covered his jaw and cheeks. His firm mouth looked tight though and his eyes were distant and troubled. He had the air of someone who'd received bad news that made him sad rather than angry.

"What's wrong?" Fin asked without moving from the sofa.

Drake didn't seem surprised he'd woken. "I have to decide whether to stay here or not."

Fin's heart hurt with such violence he gasped and flinched as if struck. "You can't leave."

Drake turned those deep brown eyes on Fin. "I might have to because I don't think I can be the man you need me to be. I really don't know if I can do it."

Fin sat up and pushed the blanket off his torso. "Riddles don't help me understand and if I don't understand I can't help. I don't need you to be anything other than the man I met a few days ago." Had it really only been a few days? Drake had turned Fin's world upside down.

"Do you remember anything about falling asleep?" Drake asked in the same soft voice making Fin strain to hear him.

Fin considered the question. "No, I must have drunk too much wine."

"You had three glasses and they weren't large."

"Then I'm tired from the previous night. I'm sorry if falling asleep on your sofa is a problem."

Drake smiled, his eyes too bright. "Watching you sleep might be my new favourite hobby. Trust me, I have no intention of ever stopping you from sleeping here." Drake rose and sat on the sofa at Fin's feet. "You know you snuffle when you dream? Little huffs and puffs. Like a puppy. It's adorable." He reached up and brushed hair off Fin's brow.

Fin caught the stray fingers. Drake's strange mood confused him. He sensed Drake felt lost and exhausted but why? "What's going on? What's made you so maudlin?"

Drake stared at Saskia for a long time. "I loved a woman once, well, a lot of women over the years, but really loved someone and she was taken from me by my brother. Denied by convention, propriety, social rules, my family's rules…"

Fin didn't really want to hear about the women in Drake's life. Bi-sexual men could be a minefield of contradictions. He also didn't want Drake looking at Saskia. "But we aren't bound by rules," Fin said, testing tumultuous waters and trying to navigate them without a chart.

Drake studied their hands, fingers knotted together. "You are the very definition of perfect, Fin, but I don't think this is a good idea. I think it will lead to you being hurt very badly and I wouldn't be able to live with that. Not again. Never again." Drake rose and released his hand. "I'm going for a walk. The two of you can help yourselves to whatever you find in the kitchen. Just shut the door on the way out."

He bent, placed a soft kiss to Fin's hair and strode from the room. Fin tried to stop him but his feet were tangled in the blanket. The front door clicked shut before he freed himself. The curse he made woke Saskia with a snort.

"What? Where? Fin?"

Fin turned to look at his friend. "Men confuse the shit out of me."

She laughed. "You think they confuse you – try being a woman... What's wrong now? He seemed happy enough last night." She frowned. "Hang on – why am I in his armchair? What the fuck happened?"

Fin sat again and put his head between his hands. The moment he closed his eyes images flashed through his mind. A kaleidoscope of pictures and words tripped around inside his head, muddling with what happened the night in the grove. What was happening to him? Was this some kind of breakdown? How had things become so weird and out of control since Drake York arrived. Why did the damn man look at him with such misery and... desperate longing? Yes, desperate longing, that's what Fin felt from Drake. Yet they'd known each other all of five minutes and Fin might need something from Drake but the emotional intensity coming from the man seemed a little over the top.

Saskia moved out of her chair with a groan because of being curled up in a ball all night. She stretched and sat beside him. "Fin? What's wrong? What's happened?"

"I don't think I understand anything anymore. Do you remember falling asleep?" he asked her. Start with small things and work backwards.

She hesitated before answering. "No. One moment I was chatting, the next it's morning." She rose and opened the curtains. "Late morning. Do you have lectures today?"

"It's Saturday, Sassy."

"Oh, right. Good. Or we'd be late." She sat beside him again. "I need coffee. Where's Drake?"

"I don't know and he said we could help ourselves."

She grinned. "I like that man. Not only does he cook, but he leaves me in his well-stocked kitchen without supervision. Come on, let's get some food inside you before you melt into a puddle of self-pity." She dragged Fin into the kitchen and began making herself at home. "What did you do this time to make *mister emotional* bugger off?"

Fin sat on a stool at the breakfast bar, struggling to remain vertical. "I have no idea. I don't think he slept at all. He's..." The swirl of images and emotions inside Fin made him queasy. "He's not like other guys."

"Understatement." Saskia put bread in the toaster, then made herself familiar with the fridge's contents. "What do you remember about last night?"

"We were talking... Then – nothing. I woke up and Drake said we couldn't be together the way he wants us to be because of his family or something. He talks in riddles."

"You tried a direct question?"

"Of course. He just avoids them. Then I get lost in his voice and those big dark eyes." The heat in Fin's cheeks grew and Saskia grinned.

"You think he drugged us?" she asked as if it were an everyday occurrence.

"Do you think he had sex with us?" Fin's shock at such an idea sobered Saskia.

"No, at least not with me."

"Not with me either."

"So, he's not some freaky rapist. Good to know. What else could it be?" Her eyes were bright, focused and seeking some answer from Fin that he didn't have – did he?

He gathered his scattered thoughts. Ordered the things he knew he remembered, collected the stray words and images, then began to string a narrative together. Meanwhile Saskia made breakfast but watched him out of the corner of her eye, patient as a tiger waiting to pounce.

"At the grove something happened. He says I ate mushrooms but I know I didn't. I remember seeing him in the water, it was him, but he glowed, like a god... like the images we've seen in the books. He helped me see things, feel things in the grove that don't exist —"

"Don't they...?" Saskia mumbled.

Fin focused on her. "Then last night I remember... Words... lots of them. We talked about a shared past I couldn't have understood. I remember seeing olive trees in a glade, tall grasses, goats and Drake, naked above me – we were about to – but then another man arrived, tall and powerful, golden, breath taking. He took me from Drake and it almost drove me insane but I had a job to do..." Fin's focus remained on the images inside his head, not on the present. The images were him, but they were also someone else. He saw the flesh of his arm, soft and curved, female. The woman Drake talked about?

Saskia drew in a breath, swallowed and said, "You had to fulfil your duties as the Oracle of Apollo's temple."

Fin stared at Saskia. "What the fuck is going on?"

She shrugged and continued to putter around the kitchen while she talked. "You always were special, Fin. It's why I love you, as a friend." She sucked honey off her fingers. "Eat. You need to eat after or you'll get wobbly really fast."

"How the fuck do you know what's going on?"

She shrugged again and bit into her toast, her bright brown eyes assessing him and waiting for something to happen. "How much are you ready to hear?"

"I think I'm going to be sick." Reality pressed down on Fin and refused to allow him to escape, to run, from the train he sensed coming for him at MACH 5.

"No, you aren't going to be sick. You're going to man up and listen to me because we need Drake and we need him on our side. You are the only thing he really cares about so you must make him work with us." She pointed her toast at him. "Are you going to listen to me with an open mind?"

"Do I have much choice?"

"No, not really. It just makes it easier if you're willing to listen and it'll save me repeating myself, which I hate doing."

How well he knew that as a fact.

"Alright, I'm awake and paying attention," he said, forcing himself to eat some toast.

Saskia chewed her lip ring for a moment before deciding where to start. "Okay, I think I have the place I need. You know things were bad with my family, right?"

"Yep," he said. Her typical understatement always made him sad. Things weren't 'bad' in her parent's home they were terrible.

"So, summers were spent with my grandma. You came down for two of them."

Fin smiled. He really liked her grandma. The cottage on the coast of Devon was full of the weird and wonderful. Old Ma Sassy, Saskia was her namesake, seemed to be the best sort of grandparent. More interested in what mischief you found than whether you took your shoes off at the door. The small cottage had everything from a phoenix feather to a dragon's skull. In fact, the first belonged to a magpie's tail and the second a monitor lizard from the local wildlife centre. Still, it meant Fin hadn't been made to be the adult his parents wanted for those few precious weeks in the summer of his sixteenth and seventeenth years.

"She is great."

"She is a witch."

Fin opened his mouth to scoff, saw the warning in Saskia's expression and snapped his gob shut.

Saskia nodded in satisfaction. "She's been tutoring me. I don't go home at all now. I just go back to Devon every holiday."

Christ, he really was out of touch with her life. Guilt gnawed at him. They'd parted as friends but Ajax didn't like her so Fin dropped her. It was a shitty thing to do because Saskia didn't trust people easily and he'd let her down.

"Okay, you're a pagan —"

"No, well yes, but no and before you ask it's not Wicca either. Old Ma is full Romany. She's also from the line that comes from Persia. Her father taught her the old ways and that means she is more of a sorcerer than a witch. So I guess I am as well." Saskia munched on more toast and sipped her coffee watching him over the rim.

"How does that help?" he asked, then realised he sounded a bit lost so asked again in a firmer voice.

"I can scry the past for us and find out what happened last night. Though I think I know but before we go any further you need to see it for yourself or you'll never convince Drake you can help him."

"Me help Drake? Why would he need me?"

"Because he doesn't trust himself. He's got that whole broken warrior thing going on and we need a fighter, not a remorseful ghost."

"I'm not certain forcing him to be something he's not is a good way of gaining his co-operation."

"He's a god, he'll do as he's told, that's his job."

Fin laughed, the hysterical edge taking him by surprise. "What?" Reality slipped in a muddy puddle and smacked down on its arse in the muck making him look like a fool.

"Just give me a minute and I'll prove it."

Saskia wiped toast off her fingers and found a saucepan in the cupboard. She filled it with water to the top. Then she raided the kitchen for a candle and found the lighter for the gas hob. Fin watched her do some exercises to help relax her neck and shoulders then she began muttering in a language he didn't recognise at all. The same phrases came again and again, in a soft voice making him drowsy and heavy limbed. If it had been anyone else other than Saskia he'd have been scared.

"Look into the water, Finbarr Wiseman."

The order came from a thousand miles away and yet he heard the command and obeyed. He looked into the dark water of the saucepan and ripples appeared despite nothing touching the surface. When the ripples cleared, he saw the grove and heard the voices, he watched Drake turn into something else, the woodland creature stepping out from the mighty oak and the colours in the water. The images changed and he watched his body collapse against Drake – Ares – and how tender the bigger man was as he lay the unconscious boy on the ground.

Next came the evening before, Fin's mouth dropped open as his body assumed new movements, the way it brushed his hair off his forehead, the quirk of his mouth, the look in his eyes... The words as well. The conversation Ares had with him – no – the Oracle. Drake had been shocked, confused and ultimately despairing because he thought they could never be together. Drake loved him. Ares had loved this Phemonoe and the Oracle.

Panic rose in Fin. "No!" He pushed the saucepan hard enough to send it over the edge of the counter. The saucepan hit the tiled floor with a crash and water shot everywhere.

Saskia grunted, woken from her trance by the deluge. "Bastard." She glared at him.

"No, no... No – this isn't right, this isn't my life. This isn't real. This isn't why I have weird dreams." He started pulling at his hair and backing away from the counter.

Saskia moved from her side and caught his hands wrestling them to stillness. "Breathe, Fin. I know it's a shock but I couldn't think of another way to convince you. If I'd simply told you what was happening you've never have believed me."

"I can't do this. Whatever it is."

"Yes you can. You've been doing it for years." Her voice held a patience that usually escaped Saskia.

He glared at her, furious and scared all at once. "What the fuck are you talking about?"

"All the times you knew something was wrong and you rang me before I started cutting myself. All the times you found things I'd lost because you cared enough to make things good for me. You have no idea what it's been like for me, losing you to the walking cock. You are my best friend, Fin, and you left me." Tears stood in her eyes and it calmed him at last. Saskia never cried.

He pulled her into his body and hugged her tight. Drake's issues could wait, right now he needed to be Sassy's friend. "I'm sorry."

"I know. I've missed you."

"I've missed you as well, I just didn't know it."

Saskia shrugged and pulled on the sleeves of her jumper. "It's not all your fault. Ajax is something you couldn't fight. I just had to be here when someone strong enough came along to break his control over you. Drake is that someone. You need to trust him, talk to him and you need to seduce him."

"I need to seduce a god? Of war? Have you any idea how fucking insane that sounds? I'm an Oracle? You're a sorcerer? What the fuck is happening? I haven't stepped through a wardrobe and no one's told me – right?"

Saskia took hold of his restless hands. "You're not just an Oracle, Fin, you are *the* Oracle. You are the latest in a long line of gifted shamans, druids, priests, saints, and preachers. Some of you go mad, some never manifest the gift. You are not mad, not yet, and you are strong. You are Ares' destiny."

Fin's world imploded with a soft poof. "How do you know all this?"

The tender sympathy in her expression made Fin's eyes tear. "Because my dreams whisper secrets to me, Fin. Some I can share, others I can't. It took me a while to figure out what Drake is but once I realised – the rest fell into place."

"When did you know?" Faint, he sounded faint.

"It all started to make sense yesterday but watching him last night confirmed it. He loves you and he can't help himself."

Chapter 9

IN THE GROVE BEYOND THE university grounds the weak autumn sunlight struggled to make it through the branches, never mind penetrate the few leaves left on the trees. Drake sat on a moss-covered rock and stared at the water trickling out, his chin resting on his fist, misery coating his broad shoulders.

"At least Rodin's Thinker looked a little more cheerful."

Drake turned and watched Fin approach. His back cracked as he straightened. He'd been sat on the rock for a long time, trying to find a way out of the corner the Fates seemed to have forced him into, he had yet to achieve his objective.

"You shouldn't be here, it won't help."

Fin stopped. The wind ruffled his hair, making the dark curls kiss his cheekbones. They annoyed Drake. Everything in that moment annoyed Drake. If he could find a way to really dislike Fin, he might just be able to save the young man's life. Drake turned away and scowled at the water.

"Saskia told me everything."

"Good for her." Drake realised what that meant and alarm shot through him. "What? How the fuck does she know? She was asleep."

"Oh, so you're not an all-knowing god then, just a run of the mill god. I guess that makes sense as you haven't smote Ajax yet, or are you saving that for the finale?" Fin didn't bother hiding his sarcasm.

Drake's anger notched up. He fed the monster. "You have no idea what you're talking about."

"No, I don't, not really. One minute I'm a third-year undergrad crushing on my PhD mentor, the next I'm the fucking Oracle of Delphi and you're Ares, God of War. Oh, and let us not forget my friend is a sorcerer. Not just a pagan Wicca, but a fucking sorcerer who can scry using a saucepan."

Drake paced, moving further away from Fin as if distance could stop the pain in his chest. "It's hardly my fault."

"Then whose fault is it, Drake? What's really going on? I'd love to know. Am I going to go mad?"

Drake heard the flutter of fear in Fin's voice. Fear meant hurt and Drake promised to never hurt Fin. The anger in him vanished. A puff of smoke had more staying power than Drake's anger with Fin.

He collapsed in on himself. "Sorry."

"For what exactly?" Fin sensed his changing mood, or maybe he predicted it, and approached the rock.

Drake shuffled over and they sat side by side. Fin's warmth seeped into his cold skin. "For everything that's going to happen because I came here. For turning your world inside out. If we'd never met you wouldn't know you were a vessel for the Oracle. You would have just been really good at finding people's keys, or lost pets, or knowing where your children were when they sneak out to go to a party."

Fin laughed. "So now I have teenage children? Well, that's an achievement. Can you even have children?"

Drake looked at him in shock. "What? Me?"

"Sorry, was there someone else I wanted a chance to fall in... um..." Fin ran out of steam and his ears turned very red.

Melting the heart of a deity, no matter how dysfunctional, wasn't easy but Drake's turned into cheese fondu as he watched Fin's fingers tie themselves in nervous knots. He captured the fingers and brought them to his lips, kissing a little warmth into them.

"You must be angry," Drake murmured.

"No, not really, more disconcerted and confused. I have questions – lots of questions – but at the moment I'm not angry. I reserve the right to be angry in the future though, so don't think you're getting off lightly."

Drake leaned into Fin a little, stealing more warmth and with it comfort. "I wouldn't dare to presume anything right now."

They sat and stared at the water for a while in silence, bodies touching but lost in private thoughts.

Fin broke first. "I have questions."

"I'm sure you do." Drake didn't turn to look at him.

"What was it like? Ancient Greece? Were you really at Troy? What was Achilles like? Or Odysseus? What about when you were Mars? Did that change you? How does all this work? What am I – exactly?"

Drake smiled in spite of himself. For so long he'd hidden in the shadows, decades, centuries passing without his presence creating even a blip on time. Fin's obvious joy at finding a primary source made the past rush forwards and for once Drake found comfort in the memories.

"Achilles wanted peace, he wanted to live out his life with Patroclus. He was beautiful to look at, especially when fighting. His skin shone like dark umbra in the sun. I loved him. Odysseus?" Drake chuckled and took Fin's hand, stroking the slim, soft fingers. "He was a pain in my arse. Funny, wicked clever, a manipulator and peacemaker where possible. Watching him twist and turn under his curse wasn't easy for any of those of us who thought the whole war with Troy should never have happened."

"But you're a god of war."

"Yes, but there were more important wars to fight. Better wars. Ten years is a long time to waste on a siege. And a woman." Drake snorted. "I never thought she was that beautiful. And Paris was a shit for not giving her up."

"He loved her."

"He loved the drama."

Fin nudged his shoulder. "Guess I'll have to take your word for it."

"And yes, being Mars changed me. Every iteration changes me. I become what my worshippers need or want." Drake considered a way to explain in terms Fin might understand. "It's like I'm a computer code. The base code is there and will always be the same – like Java – but overwriting the code changes the programming. Or it can."

"Wow. That must be confusing?"

Drake shrugged. "All things change, and it happens slowly. When there were many gods of war, the concept of me existed simultaneously in many places around the world. The version you're sat with is so different to Ares it's hard to believe I'm the same creature."

"You're not a creature."

Drake's smile became sad. "I'm not human either, Fin. You need to remember that."

"Neither am I apparently."

Drake shook his head, determined to grapple that problem immediately. Mortals thinking they weren't human led to them making mistakes and ending up dead before their time. "You're wrong. You," he poked Fin in the chest, "are human, the Oracle isn't. The Oracle is eternal and has existed in many humans."

"I don't really understand how this works."

Guilt nipped at Drake despite none of this really being his fault. "You're not meant to, Fin. I shouldn't be explaining any of this but I'm way beyond playing by the rules. The rules don't really matter when you're a shade within a shadow at midday, hardly existing. It's not like they can hurt me now."

"What do you mean?"

Drake heard his companion's worry. "When the Roman Empire turned to the new religion, then turned so many other tribes the same way, it drained the concept of me and I began to fade. Other monotheistic faiths grew in strength and also sapped the reservoir. I exist only because the concept of me exists in people's minds and souls."

"But there's been so much war since then."

"Yes, and I receive a tiny amount of the current created by the chaos and violence, but the thoughts and prayers of the people involved go to their core faiths."

"Christianity and Islam?"

"You said that, I didn't," Drake said. "I do not get involved in those creeds. Neither did I encourage my worshippers to target them or the Jews. Though I didn't welcome them either, they stole what I believed was my right – the prayers of warriors. I may have started a few wars just to piss off the new faiths, but it was a long time ago and I stopped interfering early on. All things should die, Fin, even gods. Though we fade."

"What do you mean?"

Drake stared at the tree on the other side of the brook. "Without worship gods fade or merge with other deities. Like we know Celtic and Roman gods did here in Britain. I'm a bit different because my function was strong, clear and I was worshipped by every soldier in every land for millennia. I had a powerful cult for a long time. Then it vanished. In terms of my existence, it happened very fast. I had neither the wit nor understanding to fight against it and couldn't gain worshippers through the saints, angels and other things the new creeds worshipped. They were faiths of peace – at least that's the rumour," he added with a rueful twist to his smile.

"What happened then? How are you here now?"

"As I said, I am here because war still exists and warriors still pray and some of that drifts my way. More by accident than anything else I think. It's a transfer of energy, Fin, so it's a bit difficult to explain. I have been so weak for so long I hardly remember what it's like to be Ares, or Mars. During the Middle Ages, despite the wars, I almost vanished. I lived in Greece, outside a small village, and kept goats. I was half mad and very alone. I think I was like that for centuries. Then something changed. Scholars began studying the Greeks, saving the philosophers words. Studying and learning about the ancient world. Men found my statues, my fireside altars in houses, then the temples built in my name or versions of me. They wanted to understand. Their curiosity became a form of worship and I began to regain myself a little."

Fin's eyes were wide and full of excitement. "Wow, that must have been weird?"

"It was. I was so close to not existing any longer. I could almost feel my creation vanishing from the world. I have often wished since then that it had happened. Another century and I would no longer be remembered. Alas, their poking and prying brought me and some of my brethren back." He lifted a finger when Fin opened his mouth to ask questions. "And no, I'm not telling you who. I have no wish to summon any of the brethren here and we don't need Apollo taking you from me again."

"That's possible?" Fin's squeak betrayed his fear.

"Very. My brother is possessive and difficult at the best of times. But, back to my story. The Renaissance dragged me from the brink. New statues, new paintings, even a few worshippers because the new creeds were losing control among the educated elite. I became stronger, wars became bigger and empires fought all over the world like never before. However, I had begun to change. I had lived among the children of the soil for a long time. I had learned to love the gentle life of a goat and the laughter of love. I mean the love of all things, not romantic love."

He paused and tried to swallow back the tears that always overwhelmed him when he had to think about the modern world too much. "Then the Great War began. I walked the trenches, unseen on the whole, I fought with men. I watched so many die. I tried to whisper guidance to leaders but they were too dislocated from their Mother, they couldn't hear me. They couldn't hear their God either. Then the second war came. Men, women, children, died for their faith. It happened before, has happened forever, but this… This wasn't war – it was a sickness I still can't fathom. Then the children of the soil created a new goddess in my image. One of such power she overwhelmed me."

"Drake?" Fin whispered.

Drake blinked. Damn, he'd lost himself again in memories. "Sorry, dear one. She is Annihilation. I was there. I am her father. I stood in the centre of that firestorm, created by splitting the fabric of life into pieces and by doing so, changing the very nature of creation."

"She is the atom bomb?" Fin's voice trembled but his body remained very still.

Drake nodded. "She has a power even I do not fully understand. Her creation, the death she wrought, tearing apart not just people, but every living thing – every animal and plant – then staining it in agony for decades, centuries, is just wrong. It changed me as well."

Fin lay his head on Drake's shoulder as if trying to lend some support. "How has it changed you?"

Drake dropped his head to rest on Fin's and breathed in the soft scent. "I am here studying the thinkers of the past in the hope I might find a way to peace for the children of the soil. Find a way to help Mother keep you all safe and well for the future. I want to find a new creed in the wisdom of the past when everything revolved around the life and death of seasons, the light and dark of the day and night, when humanity lived with Mother – rather than trying to tame and control her."

"You want to be a new god?"

Drake laughed, tickled by the idea. "No, I want to fade away and no longer be necessary. I'm hoping that by writing I might inspire some new way of thinking that will create a being of peace or using one that already exists and giving it a new life."

"Like Christ?"

Drake shrugged. "He makes the most sense, but his words are twisted and used for wars – I fear they are now too tainted in blood. I have no answers for you, Fin, only more questions, but I am not a god of war. Not now. I don't want to fight. I have nothing to offer that can save Mother or this place." He waved a hand at the fresh spring pouring from the shallow bank in front of them.

"That's not what the Oracle said, she said —"

"The Oracle has no gender, Fin. Don't refer to them as she."

Fin gave that a moment's thought. "Oh, okay. The Oracle seems to think you have a part to play."

"The Oracle is a pain in the arse."

Fin grinned. "Like Odysseus?"

"Yes. Very much."

"Saskia said you have to help. I have to make you help."

Drake's irritation rose to match his dark mood. "Saskia has an agenda as well."

"Don't we all?" Fin asked.

The reluctant nod was all the answer Drake could give, the weight on his heart heavy again.

Fin tried another tack. "You have to agree that what the Aegis Corporation is doing to this place is wrong?"

"That's your boyfriend's —"

"Ex-boyfriend, Drake. Heavy on the *ex* part. What they are doing is wrong. They have no right to destroy this place and Saskia needs our help to stop them. I'm not asking you to kill anyone if that's what you're worried about."

Drake snorted. "I've bathed in the blood of more enemies than you can conceive of in a lifetime."

Fin stood and stalked off a short way. "Thanks for that mental image." His anger flashed hot and Drake found his pulse picking up at seeing this fighting spirit in his potential lover. "You can't tell me you're a pacifist one moment, then say something like that the next."

Drake pushed himself off the rock. Almost salivating at the thought of taming the sudden wildness in Fin. "I cannot have two opposing thoughts and principles of being simultaneously?"

"No. Not on this subject. Do you want to see this place turned into nothing more than a leaking stain taking all the beauty and peace here with it? Do you want to see the old oak die?" Fin paced in his impatience.

"No, of course not, but it's not that simple for me —"

"Yes, it is, Drake. You can help. I'm not asking the god of war to come out to play. I'm asking the man I care about to help me help my friend do something good for this community. You have a personal charisma that Saskia and I don't have, you can rally troops to a cause, you can make people march on a concept. You know you can give the world more than just sitting in a library scribing notes studied to death by every thinker since those words

~80~

were first written. Did Socrates sit and write? Or did he march the streets and challenge authority because that authority was wrong?" Fin's passion lashed like birch twigs.

"He died for his cause."

"Men die. You said that yourself. Besides, I don't think Ajax is likely to kill me because I sided with the enemy."

"I wouldn't be so sure of that," Drake said. "What if I grow to like the power given to me by people who listen and believe my words – have you any wish to see me return to what I was?" He stalked up to Fin and drew on a little of the energy he kept leashed, allowing it to lick over the smaller man.

Fin stepped back with a hint of fear in his eyes and it pleased the darkness of war...

Drake closed his eyes and snapped off the tendril. "You could not control that beast if I use my gifts to turn people here to a cause such as this one." He waved a hand at the spring again.

"Maybe you should ask Mother what she wants?" Fin stepped back into Drake's space, not cowed for long by the anger. "Oh, yes, she has told you though hasn't she? Because I'm here. You're here. Saskia is here and who knows what else is lurking in the woodwork of the old building? We are here, Drake. We are here to make a difference to this place and if you sit on that rock and ponder the rights and wrongs of it, the world will vanish under your rather lovely arse. Is that what you want?"

Fin's passion and anger surprised Drake. They also warmed him, and his manhood began to stir. "You think my arse is lovely?"

"Oh for…" Fin threw his arms in the air and rolled his eyes. "Yes, Drake. You have a lovely arse."

The heat in Drake's blood increased. The power grew, feeding on itself as lust always did – lust and death. It warmed him, stoked the engine of his heart and revived his weakened soul. The darkness of war rose and smiled in hunger. Drake lost control of the shifting sands of time and place. "I should leave you alone, Oracle."

Fin took a step back, aware of a change but not what it signified. "Ares?"

The fear in Fin's gentle blue eyes shocked Drake. He drew in a sharp breath and turned away from his desire. "You need to leave."

"Drake?"

"Get away from me, Fin. The Oracle must be protected from me. Apollo was right. I will taint you if I touch you, touch the Oracle."

Fin shuddered and stumbled, the world tilting. "Ares, you are a fool. Take the boy. He wants you. Give him what he wants and become one with us. Become one with me. It is time. You are strong enough to control your base self. Trust me, Ares."

Drake moaned. The tug and tide of eons ran through him. Fin coming to disturb old memories in this place of power unpicked too much of Drake's hard-won humanity. It shred into pieces, turning to gossamer lace.

Fin's body jack-knifed and Drake rushed forwards with inhuman speed to capture him before he fell face first into the mud.

"Finbarr? Fin? Wake up, dear heart. Please." He held the smaller man tight to his chest, his palm cradling Fin's head, the dark curls snaking through his fingers. So soft, smelling of lemons grown in the sun of Greece. Drake bent his head over Fin's and inhaled the zesty musk.

"Drake?" whispered the stirring angel in his arms.

"I'm here, dear one. I'm here." He stroked Fin's soft cheek. "It seems I have been ordered by the Oracle to kiss you."

"Then perhaps you should."

"I want to do so much more than that."

Fin took back a little of his weight but didn't move from Drake's embrace. "You can, you will."

The young man rose from Drake's arms, stepped closer and those piercing blue eyes stared into Drake's lonely heart. Drake's breathing formed shallow puffs of white in the cooling autumn air, but his body prickled, as if doused in the heat of a Grecian summer. The scent of old oak and warm olive mixed in his mind, captured and joining the unique smell of citrus and warm books that infused Fin.

When soft lips brushed Drake's he shuddered, a quivering terror of desperate longing and need making him weak in front of this child of the soil who had arrested his attention the moment they met. Drake dared to reach out and capture Fin's slim hips, drawing him closer, turning the petal soft kisses into something firmer, more grounded and real.

Their lips sealed, parted and tongue's brushed, explored, tasted, invited. Drake's hands began to explore the strange new landscape of Fin's slim body and he felt Fin reciprocate with almost virginal curiosity. Drake's masculine body was only the second the young man had known.

SOME PART OF FIN'S MIND managed to register one fact while Drake took possessive control of his mouth and body – no one had ever kissed him like this before. The tender ownership of each moment of their intimacy shocked Fin. He never knew it could feel like this; powerful, intense, compassionate and giving. This must be what every sappy movie he'd ever been forced to watch tried to capture.

This was magic.

Drake's larger body dominated with a presence of protection rather than threat. Ajax always made Fin feel like he needed to worry and maybe even be fearful of the next stage. Drake made him crave what would come next. Fin didn't have much experience with anyone. Saskia had been his first and only woman, Ajax his first male lover, so this new territory blew him away. When Drake finished exploring his mouth, drawing forth small whimpers of need from Fin, he moved on to Fin's neck.

"Drake, Drake, I think, I think you need to stop."

Drake nosed at the tender spot he'd been mauling in a way that made Fin's knees go weak. "Why?"

"Because I asked."

Drake drew back in an instant, concern flashing through the passion in his dark eyes. "Fin, I'm sorry. Did I do something wrong? Did I hurt you? Was I too rough?"

He looked on the verge of panic until Fin gripped his face and planted a soft kiss on his swollen lips. "No, none of those things, but if you keep chewing on my neck I'm going to make a mess in my jeans. I've never been so close to coming without someone touching me and I think our first time should be somewhere a little drier and warmer?"

The smile that broke over Drake's face eclipsed the sun in Fin's mind. Drake gazed into his face, brushed his fingers through the tangle of hair and kissed his cheeks and nose. "Then I shall take you home and make love to you for hours."

"Not sure I'll last a minute if you keep making me feel like this," Fin said, unable to hide the tremor in his voice. The physical sensations were overwhelmed by the emotional ones, he had never guessed a kiss could open his heart so wide and it scared him. Drake must have sensed something of the turmoil because he coaxed Fin's head to his chest, tucking him under his chin and just stood, holding him close until the emotional mayhem subsided a little.

"Come, I'll walk you home. We have time, Fin, and I'm not interested in pushing you further than you can go. I will wait forever. I have waited forever, just to hold you."

Fin remained wrapped in Drake's warmth and said, "You're making it sound like you've been waiting just for me."

"Dear one, I have. I loved Phemonoe deeply. The creature I was in that time could not be controlled except by her gentle hand. Then I lost her and I have rarely, if ever, loved as deeply since."

Fin heard so much sadness and quiet acceptance in Drake it stole his breath for a moment – to be loved that deeply that you weren't forgotten for eons...

Fin looked up. "So it's the Oracle you love?"

Drake studied him, taking the question seriously. "I don't think that's it. I've been sat here trying to work it out. I think the Oracle might choose a particular soul to make its home and those are the ones I'm drawn to most? Does that mean I care more for them than you? No. I don't believe so. I think the Oracle drew me here, to you, but the Oracle is you, Finbarr, that is something we both need. Me and the Oracle. You are the magic ingredient in this equation."

Fin nodded and grinned. "Like a cosmic pizza? I can live with that."

Drake laughed. "Cosmic pizza... Yes, I can understand that concept."

Fin took Drake's hand, laced their fingers together and they began walking out of the grove.

Saskia

SASKIA SAT IN THE WEAK autumn sunshine and tried to soak it in as much as possible. The wooden bench under her arse remained damp from the night before, but she needed to feel the light. Last night had taken it out of her, despite sleeping through so much of it. Trying to help Fin and Drake find their path through the labyrinth of love wasn't easy. Scrying also took it out of her. However, she'd really enjoyed Fin's amazement at her growing talents. Her growing pride would be her undoing though if she didn't behave herself.

Two figures crossed the playing field from the direction of the grove, and she recognised them as Fin and Drake. A small twinge of loss coloured her joy at their obvious union as she wondered if she'd ever find her match in the world. Though so far so good on making certain all the players in this drama were in their required locations. Fin might be the Oracle but she had foresight and it showed her things would soon be coming to a pivotal moment. The world would either be better or worse for the coming conflict between the old god and the new soul eaters.

She watched Ajax and his cronies coming from the student halls behind the Union building, laughing and joking. One of them pointed towards the happy couple and Ajax stopped dead in his tracks.

Saskia allowed herself a wolfish grin. "That's right, walking cock, read it and weep. The god of war has stolen your toy and run off with it."

Ajax broke off from his pack of hounds and started to stride across the lawn towards the happy couple.

She jumped off the table. "I don't think so, fucker." Taking a sharp angle, Saskia moved to intercept Ajax. A short jog made sure she stood under a tree but in sight of the CCTV camera outside the Union bar.

"Looks like the walking cock has lost his chew toy," she called out.

Ajax turned at the sound of her voice. "Fuck you, witch."

Saskia laughed, a gleeful joy in Ajax's confusion making her reckless. "You have no idea, do you?"

"What?" He rounded on her, suitably diverted from his original objective.

"You have no idea. Fin's falling in love with Drake and you can't stop it from happening. You're not going to be able to feed off him anymore, soul eater." She'd waited months for this moment.

Ajax stormed towards her, glowering, rage pouring forth in waves, so powerful she could almost see them as well as feel them. "What the fuck are you talking about, bitch?"

Saskia allowed the moment to stretch. She took in his balled fists, flushed face, tense shoulders and knew she had pushed enough buttons. "You, the worst kind of emotional vampire out there. You've been feeding off Fin for months, but he now has Drake. Who is strong, kind, giving and will eradicate your power over Finbarr. No more food. No more direct connection to the Mother. You'll have to go back to taking sips from those foolish enough to be around you rather than bathing in the fountain Fin supplied."

"He'll come back." Ajax's words snapped out of his mouth like strikes from a riding crop.

She shook her head. "No, he won't. You willing to try to make him? You really want to face down Drake? Do you know who he is? Really is? You're no match for him, soul eater."

Ajax lashed out, the backhanded strike taking Saskia by complete surprise even though she knew it coming. She gasped, stumbled sideways and fell. It had been years since she'd last been hit by a man. Her vision turned spotty for a few seconds and her brain hurt.

"Shut your fucking mouth, witch, before I have you burnt at the fucking stake."

Saskia pushed herself off the ground, her cheek, jaw and eye smarting. "You are going to regret that, soul eater." She pointed at the CCTV camera watching over them, its red light shining in warning. "Good luck getting Daddy to bail you out of this act of violence."

For a moment she saw fear flicker in the back of Ajax's eyes but it didn't last beyond the few heartbeats their eyes locked. Ajax turned away and stormed back to his cohort, but Saskia watched in satisfaction as four of them looked at her, said something to their pack leader and left.

She waggled her jaw about and felt the bruise already coming to the surface. "Mission accomplished." Maybe not the best way of beginning to unpick Ajax's power in the university but it had worked. Feeling a lightness to her spirit she knew she'd have to hide if she wanted to play the victim, she returned to the Student Union to go in search of someone who could deal with the terrible crime of gender-based violence.

Chapter 10

DRAKE AND FIN ARRIVED AT the flat. Drake managed to get the door open, and both of them through it, before Fin shoved him against the wall. Having Fin in his arms unravelled Drake's self-control. The gentle humanity he nurtured with considerable effort on his part began to unpick, stitch by careful stitch. Fin's lips and teeth were exploring parts of his neck no one had touched in a long time. They were rubbing against each other and the promise of Fin's hard cock in his mouth or other more intimate places drove Drake to the edge.

He put his hands under Fin's tight arse and lifted. Fin grunted but wrapped his arms and legs around Drake like a vine and Drake managed to reach the lounge. They tumbled onto the sofa and ground against each other, yanking at clothing. The first moment their naked flesh touched Drake stilled.

"Damn, Fin, you're going to break me."

Fin now lay over Drake and grinned, his eyes glazed and dark with desire. "You know that's the plan, right? I'm going to drive you into a state of relentless need and make you promise me the world just so you can come all over me."

Drake moaned, his heart soaring even as his loins dropped into the darkest pit of sin imaginable. "Gods, and he likes to talk dirty. I'm doomed. Totally doomed."

Fin lowered his mouth to Drake's dark nipple and sucked hard making

Drake arch and cry out. Fin popped his mouth off and said, "I'm sure you'll get through it, big man."

Drake wasn't so sure as Fin's hand pushed under the open buttons of his jeans and gripped his cock for the first time. Drake loved everything about sex. Always had, the battleground of intimacy a magical realm he could use to dominate or submit without ego being involved. He could just surrender to need and give in to the emotions of the moment. This though, with Fin, burned to the core of him. Every nerve and fibre of his body lit with sparks and fire, all bending towards the younger, smaller man.

Fin held the source of wild flame in his hand, just as Prometheus had gifted, and drew all of Drake into that magical place. Drake realised he'd begun to babble words, ancient words in a language lost to all but the scholars. Fin slipped down his body and worked off his boots and jeans before pulling Drake's body free of the remains of his clothes. Drake just lay on the sofa and watched the slim strong body be revealed to him as Fin stripped.

Fin stood before him, proud cock jutting out of dark tight curls. Drake licked his lips, salivating with the need to taste. He glanced up at Fin's beautiful face and hit pause in his head. He saw a sudden weariness in his lover's eyes.

"Come to me, dear heart." He held out his hand for Fin.

"You've made love to goddesses…" Fin whispered, and his cock started to wilt under the pressure of his doubt.

Drake shifted, rolling onto his side and propping his head on his hand. "Yes. I have. I have made love to countless men and women over the millennia." Fin turned his face away. "Can I tell you something I have learned in all that time?"

"What?" came the sullen mumble.

Drake tried not to smile but failed. This pouting self-doubt made Fin too cute. "That beauty is very much in the eye of the beholder."

Fin frowned at him.

"Come and sit with me for a moment and I'll try to explain." Drake patted the sofa near his waist.

Fin sat, body stiffer than his cock. Drake stroked his back, marvelling at the clusters of freckles over Fin's shoulders. Then trailed his fingers down to Fin's slim waist. Fin stroked Drake's chest, sending shivers through him, before those slim fingers began tugging at the fine dark hair over his chest. Drake growled and struggled to find the words necessary.

"You are perfect, Finbarr. I have lovers, and I have those I once loved – there is a difference, and the latter is a far lower number. I have lived a long time and we do not love our own kind as we do the children of the soil. When we fall for someone like you it becomes a tether. A way for us to remain whole in the world we share for the time we are together. The old stories where children of the soil are changed into beasts or flora are part allegory, part fact. The children of the soil who love us have been used as pawns and weapons. It is not always safe to love a creature like me, but," he reached up to stroke Fin's hair, "I will never hurt you. I will never compare you to another. You are unique and that makes you a perfect jewel to me. Something to be treasured and cared for forever."

Fin smiled at him, a shy curve of his perfect lips. "You make a good speech."

"Of course. Who do you think inspires all those kings and queens when they go in battle?" Drake's smug expression made Fin's eyes sparkle and he laughed.

It warmed Drake and he coaxed Fin down to lie on the sofa under his bigger body. He started with soft kisses over Fin's face and neck, worrying at the sensitive places to make Fin squirm and thrust against his thick thigh. Experienced hands explored their new playground and found it inspiring. He worked his way down, licking the lemony musk off Fin's soft flesh and biting into the bone. Fin pushed his hips up to Drake's lips in blind need of something more and Drake, knowing they had time to tease and explore in the future, took Fin's cock deep in one smooth movement.

"Oh, fucking hell," Fin shouted, fingers tightening painfully in Drake's hair.

Drake hummed low and long, making his mouth and throat vibrate. He cupped Fin's balls and stroked the soft skin just behind but left the sweet pucker alone for now. He wouldn't push inside, not this time, that was a privilege he wanted to earn – he wanted them to be equals.

Fin started to thrust with little control over his body. Head thrashing from side to side, fingers hard in Drake's shoulder and hair. With almost no warning Drake felt Fin tighten, shout, his cock swelling even more, making his jaw ache before hot bitterness flooded his mouth. Drake drank and groaned as he tugged on his cock a few times. He shuddered at the violence and speed of his orgasm, his white seed covering his hand and belly.

When the orgasm started to ebb he remained buried in Fin's groin enjoying the soft sounds of recovery his lover made. Light and love, he'd not enjoyed a release that powerful in a long time. He suckled on Fin's softening cock.

Without warning Fin's body bucked hard enough to smash his jaw shut. Drake only just managed to pull away from the precious cock before serious damage might have changed their fates.

"What in Hades?"

Drake rose off the lean body as Fin's back continued to arch. His hands turned into claws, every muscle and tendon stood out, his beautiful face a rictus mask of agony.

"Fin! Finbarr?" Drake grabbed Fin's shoulders trying to hold his tortured body.

A sound, a high keening of pain, beyond anything heard in nature, crawled out of Fin and over Drake.

"No... No... Come back to me... Oh, no, please, Fin, fight it – whatever it is – fight..."

Tears leaked from Fin's eyes and slipped down the sides of his reddened, rigid face. Drake lunged over the taut body and reached for his phone. He flipped through the screen, cursing his messy fingers and hit Saskia's number.

"I need you!" he screamed down the line the moment he heard it connect.

"Drake?"

"Now! Get here now, I need you."

"Coming."

Drake dropped his phone to the floor. Fin's breathing came in pants. He should call an ambulance, but he knew it wouldn't matter – no doctor could cure this or prevent it. Drake lifted Fin's body off the sofa, mindful of the straining limbs and carried him into the bedroom.

"Oracle? Oracle? Can you hear me? It is Ares and I summon you to the surface... I am calling you to me. Oracle, I am the god of war. You must hear me. I command you to come."

Nothing.

He tried it in Latin, then ancient Greek. At that Fin's body began to shudder and foam started to form on his lips. Drake heard the front door open and close.

"I'm here!" he called out.

Saskia rushed into the bedroom. "Oh, fuck, you're naked."

Drake glanced at her. "Seriously? Get over here and help. Do something. You're a sorcerer – save him."

Saskia hurried to the bed and gasped. "He needs a hospital, it looks like epilepsy."

"Does he have epilepsy?"

"No, or he didn't when we were together."

"Then this isn't that, it's something else. I'm trying to reach the Oracle but it's like calling a busy line. I can't get through."

Saskia ripped off her oversized army jacket and gripped Fin's head. She closed her eyes for a moment before she yelped and stumbled back. "Shit." She shook her hands out, palms stinging. "You have to get in there, I can't do anything. The curse is too strong. I'd need weeks to work through the pain."

"He doesn't have weeks."

"No. He has minutes. You need to bulldoze his brain into sleep."

Drake opened his mouth to argue. He wasn't a healer. He didn't have the grace to finesse a human body or soul. He ripped people apart, he didn't repair them.

"Listen to me," Saskia snapped grabbing his face. "You have one choice – save Fin. Do whatever you must in this moment. It doesn't matter if you fuck it up because he's going to die if you don't do something. Save Fin, Drake. Save the Oracle, Ares. Do something."

Drake broke from her hold, opened his bedside drawer and removed a small wooden chest. He flipped the lid and removed a wooden handled bronze bladed knife. The entire object was no more than the length of his hand and weighed almost nothing but he'd owned it forever, a gift from the Oracle, from Phemonoe. Apollo didn't know he had it in his possession and Drake didn't plan on that changing.

Drake closed his eyes and began a litany in Greek, the words coming easily from memories still fresh even after all the centuries he'd lost his mind. The smell of sun baked earth, hot stone, the warm rough bark of the olive trees, brown grasses that were so beautiful in the spring after the rains, and crystal clean water in streams trickling among the trees and their bounty of bitter olives or sweet figs. Drake summoned it all and breathed power into the blade for the first time in eons.

With a firm hand he placed the sharp edge against Fin's breastbone, just under his throat, and drew down. The shallow wound filled with blood. He took the blade and opened his palm with one much deeper cut, the blood flowed and he held it over the slice in his lover's chest. Red mingled with red. He handed the knife to Saskia.

She swallowed hard and fear made her eyes big and bright. "Blood magic is a bit beyond me."

"Do it." He would make her if she didn't obey.

Saskia nodded. She cut her hand open, gasping at the sharp pain and held the open wound over Fin's chest, dropping blood into the stream falling from Drake's hand. He gripped her palm, then flattened both their hands over Fin's chest, smearing blood over the pale skin and shouted a final command.

Fin's body relaxed and he drew in a shuddering breath. His eyes opened, they were dilated and dark. "Save us, Ares," croaked the Oracle. "We will hold him to life as long as we can but he needs you."

"This isn't because I made love to you?" Drake asked, fear rendering his words a broken mass of syllables in a language only they could understand.

"No, dear one. Never. This isn't your doing. Ares, we can't hold on to this world. We have to save him…"

"Go, go, Oracle. I will find you."

"Love…" was the last sound he heard from Fin's pale lips.

Chapter 11

DRAKE AND SASKIA SAT IN the lounge, blood cleaned off and Drake in jeans and t-shirt more for her benefit than his modesty. Fin now seemed trapped in sleep and his wound had been bathed and dressed.

Drake noticed his hand shook as he swallowed the brandy he'd poured for himself and Saskia. She watched him with wide eyes, her entire body quivering in shock.

"If you're looking for answers I don't have them," he said.

"Well, we need them."

"Agreed." He rose and poured himself another large measure. The warmth from the strong spirit didn't touch his soul.

"I take it the two of you were enjoying yourselves?"

He nodded, then frowned as he looked at her. "What happened to your face?"

She managed a half grimace and touched the deepening bruise. "Wow, I'd forgotten. I thought it would be the only dramatic thing to happen this week. Ajax hit me." Her careless statement might well have been cannon shot smacking a castle wall.

Drake rose and snarled. Brandy sloshed over his hand soaking into the bandage and making the wound sting. "I'll kill him."

"Slow down, big man. I baited him into it and the university are likely to throw him out because of it. I'm hoping the video camera evidence I managed to arrange will be all the proof they need. I was on my way to the police station to make a statement."

Drake looked at her in astonishment. "Why the hell did you let him hit you?" Drake's outrage didn't lessen but a healthy dose of confusion, on top of the strange day he'd already had, calmed him enough not to start ripping the town apart looking for Ajax.

Saskia shrugged. "No big deal. It's not the first time I've been given a slap and probably won't be the last with my mouth."

He'd sensed this vulnerability in her from the moment they met. A powerful woman-in-waiting, but one who had been under the control of a vicious brute, maybe more than one.

"No big deal?" Drake put his glass down and caught one of her wrists. She tried to pull back but he kept a firm hold, turning it over. Dozens of old scars littered her forearm, most across the limb but one thick scar ran up her arm. He dropped to his knees in shame and grief. "Oh, Saskia. I'm sorry."

She stiffened and tugged on her arm. "Not your fault, big man. Now can I have my arm back please?"

He released her hand, a sense of helplessness and fury battling with the need to allow Saskia space to be in control. Drake fought to remain calm, at least on the outside. "Anyone else I need to kill for you?"

A sniff and a tight nod. "Not right now, but I'll keep it in mind for the future."

"Do that. You have my protection now, sorcerer. That's no small gift. Use it." He pinned her to the chair with his gaze.

Saskia again made a tight nod and covered her arm with her sleeve. "Can we talk about what the hell just happened?"

Drake sat, the energy draining out of him at last the moment his mind returned to Fin. "Fuck knows."

"I don't understand. You've never seen this before?" she asked.

"Have I ever seen a lover have a fit like that after we've had sex? No, witch, I haven't. I don't usually make my lovers sick." Drake rubbed his hands over his face and growled.

"Alright, no need to get personal," Saskia muttered. "What were you speaking?"

Drake sighed and sat back on the sofa, closing his eyes in a quest for peace which would never come while Fin lay so still, so silent. "Enochian. It's the only way I could think to ground him to his body. It's like his soul is turning into lace. Bits of it drifting off. The Oracle understands the language and I managed to call them from the deep. Summoning Oracle is never a good idea – they come to you. I've never done it before and I hate using the language because others can hear, and I don't want to summon more chaos to this place. If my kind start showing up at the university then things will become messy. We can't be trusted to behave if too many of us are in the same place. I've no wish to become what I was because they are here."

"The language of angels to save your angel."

Drake managed a sad smile. "Something like that."

"Tell me more about the soul shredding. What did you see?" Saskia asked.

"What do you know?" He suspected she held something back.

She shook her head. "Not until you give me more. I don't want to give you more of an imperative to hang someone until necessary."

Drake snorted. "I won't be hanging anyone. I'll rip them limb from limb when I find out who did this to my boy."

"Thanks for that image," she muttered.

"Alright, for the sake of argument, I'll explain what I saw and why I did what I did. Blood magic is the most powerful there is – you and me, even in my current state, are strong, powerful. Pulling the Oracle into the mix just added more spice to the mix. By combining the life force of the three of us I could create a barrier around Fin even if I couldn't call him back." Drake stared into the dead fire. "And don't think I didn't try, but whatever has hold of Finbarr's soul, it won't let go."

Saskia's brown eyes were wide and bright, taking in all the information. Drake wondered how wise it was to explain deep magic to someone so young and inexperienced. Saskia already had more knowledge than she should and to give her more gave her more control and power. Knowing gods walked the land and that the language of angels could be used in blood magic was a heady combination for a child of the soil.

She snapped Drake's attention back to the present when she asked, "Will Fin get his soul back?"

Drake shrugged. "Until I find out what's going on, I don't know. If I can't get it back, he'll either be soulless and therefore a shell of a human with no emotion, or mad, and he'll never go into the underworld – his soul will be trapped in this world forever. Unless he's already there of course." The thought of Fin dead or dying caused such pain Drake gasped and rubbed his chest.

"Can you ask if he's there?"

"Disturb Thanatos or worse the Keres?" Drake shook his head. "No. War, death, we've travelled together too many times to be safe. Besides, I wouldn't know where to find him. The idea of the afterlife has changed so much I'm not sure what remains of my old comrade or his disturbing sisters."

"What about Hades?"

Drake laughed. A cruel and bitter sound, so sharp he had to stop before he cut Saskia. "No. You don't want one of them involved."

"Them?"

"The fathers and mothers to us."

A knock at the front door disturbed them. "Leave it." Drake poured himself another drink. The knocking continued and Drake's phone began to ring.

Saskia picked it up. She frowned. "Dr Moran."

Drake rose took the phone and swiped to answer. "Dr Moran now isn't a good —"

"Open the door, Mr York." Dr Moran hung up before he could reply.

Drake stared at the phone for a moment. He went to the door and opened it. The small woman pushed past him and walked into the lounge.

"Where is the boy?" she asked.

Drake opened his mouth but Saskia said, "What the fuck are you doing here?"

Dr Moran turned to look at her and the energy in the room shifted. Drake moved to stand between the women and stared at his tutor. The dawning realisation as to how much he'd fucked up hit him at last. His instincts on the day they'd met told him Dr Moran hid something from him but he had no idea it was this serious. "Oh, shit. Cerberus."

Her eyes shone like new pennies in the light and made her feral for a moment. "I wondered when you'd realise. Foolish godling," she snapped at him, more terrier than hound in that moment. "What have you done to my best student? You have always been driven by your lusts."

Drake withered under her stare and authority. For the first time in centuries the stroppy child inside him, not the man, wanted someone to side with him, not just scold him. "It's not lust – I love him."

Dr Moran, *Cerberus*, snorted, then sniffed the air. She turned away from Drake and followed her nose. He trailed after her, not at all surprised when she found his bedroom and the sleeping Fin. He watched as she took his hand and closed her eyes for a moment, sensing, delving, questing for answers inside the child of the soil.

"Is this safe?" Saskia asked, touching Drake for the first time.

He looked down at the young woman. "If you're asking me if she'll eat him then no, I doubt it, but is the person or thing she decides to hunt safe? That's a no. I've hunted with Cerberus more than once. War and death, little witch. War and death. We are one and the same."

"Sadly," stated Dr Moran. She sat on Drake's bed and pushed back Fin's hair. "I came here to live in peace teaching the children of the soil something of what the world used to be like, but then *they* arrived." A growl, lower than any a mortal being could make rumbled out of the small middle-aged woman.

"The soul eaters?" Saskia whispered.

"Indeed. You always were a sharp one, Saskia." She patted Fin's hand and looked up at Drake. "We need to put a stop to them, Ares. He's one of my best students. I want him back."

"Soul eaters? Is that what I'm feeling when I'm around the walking cock?" Drake asked Saskia.

"The what?" Dr Moran asked, placing Fin's hand back on the covers.

"Ajax, walking cock," Saskia said as she returned to the lounge.

Drake gazed at Fin. "She doesn't like Ajax."

"I don't blame her. I'm not fond of him. Smells bad."

"Like death bad?"

"Worse. Far worse than any corruption I've scented in a child of the soil and that's saying something."

Drake nodded. They had both stood in the presence of mortal evil over the years. "It's good to see you by the way."

"Liar."

He chuckled. "Maybe. I've been alone a long time."

She stood and approached him. Drake pressed himself back into the doorway without really being aware of what he was doing until his spine hit the brickwork. Cerberus was not a creature to be crossed.

His tutor sniffed him and huffed. "You've been speaking naughty words and doing blood magic. That's what woke me from my afternoon nap."

"At least it wasn't our noisy sex."

Dr Moran's eyes lit up for a moment, the amber colour a long way from human. "Oh, I haven't watched a god fuck for eons. It's always such fun."

"Go, dog breath. I'm not entertaining you or any other of your kind." He meant the creatures of gods, denizens of the other worlds revolving around their earthly one.

Dr Moran's mouth twitched in humour. "You never used to be so picky."

"I've learned some discretion."

She muttered something he didn't catch.

With one more long look at Fin lying in his bed, Drake shut the door trying to find a way to calm his weighted and broken heart. Soul eaters? What the hell were soul eaters?

FIN WOKE, HIS EYES OPENED and the world came into painful focus, but he didn't recognise any of it. He sat bolt upright. "Drake?" Fear slithered along his skin.

The bed he occupied was of simple construction. Wooden planks with posts at the four corners, covered in woollen blankets and sheepskin. The room itself was small, maybe two metres wide and three long. White washed walls and a simple wooden door. The ceiling seemed to be constructed of beams with some kind of thick reed layered under flat looking stone, probably slate. A three-legged stool stood nearby and a bucket sat in the corner away from the bed. A small, high window let in pale light but not a view.

He looked down at his body. He no longer wore jeans and a shirt, but some kind of cloth nappy.

Fin's heart pounded as his bare feet touched a smooth earthen floor and he opened the door using a rope handle to peer outside. He looked at an olive grove. Sand coloured stones, sparse tufts of brown grass, plants that looked like they might be herbs, and the trees with their grey brown twisting trunks and narrow dark green leaves. The air didn't move, the temperature warmed him, and he couldn't smell anything other than fresh air and a wafting of herbs.

"Hello?" he called.

"Ah, you're awake."

Fin yelped and jumped sidewise spooked by the new arrival.

A wide grin spread over a young face. The goat the person milked bleated but continued to chew on the grass.

"Who are you?"

"Oracle."

Oracle, the genderless hitchhiker in his head. They were androgynous to look at, slim, youthful, dark complexion, covered in a simple toga of white, hair cut short, face neither male nor female.

"Where am I?" Fin asked, well out of arm's reach.

"Somewhere safe – for the moment at least. Your physical body is in Ares' possession. Due to his blood magic I managed to bring you here. This is where I," Oracle shrugged as if looking for a definition, "exist if you will, inside my companions. I like it, it's simple."

Fin glanced around him again. "Erm, yes, it's very nice. Thank you for inviting me."

Oracle shrugged again as if the matter was neither here or there. Their hands kept milking the goat, the squirt the only real sound other than the buzz of insects and occasional tweet from a bird.

"What do you mean by blood magic?" Fin asked.

"Hmm, yes, that's not so good. The only thing to do under the circumstances. You were dying and Ares —"

"Drake, he prefers Drake."

Oracle opted for a single shoulder shrug this time. "If you like. Drake decided you had to be saved. He's very attached to you already. You should know that can be difficult. It broke the last companion he and I lived with."

"Phemonoe?"

Oracle nodded and smiled, they seemed to be pleased Fin understood. He didn't understand, not really. He wondered if this was some kind of psychotic break.

"Drake told me Apollo took Phemonoe away because you were to be protected?"

Oracle cocked their head. "Yes, you could say that. Or you could say Apollo didn't want Ares to have the power of prophecy in his bed. Apollo controlled me for a very long time. Centuries."

"But not now?" Fin approached Oracle, who sat on another simple three-legged stool.

"No, not now. Not at the moment. At the moment we are free and we are happy to have Ares' company again."

Fin shook his head, there didn't seem to be much point in reminding Oracle, Ares had morphed into Drake and Drake didn't seem to want to be Ares any more. He seemed to want something more out of his existence than bloodshed and chaos.

"Can you predict how all this is going to work out?" Fin asked.

"Prophecy isn't the same as foresight and no, I don't know how all this will work out. Not at the moment." They cocked their head and frowned.

"Which is odd come to think of it but that's just how these things work – or don't work – depending…"

Fin's sense of confusion and apprehension continued to rise. Too much had happened in too short a time to deal with this new twist. "You mentioned blood magic…" His voice faded into a bleak silence.

Oracle smiled. Every emotion displayed on their face looked practiced rather than natural. A learned response and therefore somewhat extreme and a little alarming. "Yes. A mighty spell using the sorcerer's blood as well. I wonder what effect it might have in the long-term? I can't seem to see that either – which is odd." Their expression cleared. "Maybe Apollo is right and I should not have permitted the sexual congress with a god. That would be disappointing, I rather enjoyed it."

The thought of this strange being hitchhiking his private space made Fin's bone's ache. "I don't plan on turning Drake down if that's what you want."

"No, I don't suppose you will." Oracle rose and took the bucket out from under the goat. "Would you like a drink?" They held the bucket towards Fin.

Until he'd come to a rural university he'd never been close to a cow, never mind a goat. "Um…"

"You'll like it – promise." Oracle's dark eyes were wide and innocent of guile.

"Alright." If this was happening in Fin's head, the milk would taste like normal supermarket milk because that's all his memory could give this intense delusion.

The smile on Oracle's face made it clear he'd chosen the right course of action. Oracle put the bucket down, reached over the goat and picked up a small cup of rough clay. They dipped it in the milk and held it out. Fin took it and sniffed. Pungent but not unpleasant. When he placed the cup to his mouth he tasted the warmth and thick cream of real milk. Oracle was right, he really liked it. A strange buzz in his blood made him feel as if he had connected to something fundamental, an essence to the world. It also became clear it was not a delusion because it tasted nothing like milk from the supermarket. Did that make this real? Maybe more real than the world he'd left behind?

"A connection to Mother," the Oracle said without him having to say a word. "Many children of the soil feel it when they do something with a direct link to the animal or plant they consume that's unique and pure. It's like coming home is it not?"

Fin smiled and drank a little more, the rich pungent taste easy to like now. "Yes, that's exactly what it's like."

Oracle nodded, seemingly satisfied with his answer. "Come, we'll have some more with olive bread."

Fin watched Oracle open the door to the simple room he'd woken up in with some confusion, but when he started to follow, he saw the room no longer contained a bed. It now looked like a simple peasant's central room from any century in the last four or five thousand years. A roughhewn table dominated with benches on either side, all clean and pale. A hearth sat in the centre of one wall, the fire in embers and giving out little heat but adding something cosy to the room. An area which could be described as a kitchen took up the space where his bed had been. The room also seemed larger and a window now looked out on the trees and the goat, still tied to the house. Fin made no comment, deciding to roll with the weird for now at least.

Oracle waved at him to sit, so he did, and watched as they prepared a simple meal of olive bread, goat's cheese and more milk.

"How long will I be here?" Fin asked.

Oracle shrugged, their favourite physical descriptive it seemed. "Don't know. Besides, time is a little confusing here. Sometimes I've moved companions several times and never known until I see different fashions or skin colours. It can be confusing."

"I'm sure it can." Fin pulled off a chunk of bread. Gritty flour, bitter olives but also fulfilling. He chewed it far more than he would a slice from the supermarket. "Can I do anything to help Drake – Ares?"

Oracle smiled again and Fin decided it was an alarming occurrence no matter how normal Oracle tried to be. "Yes. There are things you can do. Not dying is a good idea. I think that might tip Ares into behaving rather badly. I don't think Europe needs another war."

Fin choked on his bread. "Erm, no, that wouldn't be wise. Staying alive is a good thing. How do I do that here? Am I safe?"

Again with the shrug. "Not sure I'd use the term safe. I've never had a companion here before so I don't know what I'm doing. A little unnerving for a being as old as I am."

"I guess so," Fin said.

"Dip the bread in the milk, it's lovely." Oracle offered more milk. Fin did as instructed. Weird but it worked. "You might be safe, providing the soul eaters don't find us."

Soul eaters? That didn't sound like something Fin wanted in his life. "What happens if they do?"

"Then they will finish what they started and we will both be destroyed." Oracle didn't look concerned at this turn of events.

Fin's alarm though shot off the scale. "What? What does that mean? Can I have a little more detail? What the fuck are soul eaters?"

Oracle placed both hands flat on the smooth but unpolished surface of the table. "I shall try to explain. A soul eater, that unpleasant young man you saw fit to take to your bed, has been feeding on you – on us. He knew you were something special because he could smell it, as he did with your friend the sorcerer, but you were easier for him to catch. It is why he wanted you separated. She can sense the darkness in him."

Fin detected a hint of disapproval in Oracle's gaze and tried to hide his amusement. "You're talking about Ajax?" Fin would have laughed at the thought, but instinct kept him quiet and so many things began to fall off the cliff and into place. "Okay, Ajax is bad and I'm an easy lay, but what's he doing? What is a soul eater? I don't remember them from Greek myths."

Oracle shook their head. "No, they are not a part of our pantheon. They originated in the new world and travelled back to Europe on the ships to find rich pickings among the remains of the old faiths before moving on to the priests of the new ones."

"I don't understand."

"They suck the souls from the children of the soil and those who have brushed against the power of the gods are the most tasty. They give the soul eaters more life, more power, more time to corrupt Mother. They want nothing more than to feed but they have learned to hide in plain sight. They have become like you."

"They're like vampires?"

The Oracle looked confused for a moment, as if scouring an internal database for information, before giving a single strong nod downwards. "Yes, like that, like vampires, only they suck on souls not on blood, though they like that as well."

The milk churned in Fin's stomach at the thought. "What do I do to stop it from happening?"

Oracle gazed out of the window, now behind Fin's left shoulder. "I don't know, but one of them is trying to complete the ritual to gain the power you and I share."

"That doesn't sound like a good idea, Oracle."

Their face fell and became sad. "No. It isn't a good idea. It would make it hard for Ares to kill them because he is very weak. He is soft like pudding in comparison to what he used to feel like."

"Well, I like this version of him. I'm fairly sure any other version would scare me witless."

"I'm sure you are right, companion. Children of the soil are very different now to what they once were."

Fin's sense of justice made him want to defend Drake. When they'd been wrapped up in their passion nothing about Drake felt soft like pudding. Maybe he was different to the being Oracle remembered but Drake didn't seem to like the version of himself that had been Ares, and Fin needed to trust that Drake could solve this problem, not Ares.

"We have to do something to help them save us from these soul eaters." Fin knocked on the table top to draw Oracle's attention away from the window.

The distant stillness that wrapped around the Oracle every time they stopped moving or speaking broke again. Oracle said, "Yes. It would be wise to help."

Frustration burned through Fin and he realised Oracle didn't have a clue as to how to stop the soul eaters. Was it because they came from a different cosmology? Did these different beings, conjured it seemed from humanity's desire to explain the world, understand that different cultures had different monsters? Drake understood but Oracle wasn't a god and didn't seem to function in the same way.

"I can't believe this is happening to me," Fin muttered and rubbed his chest. He didn't know why but it hurt now, right in the centre of his solar plexus. Was that where Ajax was pulling at his soul? How could he stop it? Visualisation seemed a tad too passive and New Age considering he was dealing with ancient gods and monsters. "Is there another name for these soul eaters?" he asked Oracle.

"What do you mean?"

Fin considered how best to put his thoughts together so Oracle could give him a clear answer. "Ares is known to me as Drake. I assume there are others like him walking the earth, walking Mother?" Oracle nodded in their precise manner. "Alright, what if the soul eaters are really something you know but have changed? Like Ares has? What if they are something you know how to fight, Oracle?"

"I don't fight."

Fin closed his eyes and begged for patience. "No, you'd rather milk goats, that much is clear. But I have to fight so I need your help."

Oracle seemed hurt by Fin's comment, their face clouded and unhappy. "I suppose they can be likened to some witches, but most resemble succubae and incubi. Or even better the empusai." The Oracle smiled, as if that would answer all their problems.

This didn't feel like good news to Fin but at least he'd heard of them. He knew from experience that Ajax's sexual appetite rendered him weak and unable to think clearly for long periods of time. It's why he'd stayed with the controlling prick for so long. Too weak to leave until Drake turned up. "Good, so how do we kill one of them? Or at least stop them."

Oracle moved to lift their shoulders again. Fin pointed a finger and said, "Don't. No shrug allowed. I want to know, Oracle. There must be something we can do to help the others."

The Oracle sighed and returned their gaze to the window. "Maybe," they murmured.

Chapter 12

DRAKE RAN HIS FINGERS THROUGH his hair and groaned. Dr Moran stalked around his home and Saskia watched her with big eyes, knees tucked to her chest as if afraid the older woman might turn into a three headed hound of hell at the drop of a hat. Drake needed an army to obey him right now, not an overgrown dog and a delinquent witch.

"An army..." Drake whispered, the glimmer of plan beginning to take shape. "We need to stop the Aegis Corporation, and we need stop Fin's soul from being sucked dry. These two things are happening at the same time and being perpetrated by the same family. A war on two fronts."

"Don't we need to figure out how to kill soul eaters?" Saskia asked.

Dr Moran waved away her concerns. "Everything dies when you bite out its throat."

Saskia went pale. Drake decided to intervene before his presence turned Dr Moran back into Cerberus permanently. "No throats until we know what we're dealing with and we know we won't be left with bodies. I don't have the ability to sway a police investigation or the ability to ferry them away and no, you're not devouring them." He stared Dr Moran down.

The old dog dropped her gaze in submission.

"How and why are you a professor at our university?" Saskia asked.

Drake realised the young woman had reached the end of her tolerance for weird and couldn't move beyond Dr Moran being Cerberus – guardian of the underworld. If she didn't move past it, and soon, she wouldn't be any use to Drake.

Dr Moran sat and Drake couldn't help but think about no pets on the furniture rule in his contract with the landlady.

The lecturer in Dr Moran took over when she started to explain, "Once the children of the soil started to forget about Hades and created their demons and devils I slipped away from the gates, crossed the Styx and made my way to the surface once again. Hercules took me out the first time and it was terrible. I knew what to expect the second time so I adjusted slowly. The hell hounds, created by those who took demonology to extremes, grabbed my place and I was happy to let them, naughty puppies that they are."

Drake found himself interested despite his desperate need to save Fin. "Why take the form of a mortal and learn to be a professor?"

Dr Moran looked at him with her strange amber eyes. "Why not? I found with a little practice I shift forms like any other lycanthrope. This form stops me being pestered by males and I like learning. You *can* teach an old dog new tricks, Ares. You know that better than most. You just have to be patient. I have time to learn all sorts. This place has been kind to me because of the sacred sites hereabouts and I love the room to roam without all that nasty heat further south or the cold further north."

Drake had an almost irresistible urge to pat Dr Moran's head. As if able to read his mind she fixed him with a stare so fierce he mumbled about more tea and vanished to the kitchen. Saskia joined him.

"She scares me."

"It's not Cerberus you need to worry about. I think Dr Moran is more scary myself. Cerberus is not violent unless you go against the laws of Mother, so leaving the underworld is not permitted. If she bites you then expect a nasty death, she created Wolf's Bane."

Saskia's eyes widened further. "Really? That's aconite, that's on my list of favourite poisons."

Drake raised an eyebrow. "You have a list?"

"Doesn't everyone?" she asked all sweetness and bright smiles.

Drake rolled his eyes and carried tea back into the lounge. "What can you tell me about soul eaters?"

Dr Moran sucked air over her teeth. "They were once known in Europe as empusai and fed on blood, bones and the souls of men. My guess is they have morphed just as the rest of us have but retain their essential elements, so we have a 'family' here and they devour souls of power if they can get those foolish children to have sex with them. Finbarr Wiseman is clearly not living up to his name and being one of those foolish enough to fall for their seduction."

Drake bridled at this a little. "It's not like you stopped him."

"I tried. I told him Ajax wouldn't be good for him. Ever tried stopping a young man from making a silly mistake over a serial seducer, Ares?"

Drake felt his skin flush red. "Point taken."

"Thought so."

"How do I kill them?"

Dr Moran shook her head. "You don't want to kill them. You need to stop them. If you kill them there's a chance they'll take Finbarr with them. If you stop them, you might get him back, then you can destroy them – which is different to just killing their mortal forms."

Drake growled in frustration and ran his fingers through his thick hair tugging it through the tangles. "Can't anything be simple?"

Dr Moran chuckled. "When has any of this nonsense been simple?"

"How do we get Fin back? That's all I'm interested in at the moment." Drake sat on the sofa and watched Dr Moran pace around his room, picking things up and sniffing them. How she managed to hide her nature from other people he had no idea, or maybe she just found his presence reassuring and could be herself a little more than usual.

"We know Ajax is the one pulling on Fin but we need to see if anyone else is helping him. I've met his 'parents' at university functions and they smell bad, like acid from a battery, but they don't know me and I'd like to keep it that way. They have great wealth and control over the entire town."

"We need to see who or what is controlling this spell of theirs." His attention turned to Saskia, as did Dr Moran's. She wilted a little under the scrutiny.

"I… um… I'm not sure…"

"You gave Fin my location in the grove."

"That was easy."

Drake raised an eyebrow. Nothing about scrying that well was easy. "You can track this spell they are using and find out where it comes from?"

Saskia began picking at a hole in her jumper. "Maybe."

"Maybe's don't work in battle," Drake snapped.

Dr Moran snorted. "No, because you never took a risk in battle."

Fed up with the sniping from the chorus Drake bit back. "Listen, you old dog, you can either support me or you can fuck off back to your kennel."

Dr Moran raised her head. "Less of the old and I'm not a dog, I'm a hound."

"I'll do it," Saskia broke through their bickering. "But just so you know, I'm doing this for Fin not for you two."

Drake smiled. "Good, I like getting my own way. Come on, I can do better than a saucepan for scrying."

He led the way to a small room at the back of the apartment. What would normally be a single bedroom contained a desk, computer and piles of books from the library and local bookshops. Drake might not move around the world with many belongings but once he settled he did love to collect things, they helped locate him in the present and his chosen community.

"There are some things I've found over the years and some I've never managed to lose or they found their way back to me so I've kept them safe," he said, dropping to his knees and rummaging on a shelf. "Found it." He rose and held a small bowl made of metal with inscriptions and image covering the surfaces both inside and out.

He gave it to Saskia while Dr Moran rifled through his books.

Saskia turned it in her hands. "It's beautiful."

"I've owned that for a very long time. Lost it over the years, but it always finds its way back to me. The story is of Selene and Endymion. I think it'll give you a very clear image. Do you think we should use wood ash and blood for the scrying?" he asked Dr Moran.

She lifted her eyes from the book in her hands. "Where did you find this? I've been looking for years."

Drake's eyes narrowed. "Concentrate, please."

Dr Moran took the bowl from Saskia and turned it in her hands. "I think water will do, let's not draw them back by using our blood. If we had a lamb or a calf I'd say use them, but we don't, unless there are stray children we could use?"

Saskia made a small sound of protest.

Drake reached out and lay a hand on her shoulder. "She's joking. We don't sacrifice children. We have never done that."

Dr Moran muttered. "Tell that to Agamemnon."

Drake bowed his head. "I tried to stop that foolishness."

Removing the scrying bowl from Dr Moran's hands, Saskia backed out of the room. "Listen, guys, if you want me to do this, you need to keep the ancient politics out of my head. I'm having a hard enough time hanging on to reality as it is and listening to you two talk about stories of myth as though they happened yesterday isn't helping."

"Of course, sorry. It's been a long time since I've been around my kind," Drake tried to sound reassuring but he watched the cracks beginning in Saskia's self-control. She took a deep breath that seemed to help a little and they returned to the kitchen.

"What do you need?" he asked the young sorcerer.

"Quiet." She ran the bowl under the tap and filled it with water almost to the top. The bowl looked larger in her small hands, but she held it easily, the intricate design and fine metal decoration making its weight insignificant. The surfaces of the kitchen were clean so she placed the bowl down. "I could do with some candles and incense."

Drake went to fetch both from the lounge area of the large room. They placed the candles either side of the bowl and the incense at the top, Saskia forming the fourth point of the circle.

She washed her hands and face, lit the candles while muttering under her breath and then the incense, wafting the smoke over the bowl to help combine fire, air and water. Drake watched her with interest, impressed with her professionalism. Whoever taught her knew what they were doing. The element of earth would be the scryer in this instance because they didn't want to tether Saskia's vision to a specific thing.

Words continued to flow out of the young woman and she gripped the sides of the bowl with her eyes screwed shut. Her voice grew louder and the water began to vibrate. Drake peered over her shoulder, as did Dr Moran and he smiled as a picture started to form.

"You are strong, young one," he murmured in approval.

The water formed little wavelets that spat over the edges of the bowl for a moment before it settled with preternatural speed to stillness. Ajax sat in a room that looked like every jock's bedroom the world over. He was cross-legged on the floor, naked, and staring into a full-length mirror. His cock stood proud between his thighs and a look of intense concentration marred his handsome face.

"Got you, fucker," Drake snarled. "He's using the mirror as a channel into the other realm to pull on Fin's spirit."

"That means he'll break through the defences you raised to keep Fin with the Oracle," Dr Moran said.

Drake grunted, well aware of Fin's vulnerability and his failure to protect the young man. He placed a hand on Saskia's shoulder and pushed just a little. She stiffened and the vision deepened. Ajax's physical form shifted and, in its place, squatted a dark form of long limbs and fattened body. Greenish-black skin covered the creature, and its face was flat except for a stump for a nose with long slits like a vampire bat, the eyes like those of a shark, dead black and emotionless. The head had no hair and the ears were more like suggestions than things of purpose. The hands were oversized and the feet too small. The fingers long and twitching as it dragged a thin ribbon of gold into its open mouth. The creature's black tongue flicked and swished over the ribbon, its sharp and widely spaced teeth glistening with drool.

Thick lips were also wet and covered in a sheen of gold. The belly of the creature stood proud and full.

"Fuck, that's ugly." Dr Moran turned away.

"He's still pulling on Fin despite the work we did."

"Why isn't Oracle helping him fight?" She looked up at Drake, concern in her amber eyes.

"Oracle doesn't fight. They are not designed for it. They don't know how or why it's necessary. Their host dies and they move on, that's all they know. They don't fight for their companions." The fingers of fear trailed cold over Drake's back making him shiver. "We need to break that mirror and the creature's ties to Fin."

"I suggest you draw the sorcerer back or it will sense her," Dr Moran said.

Drake removed his hand from Saskia's shoulder and she jerked hard, the water in the bowl spilling over her hands. The image vanished and she wobbled until Drake looped an arm around her waist. "I've got you."

"Get the fuck off me." Saskia pushed him away, fury snapping in her eyes and twisting her mouth. "What the fuck did you do to make me see that fucking monster? It felt like being covered in acid and it stank."

"Oops, someone's over it. The witch seen through your charms already, Ares?" Dr Moran retreated from the kitchen and walked around the island to the lounge.

Drake glared at her but spoke to Saskia, "Sorry. I had no choice. I've never seen a soul eater. I needed a clear vision of what we're dealing with and how it's draining Fin."

Saskia rubbed her shoulder where he'd held it. "Next time, ask. I am not your toy to be used at your convenience."

"As you wish, sorcerer," Drake said. He bowed his head in a gesture of supplication. Her skills were powerful and he'd pushed her further than her training allowed, it would have been painful. He needed Saskia and forcing her against her will would only give him something else to fight. Definitely, not the plan. His remorse was genuine and still a new emotion, only learned over the last hundred years or so.

"I need a shower." She glared at him.

"Through my bedroom. Don't touch Fin on the way." He stood well back from the doorway as she walked through.

Dr Moran watched her go. "You shouldn't have done that without her consent."

"I know. I didn't think. Sorry."

"You can't command or commandeer her, Drake. It's important she feels she has free will. Times have changed."

He heard the soft warning in Dr Moran's voice. The gentle reprimand a scolding smack against his guilt gland. "I know, I'm sorry. I'll make it up to her."

"Make sure you do. So, how are we going to smash that mirror?"

Drake leaned his elbows against the kitchen island and blew out the candles but kept the incense going, its sweet musky scent reminding him of the peace he once felt in the temples of old.

"I think we are going to use Enochian to make a ward."

"But we don't have angel blood or essence and you need both for it to be truly effective."

Drake drew in a deep breath. "The essence of a god should do it don't you think?"

Dr Moran's breath hissed over her teeth. "Dangerous, Drake. Really dangerous. Enochian is the language of angels and not meant for the likes of us. We are different to them."

"The soul eater is a demon. You could see that as did I so we need to use angel knowledge to defeat it."

"Your essence and your blood will twist the ward. It'll make the damned thing unpredictable. You don't know if it'll damage Fin or Oracle."

Drake threw his hands up in the air. "What do you suggest? He's going to die anyway and I'm doing nothing at the moment."

Saskia walked back into the kitchen, water trailing over her shoulders and off her back from her dreadlocks. "My clothes smelt bad, so you can wash them. I borrowed some of yours." She glared at him as if defying him to argue. She'd chosen an old sweatshirt that fell around her thighs like a dress.

He watched her and merely nodded. "Fine, whatever you need."

Saskia huffed and sat on the chair, as far from Dr Moran as she could get, drawing her legs up to her chest, and hugged her knees. "What's happening? How do we save Fin from that thing?" She shuddered.

Dr Moran glared at Drake. "He has a plan." Her dismissive tone made it clear she didn't approve.

"We don't have time to experiment. This plan will get the job done," Drake stated.

"Yes, but at what cost? He's not just a child of the soil. He's the vessel for Oracle. You have no idea what will happen by mixing supernatural concepts so readily. It's against all the rules and advice."

"Supernatural concepts?" Drake asked.

"You know what I mean." Dr Moran rose and began pacing the room again. She huffed in frustration. "Damn it, I can't think of another way."

"What if we just kill Ajax?" Saskia asked from her corner of the room. "Can you do that?" She looked at Drake with big eyes.

It pained him for a moment. Such innocence in her thoughts. This murderous idea only meant as a way to protect her friend. However, the act of murdering a person, justified or not, weighted the scales in ways too complex for innocence to understand.

Drake understood. He knew more about taking life through an act of violence than any other being roaming the world. It certainly made his scales very heavy.

Despite, or maybe because of this he smiled, pushing against the darkness in his memories. "For you, dear lady, I will do anything, but know that murder is not always the answer. Killing that creature's mortal form won't work. Dr Moran is right, it'll just come back. We need to save Fin, then plan how to destroy them all. One step at a time, one battle at a time."

"You're not giving me a plan."

He made a decision, crossing the room he knelt in front of Saskia and placed his hands on her small knees. "You've done enough. Given enough. I'm sending you home and Dr Moran will escort you. There is no safer companion on this campus than with her as your protector."

"No, I should be here. I should help."

He bowed his head, unable to meet the gaze of a young woman with faith, hope, and optimism in every heartbeat. She believed the good and the righteous won against evil in the world. Drake's experience spoke of different things. The capricious nature of his actions in the distant past were just a mirror to the awful things his family did to so many children of the soil. Drake wanted to be better. He wanted to help the children of the soil, not manipulate them into giving power to deities who rarely deserved the prayers and faithful gifts given by communities of impoverished people. He no longer wanted to favour those with the loudest voices, the most wealth, the men with the power to wage war.

"It's not a good idea, Saskia. There are some," he searched for the word, "events that should be outside the human experience. This is one of those. I am not comfortable sharing such secrets."

Anger lifted its head and snarled at him through her eyes. "Are you saying you don't trust me?"

"She's got you there," Dr Moran piped up from behind him.

"Enough from you." He didn't turn to face the other creature in the room. "It's not that I don't trust you, Saskia —"

"You just don't think I'm worth taking into your confidence because we're all 'children of the soil' and worth nothing to you." The contempt dripping from her words like poisoned treacle made it hard to match her stare.

"You might need her, Ares."

"For fuck's sake, will you stop calling me that." He rounded on Dr Moran. "Whatever I am now, I am not that. I don't want to be that."

Dr Moran rose to meet his anger. "We can morph and change as much as we like, Ares." She poked him in the chest. "But, dear boy, we cannot change our elemental sense of self."

"You are wrong." She had to be wrong. Drake desperately needed her to be wrong.

"We're wasting time." Saskia rose from the chair. "I'm helping. I have to help."

He looked at the tiny girl, her dreadlocks hanging over her shoulder, his oversized sweatshirt leaving her thin knees exposed, and her bony clavicle. He thought about the scars on her arm and all the pain she'd endured to cause them. Saskia might have an innocent soul but her heart knew how scary the world truly was and she still wanted to face danger and fight. Did he have the right to deny her the battle ahead?

He rubbed his face, exhausted by the ramifications of his decisions. A firm hand grasped his arm and he looked at Dr Moran. "Free will, Drake. That's all you can give them in the end."

The weight of Saskia's fate dropped onto his shoulders and he felt them bow even further. Children of the soil should have the right to choose, especially when they were working with or against children of the heavens and children of the underworld.

"Very well, this is what's going to happen."

Chapter 13

DRAKE LIFTED FIN'S INERT BODY and carried it outside. The ground floor apartment came with a small and well-tended garden. The upstairs rooms were unoccupied so Drake didn't fear being overlooked. Saskia lay a blanket on the grass and Drake placed Fin down with tender care. He looked too pale and his breathing came in fits and starts. They didn't have long. Drake brushed the soft hair back and brought the cooling hand to his lips.

"I'm so sorry."

Dr Moran squeezed his shoulder. "If you hadn't arrived Fin would have been dead by Easter. I can't stop the soul eaters; I just try to warn those who will listen from associating with them. I never wanted to draw attention to myself for fear they would come after me. I like it here, but it does come with side-effects."

Drake pressed Fin's hand back on his chest and rose, ignoring the older woman. She could have done something other than give Fin some vague warning about Ajax being a bad apple. Turning Fin into a victim because she didn't want to expose herself to danger made Drake angry.

"Let's do this." He removed the bronze dagger again. "Are you clear on what's going to happen?" He looked to Saskia for confirmation.

She nodded, her mouth a grim line. "You're going to form a warding sigil on the ground with your blood, then you're going to stab yourself and pour your essence into it, bringing life to the magic. When the ward is alive and bright, I stem the flow of power coming from you because you'll be busy controlling the energies created and driving them at Ajax and the mirror."

"Good, next?" he asked.

"Next, Dr Moran will pace the circle in her true form to prevent any other nasties coming into or out of the circle of power. She has your back. When I see Fin stir, hopefully his eyes opening and recognising either me or you, I draw a line through the warding symbol and break the power, leaving Ajax without a path back and yanking you out of his reach. You'll most likely faint but I'm not to worry – apparently."

Drake could see the fear in every tired line of her face. It had been a long night as they'd discussed ways of making this work and keeping everyone alive.

"Dr Moran?"

"I kill anything we haven't invited to the party. When you come back I guard you until we know it's safe." He watched as the form of the diminutive professor morphed into the huge hound of legend. Saskia gasped in shock and took several steps back into Drake. He took gentle control of her shoulders to prevent her bolting.

"Only the one head?" he asked.

The creature lifted her lip in a snarl.

"Okay, only the one head."

"She's beautiful and terrible all at once," Saskia whispered.

Drake had to agree. Cerberus was a hound, not a dog you'd have in your house, or a wolf. A heavily muscled sleek creature coloured a thousand shades of bronze and copper with huge shoulders, wide head, upright ears and broad muzzle. A tail, slim in comparison to a wolf's, wagged.

"You win, Cerberus – I'm impressed." Drake released Saskia when he realised the young witch wouldn't run screaming to the nut house demanding to be let in.

The hound dipped her vast head.

"Good. Let's get this done. Dawn is close at hand and we'll use that to give us the boost required to reach out. Questions?"

"One," Saskia said holding up her finger, "why shouldn't you use angel magic? Aren't you just another iteration of the warrior angel Michael?"

"That's two questions I don't have time to answer but the short version is, no. We are not angels – nor do we wish to be. If there are no other questions let's get on with it."

Drake closed his eyes. He drew in a deep and slow breath, concentrating on his heartbeat, like any good modern sniper with a target in their sight. He slowed his racing thoughts. He concentrated on the intent of their actions. He visualised the outcome he wanted. He spent time building all these blocks and laying the foundations of the hardest battle he'd fought for a long time.

Far more at ease with a sword or a bow or a gun than with these dark elemental forces, it took patience to push his fears and doubts to one side. In the end he used the feel of the grass under his naked feet, the soft soil under that, and the smell of the ageing night bringing the sounds of owls, foxes and snuffling hedgehogs looking for places to nest. The air tickled his face, shifted through his fingers and eventually brought Fin's sweet scent to his nose. Citrus and old books, that's how Fin smelt to Drake.

He sought the words he needed for the enchantment and they came easily to his tongue. Enochian tasted of old elemental forces more powerful than anything Drake felt comfortable using. He spoke with care, the words leaving brands of a taste like scotch bonnet chillies on his tongue and the insides of his cheeks and throat. As he spoke he walked around Fin's body in a circle, digging his toes into the ground with each stride. Once around clockwise. He turned, lifted the dagger to the east and the rising sun before stabbing the blade into his left arm and cutting down in one swift movement. Muscles tore, blood vessels opened and Saskia gasped. The pain further grounded Drake and he pushed it into the ground as an offering in itself to Mother, begging for her protection while they performed these dark rites.

He walked anti-clockwise and poured his blood over his feet, the heat vivid against the cool damp grass. The words continued to flow and he walked over Fin's body, drawing the sigil with each step, the blood trailing off his fingers. From north to south, east to west and back to his origin.

Meeting Saskia's pale but implacable face he nodded and she echoed his movement. They were ready. Drake fixed his gaze on Fin's still and beautiful face. He lifted the dagger in both hands and plunged it into his solar plexus before ripping it downwards. In a mortal being their intestines would now be a pile of steaming offal in the cold dawn. Drake wasn't mortal and despite being a weak god he had enough skill and power to save this one man from the dark. His knees buckled and he dropped to the ground. The words stuttered. A huge dark shape took up residence at the northern part of the circle and stared at him with vivid amber eyes. He took his courage from Cerberus and picked up the litany, pushing the terrible pain back, further back.

Golden light, brighter than Fin's, poured from the wounded and opened soul of a god. It hit the blood sacrifice. The light raced around the circle, a flame devouring the blood as if it were petrol. Drake emptied his soul into the angelic circle. He pictured the soul eater and his mirror as seen in the scrying and raised his voice, dagger dripping blood and gold from the ancient bronze blade.

Mother took notice. The wind lashed at the trees the moment the sun broke over the horizon hitting the god of war.

Drake's entire form shifted. His academic persona vanished and, in its place, knelt a creature of masculine perfection clothed in intricate armour. He roared his defiance.

"Nothing will take this child of the soil from me." With a hand outstretched Ares grabbed at the vision of Ajax, grabbed at the body of the soul eater, several miles away, and snapped his fist closed.

The dawn screamed in pain. Crows took to the fading night. Murder after murder rose from the treetops adding their mournful wild chorus and the wind rose still further. Cerberus lifted her vast jaws and howled, every dog and fox in the valley answering her cry.

Ares saw the soul eater snap its mouth shut in shock. Its dead black eyes widened. It stared into the mirror, seeing Ares clearly. He grinned, savage and terrible. The soul eater, Ajax, scrambled backwards, away from the mirror. Ares stepped out of the mirror, the surface shattering around him, showering Ajax in glass.

"Your time here is done." Ares lifted the shocked Ajax off his feet and threw him against the wall. The impact dented the plasterboard and Ajax collapsed onto the bed.

"Who?" Ajax asked, eyes wide with shock and fear.

Ares towered over the cowering monster. "I will destroy you. This is your one warning. Leave this place. Leave Finbarr Wiseman alone."

Back on the ground in the garden Drake flexed his fist. The body of Ajax arched on the bed and he screamed.

Fin jerked hard on the ground and sat bolt upright.

Saskia, as good as her promise, rushed to Ares' side and pressed a towel to the hole in his guts, stemming the flow of power into the circle. With the energy cut off, Ares vanished from Ajax's bedroom and returned to the garden in a snap so harsh Drake swayed and hit the ground. Saskia rubbed at the sigil with her foot and broke the power of the spell. The wind died. The crows settled. The dawn painted her colours over the sky in silence and everyone asleep in the town and university rolled over from disturbing dreams and slept in peace once more.

Chapter 14

"DRAKE." FIN'S FIRST THOUGHT DROVE him upright. The night sky had faded to purple and the east showed the promise of safety in daylight. Fin felt something sticky over his chest but didn't have time to check. He saw Drake just a few metres in front of him, on his knees, swaying as Saskia held a soaked towel to his guts and tried to stem the bleeding in Drake's arm. *What the hell was going on?*

A huge hound came out of the shadows. "Holy fucking shit balls," Fin cried out.

Its head far exceeded anything he'd ever seen on the Discovery Channel; the ears were upright and swept back to fine points. Did dogs even come this large? The amber eyes didn't hold any hostility but he scrambled to reach Drake.

"What the fuck is going on?" he asked.

"Fin, meet Cerberus. Just help me stop Drake bleeding out, would you?" Saskia ordered, shoving another towel into his arms. "I thought when he had stopped the spell he'd heal. Why can't he heal?" She looked over Fin's shoulder at the four-legged beast.

A low rumble became words. "Too weak."

Fin started in surprise. The vast hound talked? What the fuck was happening in his life?

Saskia moaned. "Great. Just fucking great. You need to help me get him inside before the neighbours wake up." Saskia wriggled under Drake's arm and Fin took the other one after tying off the bandage.

"We need a hospital." Fin's mind galloped, trying to join together dots he didn't have, to understand what the hell was happening in this perfectly normal garden.

Saskia looked at him with contempt. "Yeah, hospital, that sounds like a great plan. 'I know there is golden light flowing out of this stabbing victim, Doctor, but he's a god so it's perfectly normal. Can't you just stitch him up and we'll be on our way?' On three we lift."

They struggled but between them they managed to help Drake stand and stumble into the apartment. "Need rest." The words were barely there but they continued their journey into Drake's bedroom and lay him on the bed. The vast dog padded around sniffing then left the room.

"Saskia, what's going on?" Fin asked.

"We just have to stop his essence from flooding out. That includes his blood."

A new voice said, "Let me help."

Fin turned in surprise. "Dr Moran?"

"Finbarr Wiseman."

"Where?" The last thing he remembered he'd been in Drake's arms, the post orgasm bliss rising through him.

Saskia huffed. "Not now, Fin, concentrate on Drake before we lose him. Can you heal him?" She looked at Dr Moran.

"Not really my area of expertise I'm afraid. I tend to specialise in keeping souls out of bodies, not keeping them in." She pushed at Fin's shoulder and he moved.

"I don't understand what's going on."

Drake's hand flexed in his and Fin looked into the dark eyes. "Hold me. Tell me you care."

Fin's eyes widened. "Shit, of course. Worship." His entire mind lit up like an Olympic torch.

"What?" Saskia asked, still pressing down on the wound in Drake's stomach. It leaked but it wasn't blood, something dark and almost oily now slid out.

"Sacrifice," Dr Moran cried out. "Of course, well done, Ares. Well done." She began to mutter under her breath.

Fin looked at her, aghast. "You know?"

"Not now," Saskia muttered again. "I'll explain everything – but not now."

Dr Moran looked over at Fin. "Right, you need to lie down next to him, curl around him, do whatever it takes to keep him awake. Saskia you're coming with me, we need to find something to sacrifice."

"I'm vegan."

"Now is not the time, girl. Come."

"Fucking hell..." Saskia climbed off the bed and followed Dr Moran.

Fin realised he had blood all over his body but there seemed to be blood just about everywhere. "What happened, Drake?"

"Ajax tried to kill you. I made him stop. I'm so cold, Fin. Talk to me..." The dark eyes weren't focusing on Fin's face and Drake's skin appeared waxy, like the embalmed death masks Fin had seen in the museums.

"Alright, I'm here. I'm not going to leave you." Fin lay down. He took Drake's large and cold hand in his, opting to ignore the blood seeping through the towel. Instinct drove his actions, probably those of Oracle. "Do you know what it was like the first time I saw you? The moment I saw you in that chair by the receptionist desk I knew I wanted you. Thoughts of being in a relationship with Ajax drifted away on smoke. You are the most beautiful man I've ever seen."

Drake took his first deep breath. "I fucking hate you have to do this to save me. It makes me feel pathetic."

"You hate the fact that you need help? Everyone needs help, Drake. You helped me, it only seems fair."

No response and Fin knew, just knew the answer lay far deeper, looked much darker, than Drake feeling vulnerable in a moment of weakness brought on by battle injuries.

Fin's sudden awareness of Drake's reality made him ask, "Is it because you need to be worshipped to exist?"

Drake nodded. His eyes so dark they were black, the whites red from exhaustion.

This mystified Fin until he realised what it meant. Drake couldn't exist without people adoring him. It meant he had to be perfect in their eyes. Be the personification of war that *they* wanted him to be rather than the person he wanted to be – because he wasn't a man. He was a myth, a creation of imagination made manifest.

He didn't know what to say. How could a being, as powerful as a god, hate the very thing they represented? How could he reconcile the energy given to him by those obsessed with his bounty in battle with what he wanted to be – an academic this time, a goat farmer before, maybe other things in times gone by? Nothing Fin had in his limited arsenal of life experience could give him a way to make this right for Drake.

Slumping into silence, Fin curled around Drake and whispered, "The man I met in the hall that day, the one who smiled at me the moment he saw me, he's the one I..." Fin stumbled, too soon, much too soon. "He's the one I want to spend time with, he's the one I want to know. He is funny, kind, generous, clever and so tender with me. That man went to battle for me, not the warrior of old, not Ares, but Drake. Drake York is my hero."

Looking into Drake's face Fin watched tears well in the dark eyes. Their noses were almost touching. "You're supposed to be feeding Ares." Fin had to strain to hear Drake's whispered words.

"It's not Ares that's important to me, Drake." Fin reached up and traced the sharp, hard jawline, stubble pricking his fingertips. He stole a kiss.

The tears on Drake's eyelashes fell. "No one has ever said that to me. My entire existence it's all about the war and bloodshed."

"Then the world is full of foolish creatures, because you can be so much more. You understand the very essence of violence and how it motivates those who feed off its chaos. War does so much damage, so much harm to nations, to people but it's inescapable apparently. We are bent on destruction, just as we are on sex and food. It's just another aspect to humanity. There's nothing you can do to change human nature."

Drake managed a small chuckle. "There is that, my wise young friend." Fin watched Drake blink as if fighting sleep. "You know, most nations believe they are doing only good by waging war. The Romans didn't think it was wrong to wage war. They believed their way of living was the best way. Their laws, their towns and cities, so much more civilised than the rest of the world. I believed it to in those days."

"You don't now?" Fin asked, his interest genuine. How often did you get to ask a god questions about existence?

"No. The children of the soil need to stop fighting and squabbling over resources or whose god is best. Mother needs peace and help to survive. I know this but still I will have to fight to make it happen. I will have to cause death and destruction. How can I exist in this dual state, having to kill to find the peace Mother needs, the peace we all need?"

Fin watched the effect of Drake's words, the pain in his face, in his soul. The terrible anguish. The knowledge he would never escape the weight of his existence and he'd carry the burden throughout time, until humanity either stopped fighting or died out.

"Sleep, Drake. This will be easier to bear after you sleep." Fin stroked the broad forehead, pushing back the tangle of black hair. The dark eyes closed and his breathing evened out. Fin remained, lying beside his broken lover and just trying to imagine the toll of his grief. It made him weep in sympathy and it hurt to know he could do nothing to protect Drake. Nothing.

At some point the door to their room opened. "Fin?" Saskia whispered.

"Here." He removed his hand from Drake's and wriggled off the bed, making sure he didn't wake the sleeping figure.

When he reached the lounge he found Dr Moran and Saskia. A cat box sat on the kitchen unit. It held a cat.

"What is that?" he asked.

Both women looked at him. Dr Moran shrugged. Saskia dropped her eyes to the ground.

"Sacrifice."

The cat meowed.

"What?"

"We don't have time to find a calf," Dr Moran said. "A cat will do."

"A cat most certainly won't do," Fin told her and he rounded on Saskia, "I can't believe you went along with this."

"She says it's the only way."

"She's a hell hound. Of course she can sacrifice a cat." Fin moved away from the poor creature who looked at him with big green eyes. The cat's fur looked wet, a pretty little tabby thing.

"I'm not a hell hound. They are quite different and the species of the animal is not my preference it's expedient to use a cat, there are a lot of them around and they are stupid enough to get caught."

"I can tell you one thing for certain, Drake's not going to thank you for killing an innocent creature in his name. You can take the poor thing back where you found it and think of another way to help him." He approached Saskia. "I'm ashamed of you."

Saskia looked at Dr Moran who now sat in the large armchair, wearing a mask of indifference. "Have you tried to say no to her? She's terrifying."

They both studied the older woman. Saskia had a point, Fin found Dr Moran scary before he knew she was Cerberus, now he knew, he had a feeling his essays would be considerably better.

"What about a libation?" he asked his tutor.

"A libation of blood is the best," she said. "That's what the sacrifice is all about."

"He really won't want you to do this. We can't kill a cat for him."

"He's gone soft."

"He's changing, you might want to remember that," Fin snapped, knowing they were running out of time.

"We have the bowl he gave me for the scrying. We could use that and put something of value inside."

"Like what?"

They both looked to Dr Moran who sighed. "Okay, you can use anything really, but wine, beer maybe, olive oil, even rice or grains. It depends what you want to do. If we're trying to heal his soul…"

"Ambrosia?" asked Fin.

Dr Moran snorted. "No. You can't do that, you don't have enough to spare." When she saw their confusion she said, "Ambrosia is a mortal's soul. You give it to the gods to feed on through worship. They drink it. Making it a substance to consume is a metaphor."

"Fuck me this is confusing," Saskia muttered. "Okay, but honey is defined as an ambrosia and if we believe it can help it will – right? We set up an altar, find a physical representation of Ares or Mars or whatever, and we can…" she pulled a face, "pray to it."

Dr Moran shrugged. "It might give him enough, though I'd use wine."

They set to work.

Saskia found the bowl she'd used for the scrying. Dr Moran raided Drake's office and found a small but perfect bronze statue muttering, "The vanity of the man." Fin found wine in Drake's fridge but instinct told him it wouldn't be enough. He had the fastest shower in history to clean off the last of the blood and mess before he slung on his coat and marched to the nearest supermarket.

The doors were just opening as he arrived. Students rarely managed to make it this early unless they were under the influence of the munchies so the two members of staff nearest the doors eyed him with caution. Fin didn't think buying wine this early would enhance his reputation as a good customer, but it didn't stop him standing and staring at the wide variety available.

"How the hell do I choose the right one?" he muttered. Taking out his phone he searched the web for 'best wine to use in a ritual'. Strangely the web didn't have much to say on the subject that was helpful but the number of sponsored ads made his brain hurt.

A man walked in whistling and approached the wine selection as well. "Good morning," he said with a wide smile on his hawkish face.

"Morning." Fin's eyes dropped to the man's throat; he wore a vicar's white collar.

"Not for me obviously," the man said and winked. "For the man upstairs." He pointed to the ceiling and chuckled at his own joke. He took a few bottles off the shelf and still whistling went to pay for them.

"Fuck it, if it's good enough for Him, it's good enough for Ares." Fin took a few bottles of the same brand, paid, and hurried back to the apartment.

He found the women in the back garden. They had moved an iron bench to the centre of the small, winter dark lawn. Saskia wove the stems of daisies and grasses together to make a long necklace and they had two bowls, the small one Drake had given to Saskia and a larger one Dr Moran had in her office.

They were arguing over who should do the prayer.

Fin didn't think they had time to be arguing over who or in what language. "I'll do it. This is my fault. I need to make this right and I'm the one emotionally involved." He wanted to say 'I'm his boyfriend' but somehow that didn't seem to fit and Drake had never mentioned anything about their relationship status.

"With respect, Finbarr, I can perform the ritual in his original language and we've been, if not friends, then colleagues a very long time." Dr Moran's amber eyes were calm and focused.

Fin felt anything but calm and focused. "The Oracle —"

"Probably shouldn't be invoked under these circumstances."

Christ, there was so much of Drake's life he would never understand. How could he? Fin nodded and handed over the wine.

Dr Moran paused, she closed her eyes, drew in and released a few breaths, then opened her eyes. They shone deeper in colour than usual and Fin could swear she almost glowed with vitality. Her words began as a whisper on the soft wind and she walked towards the 'altar' with slow, measured steps. Saskia took Fin's hand and drew him back, then pressed down on his shoulder so he knelt on the damp grass.

The words became stronger, more forceful and the trees echoed the strange language as the wind pushed and nudged their branches, yanking at dying leaves to toss them around the small woman and the garden bench.

Dr Moran lifted the chalice over her head, raising it to the risen sun, then to the autumnal setting moon. Her voice grew deeper and Fin's blood raced as he felt a tug on his soul. The tug turned into a steady pull and he gave into the sensation willingly. The words started to fade into the morning light and Dr Moran poured the wine over the flowers and into the offering bowl they had found, transferring the power from one vessel to the next and with it the prayer and salutations she offered.

The ceremony finished and all three occupants of the garden remained still.

"What now?" asked Fin when an eternity seemed to slip through his impatient fingers.

"Personally? I could do with another drink."

Fin turned and grinned. Drake stood in the doorway with black hair trailing over his naked shoulders, jeans slung low on his hips, and a small tabby cat in his arms.

Chapter 15

"SO LET ME GET THIS straight – you were going to give me a blood sacrifice using the cat?" Drake stood in his kitchen and looked at the three miscreants. The cat drank a bowl of milk at his feet.

"Seemed like a good idea." Dr Moran picked leaves out of her hair.

"I'm sure it did to you," he said. "Chasing cats must be part of your exercise routine."

She looked at him and growled low in her chest. Drake decided to stop pulling her tail.

"Are you all fixed?" Saskia asked.

He wondered about the wisdom of lying to them. During the night they had unleashed a storm of consequences none of them could predict. Not least of which was the continuing threat to Fin. He gazed at his lover and made a decision. Truth always comes into the light at some point, lying to them would only place them in more danger.

"No, I'm not all fixed, but I'm strong enough to continue for now. We need a strategy though; these soul eaters are going to destroy all of us if we don't do something to control them."

"Control? We can't control them. We need to destroy them." Dr Moran began pacing the living room area. "They almost killed Fin and they took a healthy chunk out of you. If I hadn't been here to help Saskia it would have taken you months to come back to any form of strength – if you could have done it at all." Her frustration burned through the room. "Whatever you might think, Mr York, you need to go to war to end this. Mother needs you."

The anger in Drake rose on a wave of sadness and regret. "I am not going to war, Dr Moran. I suggest we all take some time to think about our actions over the coming days and plan a strategy that means we can protect ourselves and others that might fall victim to Ajax and his brethren." He fought to keep his voice even.

"Fine, if that's what you want but I'm telling you now, we should be pursuing them while we have the advantage on the field." Dr Moran drove her point home with a small but firm finger pecking at the air. She took her coat from the back of the sofa and slammed the front door on the way out.

Drake's shoulders dropped the moment the vibration from the crash dissipated. "I could do without her dramatics." He rubbed his face with both hands, trying to gather his scattering thoughts. He looked at Finbarr and Saskia. "Thank you, both of you. I am truly grateful for everything you've done to help me. It can't be easy for you to accept everything that I am and seem to need despite my best efforts. I cannot stress this enough, however, I shall not be going to war. What Dr Moran is asking from me is too much. It will destroy the man you know and create one you do not want in your lives."

Saskia pushed off the kitchen island. "Well, the immediate danger seems to have passed. I think I need some sleep, so I'll see you both around. I'm not sure Fin should be on campus alone." She looked pointedly at Drake.

"Don't worry, I'm not about to lose him now," Drake said. The exhaustion brought about by the intensity of the previous twenty-four hours still hurt, the wounds might be healed on the outside, but the insides ached. He needed alone time, like maybe a decade or two.

Saskia let herself out of the apartment and when he heard the door click shut he released a long breath, closing his eyes.

"I can look after myself, Drake." Fin's voice made Drake shiver, the confidence a false prediction.

He gathered his resources and studied the young man. Now was the time for lies. "I know, Fin. I just… I need to hold you, keep you with me, more for myself than to protect you."

Fin's eyebrow rose. "Really? I'd say 'how sweet' but we both know you're lying to me." He stepped into Drake's space and looked up. "However, I don't mind you lying to me about this so – as it's the weekend and as we are technically students – why don't we go back to bed?" Fin's hands were sitting on Drake's hips, his thumbs making circles on the soft skin of his defined and elegant 'V'.

A low growl rumbled to the surface. "You sure you want this? I really need to be inside you but I don't want to hurt you."

"The soul eater isn't going to get me now is it?"

Drake found Fin's disassociation from Ajax an interesting side effect of everything they'd endured. For a brief moment he wondered if it would last, then disregarded the thought, Fin wasn't that self-destructive.

"I don't know if I'm honest. This apparently is my new normal when talking to you – being honest." He smiled while stealing a brief kiss. "I think if you stay away from Ajax it will help. Don't let him touch you, don't talk to him if you can avoid it. I can teach you some tricks to help keep him out, maybe Saskia will have more, but blocking him from your life is now the only option to keep you safe."

"And keeping me safe is your job." Fin's eyes were bright, the warm blue a vivid shade reminiscent of a jay's bright colour.

Drake drew Fin's face closer. "Keeping you safe is my only reason to exist in this world, Finbarr Wiseman." His cock, already half hard, approved of the soft mewling sound coming from Fin as Drake took possession of his mouth. They stood in the kitchen and kissed for a long time, Fin's hands exploring Drake's naked flesh. Drake removed Fin's shirt in no time and planned to start on his jeans but feeling Fin's naked, heated skin press against his chest derailed most of his higher brain functions.

"Bed, Drake," Fin murmured against his throat, licking his ear.

"Bed."

Finbarr laughed. "You sound like a caveman."

Drake grunted, pushed Fin far enough to lower his shoulders and hooked the smaller man over his back, eliciting a yelp. Drake smacked Fin on the backside. "I'll give you caveman. I'm not quite that old."

With a sharp toss Fin landed on the middle of the large, and now clean, bed. Drake climbed over him and Fin attacked the belt buckle and buttons of his jeans while the kissing resumed.

Somehow, during the kissing, Fin ended up lying over Drake, savaging his neck. The pain sent jolts of pleasure downwards and Drake's hips bucked up seeking to claim a prize worth fighting for.

"I'm going to ride your thick cock after I've sucked you to the edge," Fin murmured against his swollen lips.

Drake grinned and pushed Fin's dark hair back. "Do I get to lie here or do I get to pound up into that tight body of yours?"

"I'll want both. Find me lube and a condom." Fin returned to savaging Drake's jaw and neck, biting the lobe of his ear before moving down.

Drake reached for the bedside drawer and found a bottle of lubrication and a box of condoms. He couldn't catch anything of course but his partner's security always lay at the fore front of his mind. If it made Fin feel more in control and safer to use condoms he could wait until the right time to fill his sweet boy's arse with lustful desire.

Not even war brought out these primal needs – to mark, to take, to claim, his lover. Drake wanted to bend Fin over and pound into him before spilling deep inside, then force himself hard again before repeating the experience only to spill all over Fin's beautiful pale flesh. Later, he promised himself, that will come later.

Right now, Fin needed control.

When the young man's mouth sucked hard on Drake's nipple he cried out and forced Fin to suck harder.

"Lube my fingers," Fin managed to say as he changed sides.

Drake squirted some of the cool fluid onto Fin's slim fingers and watched as his hand slipped down between his arse cheeks.

Drake groaned as he watched Fin push into his body and felt the effect on his nipple as Fin's mouth went slack but his tongue flicked harder over the tight nub.

"I want to see more," Drake complained.

Fin paused and looked at him for a moment, eyes dark with need. "You want to watch me finger myself?"

"Yes."

Fin grinned. "Don't move a muscle. You'll get to finger me open another time."

"Another time I'll lick you open," Drake promised.

Fin groaned but sat up, still with his fingers in his hole, he managed to turn across Drake's hips and pushed his arse back over Drake's chest. Fin balanced on one hand and his knees. Drake clutched the slim, lightly hairy, thighs.

"Oh, fuck, yes." Drake almost drooled at the sight of Fin's fingers, two of them, pushing into and out of, that tight and secret hole. Fin rocked back, his balls and cock brushing against Drake's belly, leaving lustful fluid in its wake as he fucked his fingers. The position meant Fin couldn't push deep but he worked hard to give Drake a show and when Fin licked Drake's cock he almost fell off the bed.

Drake threw his head back and groaned as Fin devoured his balls before sucking off them with an obscene sound. "I want another finger," Fin ordered.

"Bossy bottom, huh?"

"I've waited too long to enjoy sex, Drake. Make me want more." Fin eyed him before returning to his cock.

Drake poured more lube over Fin's flushed hole and pushed in, joining the fingers already there. Fin groaned and a muffled, "Fuck yes," came from Drake's groin area.

Able to go deeper Drake pushed his thick knuckle in and twisted drawing a keening wail of desire from Fin, who lost control of his fingers and they slid out. Drake pushed against his tight hole with two thicker fingers and started to fuck his beautiful, willing boy harder. When he found that soft spot inside, Fin whimpered and his bones turned liquid, his mouth slack over Drake's cock.

Drake didn't want Fin to come yet, so he worked on opening the beautiful body, making it ready for his thick, long, cock.

When Fin had enough, he smacked Drake's hand away. "Enough. I need more."

"Take it all," Drake said, watching as Fin turned around again to face him.

"I plan to, old man."

Drake laughed. "You think you can best me in the bedroom, boy?"

"Oh, yes. I believe I can."

The confidence and light inside Fin shone so bright Drake caught his breath, unable to look into such mortal divinity, but also unable to look away. He stroked the dark hair from Fin's sweaty face and traced those ruby red lips. Fin, staring back just as hard, moved Drake's cock to his entrance and still looking to Drake's awestruck face, lowered his body.

Drake watched Fin's eyes widen, his mouth fall open and his body fight to take his cock. "Slowly, sweet boy, slowly. I want this to be the best you've ever had, take whatever you need from me."

Fin reached out and placed Drake's hand over his softening cock. Drake played, drawing Fin's desire back to where it should be as Fin lifted up and down taking more with each straining effort.

"Fuck you feel so good inside me," Fin murmured. "I want you all but I don't know if I can take so much."

Drake held still, the effort almost driving him insane as Fin's tight entrance gripped him hard. "You can, sweet boy. You can take it all. I know you can. I know you want it."

"I like being your sweet boy."

"You are everything, Fin."

"You're going to come inside me."

"I am going to come deep inside you."

"I feel so stretched."

"You feel so tight."

Fin rose up and… finally dropped down into Drake's pelvis. They both paused, staring at each other. Fin began to rock and Drake dragged him down for a kiss. A soul deep kiss.

When Fin broke the kiss he straightened and closed his eyes, taking Drake deep into his body. Drake lifted his knees to give Fin something to lean against and he did, further shifting them together.

"Damn me to an eternity of this oh most wicked of the Fates," Drake cried out, clutching Fin's thighs hard enough to bruise.

"You like being used?" Fin asked, rolling his hips up a little before pushing back down.

"Yes. Yes. I like being used. I want you to use me. Fuck, yes, Fin. Use me, fuck me, hurt me, I don't fucking care, just make me feel you."

Drake knew he was revealing too much of himself but Fin just pulled at his heart with every movement of his delicious body. Working the angles he favoured Fin rocked and rode, rocked and rode. He fucked like he'd been born to take Drake's cock and watched through a gaze made heavy with lust and deeper needs, heart deep, soul deep, damn he loved his sweet boy.

Fin's movements grew faster and he bent forwards, resting his hands on Drake's chest. He dug his short nails into the thick muscles. The slim thighs were shaking with the effort and Drake knew Fin couldn't quite make it work.

With practiced ease, he rolled Fin over, remaining inside his body and pushed those sweet thighs towards Fin's shoulders. Fin groaned, "Yes, fuck me hard and deep."

"I can't hold back, sweet boy."

"Don't, old man. Fuck me."

Drake snapped his hips forward and Fin reached for his hard cock. "I want to watch you come first," Drake managed to say.

Fin nodded, breathless as Drake drove in deep. A flush of colour raced up Fin's chest and neck. Drake groaned as Fin's arse tightened further and he plundered his boy's arse and mouth as Fin came hard, covering them both in hot fluids. It tipped Drake over and it became Fin's turn to kiss Drake's slack mouth as he came deep inside that beautiful, sweet body.

Breathing deepened with time and Fin pushed Drake off, only to snuggle back into his side. They lay still, looking at each other while Drake pulled off the condom and tied it, before wrapping it in tissue to be dealt with later.

"I need to clean you up," he murmured, stroking Fin's sleepy face.

"In a minute, I'll do it."

"No, it's my duty. I want to."

Fin smiled. A coy, shy smile considering all the verbal filth he'd had pouring out of him while they'd been fucking. "That was amazing."

"I enjoyed it," Drake said with a grin.

"Oh, you enjoyed it did you?" Fin tapped Drake's nose.

Drake took hold of his finger and sucked on it. "I want round two, to make certain," he said around the digit.

"I'm fairly sure I need a rest, despite my youth," Fin told him.

Drake dragged Fin's hips close. "You sure? I can feel you stirring, sweet boy."

Fin blushed and hid his face against Drake's neck. "I think I might want your cock again, if that's what you need to hear."

Drake chuckled. "This time I'm going to town on you and I want to hear you mewling and begging for my cock."

"Is that right?"

Drake nodded. "Ever been rimmed?"

Fin's eyes widened.

"Didn't think so, shower, then food, then more sex." Drake kissed his beauty with a brief peck so they didn't become distracted again.

"You are my god in all things so I guess I must do as commanded."

"Damn straight," Drake said with a wink.

Chapter 16

THE LECTURE DRONED ON AND Fin struggled to remain awake. Staying the weekend with Drake had its downsides, mostly due to the physical exhaustion of trying to keep up with a god. His arse ached but in the most delicious way, as did most of his muscles, some of which he never knew he owned. The upside though… Fin's mind drifted back in a haze of blissful memories to that morning when Drake had once more been inside him, sliding in and out with slow, deliberate strokes over Fin's most sensitive places, encouraging him to lose all control while Drake held him safe. He'd never felt more loved. More worshipped, cherished and adored. His heart and soul were full, replete and content…

"You need to stop yawning," Roger whispered next to him.

Fin blinked. The lecture hall too warm for a Monday morning. "Sorry, long weekend." He groaned internally, knowing he'd just dropped himself in the shit.

Roger frowned. "Really? Doing what? Ajax looked like shit last night when he finally came out."

Roger the Dodger was one of Ajax's coterie and although Fin had tried to avoid sitting next to him in the small lecture theatre it hadn't worked. "Sorry." He had no idea what he was apologising for but anything to do with Ajax made Fin want to apologise. He wondered when he'd be free of the compulsion or if it would taint him forever.

"He was in a right mood as well – what happened? You two have a tiff?" Roger asked, gleeful at the prospect.

"Yeah. It's over between us. Now, I need to listen, so can you give it a rest? This lecture is basically my next essay."

The heated whispering didn't go unnoticed by Dr Moran who shot Fin such a glare he lowered his eyes to the paper and shrank in on himself.

"Fuck she's terrifying," Roger muttered.

"You have no idea, mate. No idea," Fin breathed without moving his lips.

The lecture finished and Fin managed to leave in the middle of a huddle so Dr Moran couldn't catch him alone. The prospect of dealing with her in university mode while he knew what she looked like under her human skin made him anxious. In fact being away from Drake made him anxious. Monsters lurked in the shadows now and Fin didn't know who or what to trust. He'd asked Drake about everything from vampires to ghosts and some of the answers had proved disturbing. Who wanted to know Medusa might still be walking the world in a different form?

A number of the girls were talking about the lecture, which had been about Plato and his relevance to political theory in the current climate, so Fin didn't notice Ajax until far too late.

"Finbarr, a word."

Roger stood next to his lord and master, the perfect spaniel in Fin's disparaging opinion. "No." He tried to cross the hallway so he could reach the exit.

Ajax stepped in front of him. "Yes. You owe me that much." He reached out for Fin's arm.

Fin tried to step back, well aware of Drake's repeated instructions as he lay in bed watching Fin dress that morning. "Stay away from me, Ajax. Do not touch me." He looked into Ajax's face, there were deep shadows under his eyes, lines in the corners where none had existed just days ago and was his blond hair thinner? Maybe even going grey?

Ajax managed a smile. "Listen, Fin, I'm sorry. I never meant for things to go so far. That…" His mouth twisted into a snarl. "Man —"

"You mean Drake I take it?" Fin snapped. "His name is Drake. He's the one to save my life – from you."

Roger looked between the two of them with confusion and concerned. "What's he talking about, Ajax?"

"Never fucking mind. Just go and wait over there." Ajax waved at the doorway without looking at Roger. Fin watched the weak man move away with apprehension. Ajax without an audience was always more dangerous and he was fast being isolated from the rest of the lecture group.

"I've said all I want to say to you, Ajax. Whoever or whatever you are is of no interest to me. We are over."

Ajax sneered. "You think that old god is going to be willing to accept a weak creature like you?" He leaned over Fin. "Does he know about the disgusting things you did to please me?"

A series of images Fin worked hard to forgot every single day flashed through his mind. "Fuck off."

Having struck the proverbial ball out of the park, Ajax continued. "What about all the times you begged me?"

Tears pressed against Fin's eyes and his body seemed to grow weaker even as the lines around Ajax's eyes started to fade and they brightened in victory. "That's right, Finbarr. Remember me, remember all the times I fucked you, came inside you, used you. Do you really think someone like Drake would want you if he knew it all?"

Fear made Fin's heart scream in his ears. He had to run, he needed to escape but the control Ajax held over him remained and Fin didn't know what to do, where to run, his mind seemed clothed in wool and a terrible smell – like rotten fish – floated around him. Or maybe it came from Ajax? The only man who put up with him... who —

"Finbarr Wiseman, I believe you owe me an essay on Plato and I believe Mr York has the books you need – I suggest you go and find him. Now." Dr Moran stood in the doorway of the lecture theatre with her arms crossed over chest and a firm set to her jaw. "Mr Vargas, your tutorial begins in twenty minutes I shouldn't think Professor McNab will want to be kept waiting.

Despite what you seem to think your responsibilities to your tutorials are important."

Ajax turned his glacial blue eyes on to Dr Moran and Finbarr's insides twisted. He'd watched big men shrink to nothing under that stare. Dr Moran didn't so much as flicker an eyelid. The soul eater turned and stormed out of the building, Roger a quiet shadow in his wake.

"Fin?"

Fin leaned back against the wall, fighting tears and the weakness in his legs. "How did you do that?"

Dr Moran approached him and it wasn't until she touched his arm that Fin realised he was shaking, either from fear or anger, perhaps both. Kindness made her eyes soft and Fin really wanted a hug from the older woman.

"What can I say?" she said with a smile. "My bite is actually worse than my bark and trust me, he's nothing compared to Hades in a mood." She guided Finbarr away from the exit Ajax had taken but took care not to touch. "Come on, let's get you somewhere safe and give Drake a call to come and collect you in person. It looked to me like that young man can still hurt you, which is a worry."

"It feels horrible. Like I'm covered in something nasty." Fin rubbed his chest.

"You are covered in something nasty. His nasty."

They walked together leaving the lecture area and heading to Dr Moran's office.

"Fin!"

He turned and watched Drake hurrying across the grass. Fin looked at Dr Moran. "Did you call him?"

She shook her head.

"Are you alright?" Drake asked the moment he caught up.

He reached out for Fin's jaw but Dr Moran knocked his hand away.

"I don't think that's a good idea. Ajax hijacked him outside the lecture theatre. I managed to scare him off but when he figures out I'm not just a doctor of Greek history and literature, he's going to come after me."

Drake cursed. "I thought I'd scared him away, or at least knocked him over for a while."

Fin ached to be held and have that safe feeling back again. "You have, I think he came after me because he's desperate. He looked like shit until he managed to get me to talk to him and he touched me. I tried to leave, Drake. I really did." Fin's emotions were fragile at the best of times but Ajax had scared him, really scared him. Understanding how dangerous and close to death Fin had come hadn't really sunk in until Ajax hunted him down again. It brought home the feeling of being a victim more than any other humiliation he'd endured at Ajax's hands.

The look of worry on Drake's face didn't reassure him. "Okay, we need a plan. We need to stifle whatever he's still doing. For now though, let's get you back to my place. You need some rest."

"I'm sorry."

"Hey, look at me." Fin obeyed the instruction. "You did the right thing and none of this is your fault. You didn't give permission for any of this. He took, stole, from you."

Dr Moran grunted. "Can you even give consent to a creature like that?"

"You'd be surprised..." Drake trailed off as something caught his eye. "Is that Saskia?"

Fin followed his eye line. On the playing field, a small figure with a mass of almost honey coloured dreadlocks ran over the grass.

"She's fast," Fin murmured.

The three of them moved as a single unit towards the young woman. The moment she saw them she changed direction and headed over. "They're going to destroy everything," she called out, slowing, panting and waving her arms. Fin realised she'd been crying. Nothing made Saskia cry.

Drake strode over to meet her. "What are you talking about?"

She pointed a frantic and shaking finger back the way she'd come. "They have fences going up. Notices everywhere. They are moving the bulldozers in and men with chainsaws are there. I don't even know how they have the permissions. I don't know what to do, Drake!" She threw herself at Drake's chest and his arms encircled the sobbing woman. He looked at Fin who shrugged.

"Alright, Saskia. It's alright. We'll figure it out." Drake patted her back and began guiding her up the path to the university's large gates.

"I have another lecture. You'll need to count me out for this one," Dr Moran said, peeling off from the others once they reached her office building.

"I might need your help later," Drake called out.

She gave him a pointed look. "Yes, because I have all the time in the world with papers due and end of semester reports to start, never mind the budget projections, the faculty meetings —"

Drake held his hand up in surrender. "Okay, you're busy. I'll still call if I need you though."

The glare she gave Drake made Fin wince but his lover seemed unaffected by her outrage as she stomped off. With Saskia tucked under his arm Drake continued to his home. Fin watched them for a while, a strange twisting thing in his gut making him thoroughly dislike his friend for a long moment.

Trying to shake the feeling off, he followed but it left him hollow and fragile in his heart, unable to comprehend the mix of emotions left behind by Ajax and now this – Drake's desire to protect Saskia. Having sampled Fin's limited delights did he want a woman in his bed next? Or maybe as well? It's not like Drake didn't have a world of experience and enjoying two young bodies in his bed might be just the thing for the long winter nights in the quiet university town.

Fin continued to brood until they reached Drake's apartment.

DRAKE SAT SASKIA ON THE sofa the moment they were home. "You need to shower, Fin. That'll help wash Ajax off your skin."

"I want to know what's wrong with her first," Fin stated.

The sharp tone make Drake look up. Fin stood in the doorway with his arms crossed and a scowl on his face somewhere between angry and petulant. *What have I done now?*

Drake thought about the last thirty minutes trying to understand where he'd made a mistake and the dawning realisation hit him that snuggling up to Fin's ex-girlfriend when Fin felt vulnerable might not have been the cleverest idea in the world. So much for learning to be a 'new' man.

"Why don't you go shower, I'll make Saskia some tea and we can talk once you're back. Then I can give you a proper hug." Drake risked a smile.

Fin's eyes narrowed but he left the room and Drake heard the bedroom door open and close, Fin was using the en-suite bathroom. It made him smile, the possessiveness of Fin's actions cute rather than annoying.

Saskia sat in glum silence, staring into space, missing the conversation as if her reality only had room for whatever she saw in her head. Drake left her to it for the moment and decided that maybe tea really would be the best idea. Whatever had disturbed her didn't bode well for their current situation.

He delivered her tea and sat on the large, sturdy coffee table. Fin walked in, wearing a pair of Drake's cotton 'stay at home' trousers and a t-shirt that slipped off his slim shoulder. Drake's mouth went dry at the sight. Fin smiled as he rubbed his hair dry with a towel and the t-shirt moved up to reveal how low on his hips the trousers were, the roll-ups at the hems of the legs showing off his naked feet. Drake wanted to throw him over the coffee table and see if it really was as sturdy as it looked.

"Okay, what's happened?" Drake asked Saskia, taking Fin's hand and guiding him to sit next to her so he could have physical contact.

She focused her gaze on his face. "Aegis Corporation have permission to destroy the grove, Drake. They're going to bulldoze it and donate the site to the town for a new sports development in conjunction with the university. They've been down there already with metal fences forced into the ground to isolate the place. I can feel its fear. The trees are scared, Drake. I don't know what to do. I can't fight them alone."

"How the hell did they get permission for that?" Fin whispered, shock widening his blue eyes.

"I don't know," Saskia's thin wail cut through Drake's heart.

He thought about the small fountain of water bubbling away, the old oak tree and its soul. The light, the grace, the beauty and peace to be found in such a place. All would vanish in a moment. Just one tree felled by man would upset the balance.

"What do we do?" Fin asked him.

War... Drake put his head in his hands and knew that's why he'd been called to this place. Not because Fin was the Oracle. Not because Cerberus happened to be here. Not even because souls were being devoured by unnatural means. He had been called to this place because a war needed to be fought to save Mother and *she* used all the tricks in her book to drag him to Annwn. He drew in a deep breath. If this was going to be war, it would be on his terms, not anyone else's.

"I'm not strong enough to fight. I cannot bend the children of the soil to my will and make them take to the field to defend our cause." He spoke with deliberate care, sorting through his thoughts at the same time. "If I am to do this, I will need your support and help. I will need your trust and faith in me." Now he looked at his companions. "This will require sacrifice —"

Fin shook his head. "You don't know that."

"War always requires sacrifice, Finbarr, that's the nature of war. That's the point of it – it's usually paid for in blood but I hope this time it might be different. Or at least not be the blood of those I care about."

"What do you need from us?" Saskia asked from her untidy huddle in the corner of the sofa.

Drake studied the woodland urchin and wondered how the young sorcerer could help him reach into the core of his being and fill it up enough to sway people to his cause. "Your eco-group at the university – how motivated are they? I need a realistic assessment, not one based on bravado and hope."

Saskia shrugged. "I guess I could get half of them on a march if it didn't cost them anything to attend it. So... twenty people maybe?"

Not enough, nowhere near. He needed a city's worth of people to give him the worship necessary. Sucking in that much power would change him though, he wouldn't remain Drake York – genteel academic. He'd twist into something stronger, possibly darker in this current world, and that creature, that version of him would be unpredictable.

He stared at Fin for so long the young man whispered, "What's wrong?"

Should he warn Fin? Should he explain that if he did this, if he went into direct conflict with the soul eaters then Fin would lose the man he'd come to care for and he'd be forced to watch Drake change forever?

"Don't," Fin murmured, reaching across the gap separating them and taking Drake's hand.

"Don't what?"

Fin shook his head as if reading Drake's thoughts. "Don't push me away. I can see you considering it as an option. You can't do this without me. I can keep you safe and level, Drake. Between us we'll keep control of the darkness. The call of blood and bone doesn't have to take you."

"Oracle?" Drake asked.

There had been no warning this time, one moment Fin spoke in terms a young man would use, the next the phrases were older and more mystical. He'd never seen a vessel blend with Oracle this seamlessly.

"Thanks to the soul eater's foolishness Fin and I can work more closely than before." That answered that question. "War does not always have to be battlegrounds bathed in men's blood and bone. You can find another way. You will have to find another way; this modern world will not sanction you taking up a sword. You must be cleverer than that and we shall help. You must rouse them to action by taking the fight to them. You must show them, let them feel Mother's grace and they will come, they will fight for you, Ares."

The calm assurance from the Oracle that he would survive this new twist to his endless incarnations didn't make him feel any better. He also knew his feelings were irrelevant. He had to fight, it was his destiny. Turning his back on conflicts around the world, refusing the call to arms that so many soldiers begged from him – or versions of him – cost a great deal in its own way. In fact they often made him weep as he pushed the prayers and entreats to one side, ignoring the cries of the fallen and the scared. Denying them his blessing so they could not use him as a way to sanction their crimes against others.

Cruel in its way but Drake had seen too much waste and he hoped that by denying men the gifts of his presence in their hearts, they would lay down their weapons. So far it hadn't worked. They just found other ways to fill their hearts with the need to kill. Their flags, their lines in the sand indicating one country over another, their resources. The need to be on top of the world.

The grove though, it needing saving, it had to be protected and even if he were just a man he would take up arms to protect that site. The fact that he could and would manipulate the hearts and minds of those already bent to their cause was a justifiable act of coercion he'd have to live with.

"Saskia, I need you to arrange a meeting, get as many people there as you can. I will speak. I will give their hearts the courage to fight and at the very least we'll slow down the plans of the soul eaters. Once we've slowed them, we can fight them in other ways. I need a crowd though, the bigger the better."

The look of dawning hope on the young woman's face gave Drake's heart a jolt of pain as more weight added to the burdens he already carried. He wouldn't be able to walk away from this without it scarring his conscience. Unlike the wars of old, where he and his kind played with the children of the soil to make them do their bidding, this battle would lead to a war that really mattered. The health and continuation of Mother lay at the heart of this call to arms.

"What can I do?" asked Fin.

"Go and help her. Create a stir. Use your defection from Ajax to help if necessary. Anything that draws energy away from the soul eaters and towards me will help. I need to plan and gather my resources. I can only do that alone."

Fin looked hurt. "You don't want me here?"

"I'll want you here later. We need this meeting to be tomorrow morning. We need to march on the place tomorrow at midday if possible. I'll go and see Dr Moran, get as many of the faculty involved as possible. We need to make the university see that this is wrong despite the backhanders they are obviously receiving to make this possible."

"If we could find evidence of their duplicity it would help," Fin said.

"Agreed, but that's not my objective right now. Right now I have to prevent the bulldozers from destroying the grove. Evidence can come later."

"WMDs," muttered Saskia.

"What?"

She looked abashed at Drake. "Sorry, I didn't mean anything by it. They invaded then looked for the evidence to justify their invasion."

"That's exactly what we're going to have to do but I hope we'll have considerably more success and a lot less bloodshed," Drake said, managing a smile.

"No bloodshed would be good, unless it's Ajax's," she said, her eyes flashing dark for a moment.

He couldn't help it, he really liked Saskia, her sense of justice might just carry him through to the other side of this without him losing his self-control and hurting someone.

"Reconvene here for supper tonight and we'll draw up more plans over a bottle of wine. You can't go to war without a drink, even Homer knew that."

Ajax

CLOSING HIS SHAKING FIST, AJAX Vargas tried to figure out where the last few days had gone so wrong.

A week ago he'd had Fin in the palm of his clawed hand. Ajax fed from that delicious soul daily and it just kept giving thanks to whatever hidden gift Fin didn't know about. The boy had been touched by the gods long before Drake fucking York had turned up and Ajax reaped the rewards. Now he had nothing and that... thing... that godling had taken Fin away, stealing so much from Ajax in the process he found his human shell degrading at an alarming rate.

His sister was right, Ajax had become involved with the foolish boy and his addiction would get him killed if he didn't do something dramatic.

Rising from the chair hurt and Ajax made his way downstairs with painful steps. Electra strolled in from the garden as he stood in the entrance hall debating the wisdom of interrupting his father in his study.

"Oh, brother mine, what has been done to you? I've shit turds more attractive," she said with a feral grin.

"Fuck off, Electra. I'm not in the mood."

"No, I don't suppose you are. What's happened?" She approached and frowned, waving a winter rose in his face.

He batted it away. "Don't fake concern, sister. I know you don't give a shit."

Electra opened her mouth to argue, he saw it in her eyes, then surprised him by snapping her mouth shut. "What's wrong?"

He'd not heard honesty drip from his sister's venomous lips in years. "I need to talk to Father and I'm not looking forwards to the consequences."

"Okay, what's happened?"

Fuck, he was tired. Not just because his prime food source had been ripped out of him but because he'd been alive for centuries doing the same shit over and over. Ajax lowered himself onto the stairs and sat in a heap.

"I've fucked up."

"You're in love with the boy?" she asked sitting next to him.

Ajax scoffed. "One doesn't fall in love with the cow that provides the steak you eat. No, I'm not in love with Fin. Though I want him with an unhealthy need I don't like."

"You're addicted to his essence." It wasn't a question. It should have been, but it wasn't.

Ajax merely looked at her.

Electra stared into the distance. "You know Father will remember what happened the last time you fed from the same human for too long. What he promised to do to you if it happened again."

"I know but this is bigger than me. I think the family is in danger."

"Family first." Electra entwined their fingers together and Ajax leaned into his stronger sibling.

"Hmm..."

"What kind of danger?" she asked.

He explained about the mirror, the attack, about the god coming through the glass.

"Shit," she whispered when he finished.

Electra sat preternaturally still for several long moments and Ajax waited. Although she'd never stepped between their father and Ajax directly, she'd helped him cover up his mistakes more than once over the centuries. Though owing her always cost him in the end.

"He needs warning but if you admit to being addicted to your cock warmer he'll starve you for years, not just months. I don't think you'll come back from that. You barely survived last time."

Ajax shuddered. The pain of starvation for a soul eater tore their minds and bodies. He couldn't afford to think about it, not again, never again...

"What do I do? If I go into that office looking like this, he'll know." Ajax stared at the papery skin on the back of his hand where he had contact with his sister.

Electra sighed, as though dealing with an idiot child. "Come, we'll fuck you back to health. I can share what I have taken from the local police sergeant and when you look a little more civilised we'll tell Father what happened. At least the edited highlights. Father will have a plan I'm sure. Nothing happens in this valley without his knowledge so it's likely he already knows about the godling. It's that little witch at the back of this somewhere. Fucking eco-terrorist. The faster we can deprive the locals of that fucking grove the better. It gives the human idiots too much space and peace to think."

"Keeping them stressed and rattled does make them easier to handle," Ajax muttered as Electra helped him back up the stairs.

"Maybe we can make this the grove's fault. If we say the godling attacked you during some meeting or another —"

Ajax grunted. "I may have fucked up at the uni as well. I smacked the witch in the mouth."

His sister's delighted laughter sent pleasant chills over his tormented skin. "Oh, you are a fool, brother mine. Right, we'll spin it the godling attacked you because of the grove and smacking the witch. We'll leave Fin out of it for now."

They arrived in Electra's bedroom and Ajax surrendered to his sister's cruel mercies.

Chapter 17

THE CROWD IN FRONT OF Drake was restless. He saw Dr Moran at the back flanked by several other post-graduate students, teaching assistants and at least a dozen faculty members. She'd done well, once he'd convinced her to join him in open conflict with the university. Cerberus never did like making waves. Drake studied the young faces around the Student Union building. They were outside on the large lawns with the small river at their backs. The day had a hint of the coming winter but the sky mimicked the blue of Fin's eyes, almost as if Drake had asked Apollo to shine down on their endeavour.

He hadn't asked Apollo for anything and he wouldn't. He didn't want the others anywhere near this little project. It would bring old rivalries to the surface and test loyalties. He didn't have time for the politics of his siblings and greater family. He needed control of this, to ensure it didn't leak out into the wider world. He wasn't about to turn Annwn University into the next Troy, Sparta or worse – Carthage.

For the first time in centuries Drake's nerves were getting the best of him. During countless years he'd been mired in anonymity, hiding his nature, hiding his purpose and denying his abilities to control, persuade and manipulate. He and Fin had discussed tactics for this speech long into the night, he'd even asked Oracle to help. They'd formulated a plan but looking out at those surrounding the stone table he'd be using as a platform, he wasn't convinced they'd created something passionate enough to make this happen.

Saskia had spent most of the night down at the site and reported back startlingly early to say the work was due to start later that day. They were waiting for the final permissions to come through from the regional council. She'd ceded a little of her own brand of chaos with a couple of die-hard eco-warriors by pouring petrol into diesel engines. Pouring sugar or other substances would indicate direct and illegal action which wouldn't help their cause at this point. The petrol could just be classed as an accident without evidence.

Dr Moran used her contacts at a local news network to make sure some reporters were present. She wanted them to post through social media even if they couldn't get the news onto the mainstream media because of the Aegis Corporation's control. Social media would give Drake access to many, many more souls. If they prayed for the grove then perhaps he could syphon off enough of the energy to bolster his existence.

Now, it was Drake's turn. He'd chosen his armour carefully that morning. He needed to act as a focus, so he needed to draw in the men and women who wore art and piercings on their bodies, as well as those who thought they would leave university to work in the corporate world. He couldn't afford to lose one heart or mind today. He needed to be the speechwriters of Alexander the Great, Henry V and Elizabeth I all rolled into one. The fact he'd been whispering in their ears at the time gave him hope he still remembered how to manipulate an army.

He wore dark, snug fitting blue jeans that Fin told him were flattering, with his heavy boots. A warm forest green shirt that hugged his chest and looked good tucked into his wide leather belt. His thick canvas coat of pale army khaki made him look casual, close to nature, strong without being aggressive and more urban naturalist than warmonger.

Fin had said, "Handsome enough for the women to want you, not too handsome for the men to hate you – that's what we need."

They'd left his stubble alone and the dark curls of his hair tumbled around his face and neck. Drake drew on what little power the libation from the day before gave him and stood with firm purpose first on the stone seat, then on the surface of the table, raising his hands to draw the eyes of those present and coerce silence.

The trick to making people give him the energy he needed to function as a god, came from a simple exchange. Like any star on a stage, give the audience a little of yourself and they will give you a little in return, it all came down to numbers in the end. You give out, they give back – there is one of you and ten or hundred or a thousand and more of them. All that faith, love, need, want, hope, despair, all of it comes to you and feeds your creation.

The crowd hushed.

Drake swallowed hard, nerves biting his stomach. If he failed today it would mark the ending of his existence. He would cease to be relevant and begin to fade for good. Fin stood front and centre, gazing up with total faith and adoration in his soft blue eyes. Drake smiled just for him and nodded.

"Friends. May I call you friends?"

"Fuck off," someone called from the back.

Drake repressed the urge to murder with difficulty. "I will call you friends and shall I tell you why? Because we are here for a common cause. We are here, together, on this beautiful autumn morning, to try to make a difference. Friends share their lives, their goals, their loves and their grief. Friendship is the foundation on which we base our society and that is why you are all my friends. You have all given your time to listen this morning, to help me. I am a stranger and yet you have offered me friendship by consenting to listen."

"What's a pretty boy like you going to do for us?" someone else yelled.

"First, thank you for the compliment, it's been a long time since someone called me a boy." This made a few of the women smile. "Second, why do I have to do anything for you? Is friendship a bargain? Perhaps. These factors are better left to philosophers braver than I am. What I do know is this, friendship can change the world. Truly change the world."

"What the fuck is this guy on about?" another dissenter. The crowd didn't want to hear this, he needed to change tack.

"I'll tell you what I'm on about. I want us to join together in friendship to commit an act of vandalism. I want us to be an army of friends who sing and dance our way to chaos. I want us, as a collective of like-minded individuals, to become one organism strong enough to stop what's happening right over there." He pointed to the left. "Over there are the men and machines who want to rip out the heart of our valley. They want to take Annwn's heart and burn it down so they can pour concrete and build a new sports venue for a town which already has two, they just need better access, better services, they need refurbishing and recycling."

He paused and shook his head, as if in confusion. "Isn't this what we've been so afraid of, my friends? Endless new 'stuff' rather than fixing up and improving the old? Shouldn't we be recycling all the buildings we can rather than ripping the heart out of our life-giving Mother earth?"

"Fucking hippy."

"Shut up, dickhead. He's right."

Drake took a moment, and the first faint trickles of faith began to flow towards him. "That's right, my friend," he said, looking into the young woman's eyes and watching her flush pink. "Shut them up. Fight those who stand against us. Fight those who have no wish to save the breaking heart of our dearest and most vulnerable of friends. Our only true faithful friend who gives us life, constant renewal, who knows that death is never the end, it is merely the opposite to life and life is eternal. Life. Friendship." Drake crouched down and reduced the volume of his voice trying to look each person in the eye. "Life and friendship. We need these things and the very earth we walk on, feed from, take from every moment of every day, is crying out for our help."

He rose in a swift, sharp movement, startling the people at the front. "Friends. I call on you, all of you, to feel the earth around us, to know her grief and pain. To know how much worse it will be when those machines of death rip out her heart. The noise, the stink, the foul intent of those machines will drive through our sacred spaces and tear them asunder. Can we not act as true friends and protect the innocence and grace of such spaces? Are we not responsible for being the friends she needs? She cannot ask herself. She tries in her way but we are so sliced from the natural world we no longer hear her. Our instincts are dull. Our spirits weak. But you, dear friends, want to fly with the birds, snuffle with a badger, burrow like a rabbit and know the beauty of sunlight through a green canopy of trees. If you want to know these things then we must strengthen our spirits, build our resolve, trust in our Mother and her grace. Her friendship. We must go to battle. We must go to war. We must protect her through the demonstration of the power of friendship."

A lone voice from the crowd piped up, "Stage an illegal rebellion? We'll end up with criminal records."

Drake zeroed in on the miscreant. "You'll end up with a death sentence if you don't make changes in this world. If you don't make ripples that turn into waves of change. If we don't go over those fields. If we don't stop them ripping that small grove from the face of the world forever then what's the point in our existence? To go to work in a shining tower to money and politics? What's the point in that?"

"To pay a mortgage?"

Drake pointed to the person who asked the question. "Yes. Yes, you need homes, you need jobs, you need a future but at what cost? Can we not strike a balance? Is it not better to feed our souls while we can by doing something right? Something truly good in life, before we are swallowed by our future expectations? Can we not act now as selfless people in order to say to our children – we made a difference and you can too? Does all change have to be bad? No. It's what we do with the change that can make the difference. How we manage it. And we can manage it together as friends, with each other with our Mother.

"I beg of you, I need your help today. I need you to walk with me over those fields and I need you to stop those machines, stop the chainsaws, I need the media to see what is happening here and help us fight through the courts, through the councils. I need direct action from you – now – to make our politicians listen and act. Or this is pointless. We can go back to our rooms in the campus, in the town and forget that the heart of this beautiful place is being torn apart. We can turn up our TVs and stereos and drown out the noise of her screams. Because she will scream. She will scream my friends and those screams will keep you awake at night.

"Please, please, come with me, *believe in me*. Believe we can make a difference in this place. That the ripples we create today will be tomorrow's tsunami of change for the better in our world, our environment. I am a creature of battles and war. I have created so much death. I am a product of every violent act throughout history. That is why I am stood here today. So are you all. Every one of you comes from a family who has known conflict at some point in their past. We are all warriors, we are all survivors. We are all able to take up arms, be it a pen, a banner, a sword or a gun. We are warriors and we now have a fight of such importance on our hands, happening right here in our back garden, that we must defend our castle walls and we must fight. *We* must be the new heroes. We are warriors for the environment using friendship as our shield, and love for our ever-giving Mother as our sword. Who will come with me to fight?"

During the tirade Drake's essence began to draw in the attention of the crowd, draw it in and hold it, twisting it for a moment before returning it to the crowd. The cycle repeated and repeated making the crowd listen, believe, want and crave him. They wanted to please him. They wanted to offer him their love and loyalty. The monster in their midst – feeding off them just as the soul eaters sucked Fin dry. Was he really so different to their kind? Even as the crowd cheered and called for action, even as he crowed his delight and gave the order to march, he hated himself. Hated what he was and why he existed. Drake York – a fake human for a fake world, sucking it dry.

Saskia rose on the table next to him and began a chant. He stepped down and gave the crowd over to someone who actually deserved the adulation for her courage.

Dr Moran approached. "I'm not sure invoking Dionysus was a wise move, Ares."

"I thought he was invoking the spirit of Woodstock," Fin said with a grin. "That was amazing. You are amazing. I'd follow you anywhere."

Nausea burned in Drake's gullet. "That's the problem. I give them back a little of what they give me and then they give me more."

Dr Moran narrowed her eyes. "You should be riding this wave, Drake. Why aren't you?"

He pushed out a sudden breath. "Why do you think, Cerberus?" A chill made him shiver so he did up his coat and followed the crowd now moving over the playing field towards the grove.

Chapter 18

"I DON'T UNDERSTAND, I THOUGHT this would make you feel better," Fin walked next to Drake, struggling to keep pace over the rough ground of the field. The mud sucked at his feet and clumped around his boots, though Drake moved over it easily enough.

Drake looked over the hedgerow. "I do feel better."

"You don't look like you feel better." To Fin it looked as if Drake wanted to snap and snarl at him.

"I can feel their love of what I want. I feel it bone deep. I can use it. Fight with it. Isn't that all I'm worth? Isn't that the only reason Mother wants her son here? To fight for her – to sacrifice these pawns to her end? I feel fucking marvellous." Drake further increased his stride and Fin let him surge ahead.

Dr Moran touched his arm as she caught up. "Don't worry, Fin. He'll find a balance. He loves you and that will help ground him in the present."

"What if it doesn't? I don't know if he loves me at all." Fin watched the dark head of his companion vanish among the centre of the crowd as his voice rose over them, calling them to his war.

"He loves you, never doubt that. He just doesn't want this to taint what he wants for you both. Ride the wave. It'll be intoxicating if I know Ares."

Fin frowned. He didn't want to be intoxicated by the man he knew he loved. He also knew he loved Drake York, not Ares. For a terrible moment

Fin wanted the grove gone, Saskia gone and this mission gone so he could have Drake all to himself.

They walked through the field to the looming yellow barriers, more than two metres high and thick metal, surrounding the copse of trees and its spring. Men in hard hats and high-viz coats walked around, the field already churned up. A big man in a white hard hat approached Drake, and Fin pushed his way through the crowd to join him.

"What the bloody hell are you doing here? Get off this land. It's private property." The man's bullish face turned red as he waved a clipboard at Drake.

Saskia stepped in front of Drake. "It's not private property, we're on a public footpath. These trees will have preservation orders on them and I want to see your paperwork. I have a right to request it and present it to the lawyers of concerned parties."

Fin looked at her in surprise. "Is she right?" he asked someone next to him.

The man shrugged. "Who knows, but I never want to question Sassy, she's way too clever."

It took some effort but Fin managed to hide his smile. Saskia had a fan. He'd have to let her know, the guy was cute in an earthy and earnest way.

The debate between Saskia and the foreman heated up while the protesters began fanning out over the site. Within minutes they were slipping between the barriers that hadn't been fixed in place properly and vanishing into the trees. The foreman started yelling about the police so people sat in front of the heavy machinery. Drake leapt with grace onto the hood of a bulldozer and began another rallying cry. Fin watched him but found he couldn't stand it for long.

Drake spoke all the right words, made all the right movements, he gave out the energy others needed and received it in return, Fin sensed it happening, but something inside him shrivelled the longer he stood in the crowd. It wasn't the same feeling Ajax left, a greasy suffocation he couldn't think around, rather it made Fin sad. Bleak and empty. As if he watched

Drake unwillingly prostitute himself for the sake of others. Fin didn't doubt the grove needed saving but Drake looked desperate somehow.

With every word Fin realised Drake drew further from the world he'd created, that of the gentle academic, and Drake didn't want to surrender that persona. He didn't want to pick up arms and do battle. Fin backed further away from the crowd, unable to watch the increasingly desperate plight of his lover. The others were lapping it up, they adored the warrior and even some of the workers were listening with rapt attention.

Saskia joined Drake on the hood of the large vehicle and Fin turned his back on the protest intending to return to the university.

Dr Moran stepped in front of him. "No, you can't leave. He'll need you."

Fin waved a hand in the direction of the vehicle being used as an impromptu stage. "He doesn't need me – I'm not sure what he needs but it's not me."

Her small hand closed over his wrist. "If you leave you'll lose him. Can't you feel it? He's twisting in on himself, the older versions of his psyche are fighting for dominance. He's trying to fight back while using them to whip the crowd up. It's a juggling act he'll lose if he doesn't have a reason to keep Drake York in one piece."

"It's making me feel sick, he hates himself."

Dr Moran nodded and smiled. "Good, you can feel it. That's good. It means you're closer to him than any of these 'worshippers'. When he gets down off that machine, go to him. Hold him. Let him sink into you. We don't need Ares, not really, we need Drake York. You know he used to be a god of agriculture? He became a god of war when neighbouring tribes began to fight over land and resources. He needs to remember his beginnings, not what he became later."

Fin closed his eyes and nodded his consent. He planted his feet in the thick soil and endured watching Drake fight for his survival while trying to save Mother. The day wore on and Drake moved through the crowd. The police turned up but just watched the protest and more members of the press rolled in. Saskia and Drake spoke with eloquence about the importance of saving such beautiful places, without mentioning any alternative religions or philosophies. They kept it grounded in reality, which would have made Fin laugh considering an ancient god and a sorcerer were the ones doing the talking. Unfortunately, it left him disturbed.

Eventually a large black, sleek SUV drove into the field. Fin's stomach knotted even further. Ajax's father had arrived. The CEO of the Aegis Corporation. Fin's eyes shot to Drake. He stilled, sensing an enemy and his mouth twisted into a smile of grim intent. His right hand flexed repeatedly as if looking for a weapon.

The door to the vehicle opened and Ajax's father stepped out. Tall, slim, beautifully dressed in a suit of dark cloth to contrast his blond good looks. Fin suddenly understood. The Vargas family had taken the form of the ideal American family, all of them blond and blue eyed with shining white teeth. They masqueraded as the perfect poster family for family values and in Britain they blended with perfection while standing out just enough to give them the energy they needed to feed on. Victims like him. Fin shuddered and swallowed the bile rising in his gullet.

Mr John Vargas zeroed in on Drake the moment he stepped onto the site. They stared at each other for a long time, learning and probing from a distance before the joust truly began. Fin made his way towards Drake, more anxious than ever.

"He's powerful," Drake murmured without acknowledging Fin's arrival.

"He's been the head of a large company that specialises in destruction for a very long time. He makes Ajax look like chicken feed."

"A challenge at last." Drake's eyes were bright.

He stepped forwards but Fin gripped his arm, pulling him to a stop. "Wait, please. He's going to do far more to you than Ajax did. Let me deal with him. Please, Drake. You don't have to fight him directly."

Drake growled, looking at Fin for the first time. "Are you calling me a coward?"

A terrible moment passed between them and Fin's eyes pricked with tears. A promise of violence surged over him and he shivered in fear. "No, Drake.

How can you say that? I'm just trying to protect you and the man I met – Drake York – remember him?"

"I don't need protecting." Drake pulled away from Fin's grip and strode towards John Vargas.

THE CALL OF POWER SWAMPED Drake. It swirled around him and he sucked it in by the lungful. He hadn't tasted this much worship in decades. These young people were full of life, full of integrity and passion for their cause. Awakening their inner warriors had been easy, he'd just needed to give them permission to go to war. He moved through them, accepting the touches, the smiles, and not so subtle hints from women and many of the men, that his private company would be more than desirable. Temptation drifted its lazy fingers through his libido.

The moment a large and new SUV drove onto the site things in him shifted. His right hand ached for his sword. The left for the weight of his shield. The mud under his feet turned to the sand of the near east and he smelt the heat of the sun burning that sand on the cold wind brushing his face. A hand touched his arm and he realised Finbarr stood at his side, worry and fear radiating off his young body. It annoyed Drake. A battlefield was no place for fear. A battlefield required you conquer your fear and go into the fight heedless of the dangers.

A suited man left the vehicle and Drake knew his true enemy's face at last. The boy, Ajax, had just been an appetiser this was the main course. Drake stepped out from the crowd and approached the man in the suit, mind alive with the coming fight.

Blue eyes, blond hair, slim, tall – perfect on the outside but Drake could see the monster lurking under the shell of flesh, and he smelt the taint on the air. They were two spear lengths apart and studied each other.

The suited man blinked and smiled. "It seems we have a deal that needs to be struck."

"No deal. You leave this place alone and you live. That's the only deal on my table."

The man shook his head. "I will not be leaving this place and this —" he waved a dismissive hand at the grove "– illusion of power you have conjured will not be enough to sustain you for long. I shall destroy this teat of Mother's milk you want to save so desperately and once I've done that, I'll suck the marrow from your bones. God or not, you are nothing compared to me. I have been feeding on these children of the soil for years."

"They no longer serve you, soul eater, they are under my protection and guardianship," Drake snarled.

The world shifted around the pair, landscapes moving and warping into other places as they vied for dominance in time and space. The protest faded. Only the relentless push and pull of esoteric energy mattered. Drake hadn't touched the true gifts of Mother for a long time but as he tapped into the currents under the ground, moving through the air and dancing on the light from the sun, he began to realise he'd cut too much of himself out of the world. He'd been denying his true nature for too long, wallowing in self-pity and loathing for his existence.

The other man, seen clearly as a void in Mother's creation, continued to smile. "Yes, feed Ares, son of Zeus, god of war and chaos. Become strong. The stronger you are, the better you will taste when I destroy you and mark me, son of Zeus, I shall destroy you and all your little birds that flutter about you. I'll have the dog for my hearth rug as well. You might want to warn her of that. I shall give no quarter or mercy when I strike. For now though, feed and enjoy your freedom."

Drake wanted to laugh at the arrogance of the creature before him. Did a monster like that really believe he could best a god? Nothing in this broken world could resist the power tumbling and swirling around and through Drake. He stood before this monster as he had countless others, knowing he would be victorious.

The monster bowed his head, as if to acknowledge the challenge, before climbing back in the vehicle. The moment the door shut the illusions surrounding Drake snapped off and he stumbled as reality grounded him once again.

"Drake." Fin grabbed his arm, preventing a humiliating tumble into the wet soil under their feet. "Drake?"

Fin sounded scared. It brought Drake up short. "I'm alright. I'm alright."

The young man released his arm and stepped away. "I'm going back to my room."

That focused Drake on the present. "What?"

"I don't belong here. I can't watch this happening. You should stay with Saskia, keep them safe, but I need to go. This isn't... this isn't what I want, Drake."

Pain shot through him. "You mean I'm not what you want."

"I didn't say that. I just..."

"Just what, Fin? Don't you want the essence of me tainting your world? Is that it?" Drake lashed out because nothing in the wide earth scared him more than losing Fin, his anchor, but he didn't know how to stop it from happening. The day was twisting him like corded flax.

Fin cast his bright gaze down into the churned soil of the field. "Come and find me when you're ready, Drake."

Drake stood there while Finbarr walked away, cutting a lonely figure in the waning afternoon as he crossed the winter grasses of the field to return to the university.

Dr Moran, huddled in her coat, approached him. "Well, you managed to fuck that up."

"Thanks for the solidarity."

"He's scared, Drake. He's a boy drowning in a world he can't possibly understand and you've gone all..." she wafted her hands about, "...weird on him. You need to go find him and let him bring you back to where you want to be."

"Mother needs me, isn't that what you all want from me?"

With the sun setting the men working on the site began to pack up and the foreman was on the phone.

Dr Moran shook her head. "Maybe Mother needs to learn to compromise a little when it comes to her children of the heavens. You've done your job here, at least for now, go after Finbarr and make things right, Drake. You need him."

Nothing inside Drake seemed to fit properly and his skin felt tight. His mind spun and flashed with images from too many incarnations and lifetimes. Too many people and places. He tasted foods grown in countries far from this dark loam under his feet and smelt the bitter wines poured on altars so old the stones were memories in the dust.

"I can't think, Cerberus."

"You need to go, find the boy, hold him close and don't let him go. Tell him you love him, Drake." She said his name firmly and he knew her attempts at placing pins in the timeline of his existence were meant to help locate and steady his current reality.

"I should go into the grove. See the old man."

"He won't come out to you tonight, you know that. He can't help you, Drake. Only Finbarr can and it seems to me that you might be a little scared of what that means, or you'd already be going after him."

His eyes narrowed. "You calling me a coward now, as well?"

"I never used the word," she said. "Go. I'll martial your troops here and get them home safe. Tomorrow we fight again but by then it'll be legal. I've been on the phone while you've been glad-handing all day. We have various charities and their lawyers coming in to delay things. You've done your duty to Mother for the moment," she pushed him out of the crowd, "go now – go."

Drake nodded, turned away from his battlefield of dirty machines and youthful hope, to race back to the university and Finbarr's warm, safe body.

Ajax

AJAX WATCHED FINBARR CROSS THE playing field, his father's voice echoing in his head from their brief phone conversation moments before. He'd dared to contradict the old beast by warning daddy dear that Drake York was a clear and very present danger. There would be a price to pay for that later but right now, he had a mission to complete.

Fin, huddled in his coat, head down and hands in his pockets didn't think to check his surroundings. Ajax stepped out from behind the large beech tree near Fin's building and stood in his path.

"Ajax." Fin stood in frozen shock, panic flitting over his beautiful face. He glanced around but they were alone in the dim light of the darkening autumn day. No rescuer today.

"Finbarr."

"I told you, I didn't want to see you again. You shouldn't be here."

"I came to apologise." Ajax worked hard to sound and look neutral, harmless.

"I don't believe you and it's far too late for that. I know what you are. I know what you can do to people." Fin began backing away.

Ajax realised the futility of trying to make Fin come quietly. He clapped his hands and his sister walked around from the back of the building.

"You need to come with us," Electra said to Fin.

A flash of movement in the distance caught Ajax's attention and he realised Drake York ran over the field towards them. "No more games."

He stepped close to Fin who turned to bolt into the grounds of the university. Electra reached out a hand, caressed the soft flesh of Finbarr's neck and he stumbled before his knees hit the soft grass. Ajax slipped his arms under Fin's, hauled him up and threw the smaller man over his shoulder.

"Go get the car started, before that old fool comes to find his lost love," Ajax ordered, the heat of Fin's body oddly reassuring.

"Bet you wish you could incapacity your prey with such ease," Electra said, dancing off and waggling her fingers at him.

Ajax snarled at her and she laughed. The gifts of the female of their species were far more deadly than the male if given full rein. Electra could suck the soul from a man while he slept in a narcoleptic state because she'd touched him and ordered it. The only real disadvantage for the female soul eaters was their size. They never grew in strength like their male counterparts and they didn't store power in the same way, it made them more vulnerable to starvation and physical assault. It also meant they would pair for significant periods of time in order to stay alive and healthy.

Electra could hunt and feed more easily than Ajax, but he could protect her. Tonight they would both taste the sweet soul of Finbarr Wiseman while their father dealt with Drake York.

Throwing Finbarr across the backseats of the SUV, Ajax climbed into the driver's side while Electra lifted herself into the passenger seat. "Better go, brother, before the nasty and scary godling comes to get you in the night." She made a Halloween noise and waggled her fingers.

"Fuck off, bitch. What he did to me shouldn't have been possible. That little witch, Sabrina —"

"Saskia, dearest."

"Whatever, she'll be the one responsible. I'll hunt her down after we've dealt with York and I'll fuck her while draining her dry."

Electra pouted. "No, I want her. I never get to play with the fun toys and she's a lively minx."

"Discuss it with Father," Ajax said. He focused on driving off the university grounds, refusing to think about the consequences of his confession to their patriarch. The heady scent of Finbarr filled the interior of the SUV making him dizzy.

When Ajax had confessed to his father how badly the fight with Drake had gone, what he'd done by pulling on Fin's soul even as the god made love to Ajax's possession, John Vargas had lost his temper. The beating he'd received broke many of the bones in his body and he'd lost the illusion of the human male he pretended to be. Electra had found him a quivering mess in the corner of their lounge, his long arms snapped, and ugly face distorted by fractures, abrasions and contusions. She'd fucked him back to some kind of health and he'd sucked in the souls of his sycophants to draw the illusion of Ajax Vargas back around his torn and broken body.

He deserved nothing less and did not hate his father for his punishment, rather he craved to make amends for his failures and bringing Finbarr to his father would go some way towards correcting the imbalance. Their mother had stood by and watched the punishment, telling their father when she deemed it time to stop. She never raised a hand to the children, but her wrath they feared the most because if John Vargas acted on their mother's behalf, they could be left imprisoned and broken for months before she would permit them to heal and feed again.

Ajax couldn't afford to fail. He drove home with Electra humming a chirpy and annoying tune. He glanced in the rear-view mirror several times during the journey, watching Finbarr sleep on the back seat. A strange and unfamiliar twisting sensation in his gut made it hard for Ajax to concentrate. An ache somewhere in the middle of his chest had begun the moment Finbarr had met Drake York and it grew when Ajax realised they were sleeping together. It made him angry, but a new anger he didn't understand and couldn't control.

Touching the emotions of humans often happened while they fed on the souls of the chosen, so he knew how they tasted and some of them were divine to suck down, but he didn't have a vast range of emotions himself and this new sensation made him uncomfortable. He wanted to talk to his sister about it but he knew Electra too well and sentiment wasn't one of her failings. She'd always regarded him as weak and this wouldn't help.

Fin looked so sweet asleep. Ajax had often watched him during the nights they spent together, especially at the start of their relationship. He had an innocence to him that appealed to Ajax and the old god as well it seemed. Ajax forced his hand to relax on the steering wheel. He'd have Fin back after tonight and try to make some amends for the damage he'd done to the young man. If he looked after Fin he might be able to keep him, and his soul, as food for years to come – that might be nice for a change. He'd never built a life for himself outside the family, in all the centuries they'd existed, it had just been the four of them.

Yes, that's what would happen. He'd take Finbarr away and they would live like real people for a while. It would be nice. Fin would understand why Drake had to go and forgive Ajax. He would love Ajax again and everything would be fine. Ajax repeated this to himself several times as he navigated the driveway to the house.

Chapter 19

DRAKE RACED UP THE STAIRS to Fin's room and knocked on the door. Then banged. No answer. He pressed his ear to the wood, expecting to hear the shower in the small bathroom. Nothing. He knocked again and called out. Still nothing.

"Come on, Fin, you can't be that angry with me. Please, let me talk to you. I'm really sorry I've been a prick all day. Please, just let me in and I promise I'll make it up to you," Drake said through the door.

One of the others from Fin's corridor walked past. "He's not been in there, man. I've not seen him all day."

"You sure?" Considering the stink of weed coming off the guy, Drake wasn't convinced he'd know what day it was never mind whether Fin had made it home.

"Sure I'm sure, man. I saw him out of my window with that prick he was hanging with until you showed up." The young man scrubbed his palm over his shorn hair and fiddled with his nose ring. "To be fair, it did look weird. Looked like Fin was being kidnapped. But that can't be right – right?" He looked at Drake as if he held answers able to placate an uneasy conscience.

Drake briefly considered throwing the young man off the roof of the building. Instead, he turned on his heel and raced down the stairs. "Fuck, fuck, fuck..." He yanked his phone out of his pocket, aware the sun was now setting and with the night, the power of the soul eaters would grow. Just as he was about to speed dial Saskia his phone rang with an unrecognised number. He took a breath to calm his thoughts. It didn't work.

"Where is he?" Drake barked.

A low chuckle. "Very quick, Mr York."

Drake's teeth ground together. The sultry tones of the man-creature, John Vargas, made his skin crawl with a thousand scorpions. "Where is he? You have one chance —"

"Now, now, I don't think you can go making demands on me – do you? I think we'll play by my rules. So far you've only annoyed me because you attacked my son and took away his toy, now you've interfered in my business and that requires some payment in kind."

The phone creaked in protest at Drake's crushing grip. "What do you want?" Rage boiled with such passion in his chest he saw black spots.

"I want you, Godling."

Drake's mouth dropped open as a sudden awareness of their predicament hit him. The soul eater wanted to feed on the soul of a god. The consequences of his surrender to these creatures could be catastrophic. With the charge he'd taken from the crowd earlier he might be able to fight them on open ground, but...

With a dawning realisation he'd been played, Drake understood John Vargas had allowed the protest to give him more power, more of a soul to eat.

"Where and when?" Drake asked, a snarl of words and torment.

He knew, despite the day's events, he wasn't strong enough to win. Not yet. Not now he'd returned to find Fin gone. Tears burned the backs of his eyes. He had no choice but to give them everything and hope that by doing so he'd save Finbarr and find a way to destroy the soul eaters.

"I can hear you thinking, Mr York. You know you have no choice. Tell me you understand."

"I understand."

"Say it all."

"Fuck you."

"No – say it."

The heat in Drake's body reach critical as he ground out, "I understand I have no choice."

"Very good." Drake heard the smile in Vargas' voice. "You will come here – alone. You will leave the bitch hound and the witch. You will inform no one. You will behave yourself or I will give the boy to my son and daughter. They are hungry for him, Mr York so I suggest you do as you are told like a good little deity."

Drake was going to rip out Vargas' tongue and feed it to Cerberus – slowly. "Fine."

"No bargaining?" Vargas tutted. "How disappointing. I thought you'd be harder to contain – Ares."

Drake's formal name came with such a dismissive sneer he almost crushed his phone. The line died and Drake stood there, in the gathering darkness, trying to clear the red tinge to his vision. The last time someone had roused him to this much anger Rome had burned under the power of the Vandal invasion.

He thought back to that morning, where he'd held Fin in his arms and gazed down into those soft blue eyes as they'd made love for the third time.

Fin had clutched at his arms, wrapping his legs around Drake's hips, riding each slow thrust into his body. Drake had licked the sweat off his neck and chest. Smothered his mouth and jaw in kisses. Whispered benedictions of devotion as Fin had hit his orgasm again.

Drake's heart broke even as his phone gave up its fight for life and dissolved into pieces at his feet, an unnoticed sacrifice to his grief.

He started to walk towards the grand house at the top of the town. The walk turned into a jog and before he knew it, he raced over the fields and leapt the stone walls separating the university from the countryside and his objective. The world moved so fast around him no mortal eye would ever be able to track his progress. He reached the high wall surrounding the property and rather than go over, or even use the gate, he smashed through the wall, taking out a small tree in the process.

Slowing on the manicured lawn he stood for a moment and looked up at the house. Lights were on in the downstairs, blazing over the formal garden. He glanced further up and realised storm clouds gathered overhead. The atmosphere crackled. The air as violent as his screaming mind. All he really needed to do was reach out, take the gathering storm and slam it into the house until everything turned to dust.

He'd learned though, often the hard way, that Fin would die. The soul eaters would survive as their nature dictated, and he'd lose everything. Again.

His jaw worked as he tried to think through the problem, rather than just act, but after the day he'd had the part of him that was Drake York did not hold sway. Ares, god of war, didn't plan – he acted. The impulse to charge the enemy burned through his body and it began to shift. His features grew sharper, harder and more aggressive. His hair grew longer, a black mass over his widening shoulders and thickening arms. His legs began to lengthen the muscles wider and harder than ever. His clothing shifted from jeans and jacket to armour made of bronze and leather. A helmet with a deep red crest appeared in his hand and a short bronze sword with a wooden hilt snapped into existence in his right hand.

Drake York vanished. Ares stood on the now scorched lawn and watched the world before him with death in his heart.

Chapter 20

FIN WOKE WITH THE TASTE of copper pennies on his tongue and a horrible lassitude in his limbs and eyes. He tried to focus but each effort swept nausea through his guts and brain. How did he have the hangover from hell? He didn't remember drinking. Where was Drake? He tried to track his thoughts. A vision of the protest and their argument swung into view looking like a fun house mirror through the effects of whatever made him sick.

He remembered walking over the field to his halls of residence, then...

"Ajax?" he breathed the name and a crushing sense of horror made him sob.

"Shh, it's alright, Finbarr. You are safe. I shall protect you."

A hand stroked through his hair and Fin tried to jerk away. He realised they'd tied him upright in a chair, wrists and ankles bound tight to solid wood. He lifted his head and moved it away from the nestling fingers.

"Gerrr off mmeee," he slurred.

"Shh, all will be well," Ajax repeated. "You don't need to worry. Father has everything under control. Once the godling is dealt with, we will leave here together and everything will be fine. I will make you happy, Finbarr."

A snort came from Fin's left and he rolled his head managing to look at Ajax's twin sister – Electra. She sat on the dark and shining surface of the dining table using a steak knife to clean her fingernails. The table had been laid for dinner.

"You really believe Father's going to let you take that tasty morsel for yourself? After your failures? He'll be pudding after the main meal of the godling."

Was she talking about Ares? They were using him as bait to reel in Ares? Were they mad? He'd never consent to surrender – he'd rather sacrifice Fin. Right? The god Ares was not the man Fin loved and they'd only been together such a short time, he was a mote of dust in the existence of a god.

"Father promised I could have him," Ajax snapped, his fingers tightening in Fin's hair making him grunt in pain.

Electra laughed. "Oh, brother dear, are you feeling things you shouldn't for this toy? You know he's little more than a fatted calf."

"You know nothing."

"I know a great deal, Ajax." She moved off the table and approached her brother. Fin watched in horror as she leaned into Ajax and swept her tongue over his full bottom lip. "Why don't you fuck me over the table so your pet can watch how to satisfy you?"

Ajax's eyes darkened and his breathing deepened. Fin realised they were actually considering having sex in the same room as him. Human or not, true siblings or not, he had no wish to watch them pant and heave over each other. He tested the restraints on his arms and legs – little to no give and little to no strength in his limbs.

They were now kissing and Ajax had lifted his sister onto the table's edge. She wrapped her legs around his thighs and ground against him.

Fin's vision flickered. "Oh, shit, not now," he whispered.

Reality vanished and he stood in front of the simple peasant's home on a Greek island that existed in Oracle's memory somewhere.

"Hello, Finbarr."

Fin turned in a full circle. "You have to let me go back."

Oracle smiled their all-knowing, and frankly patronising, smile. "In time. The poisons need to leave your body and it's best you are unaware of Ares' at the moment."

"He's here?" Fin shook his head. "I mean – there?" Shifting realities didn't help him understand the decisions he needed to make to save himself.

"Did you really believe he would sacrifice us?" Oracle looked amused at the thought.

"I thought he might have the good sense not to overreact."

"You clearly don't know Ares. He's not known for having a steady temper." The goat appeared from behind the building and Oracle clicked their tongue to encourage her. Oracle picked up the rope halter, placed it over the docile creature's head and took her to the milking post.

"No," Fin agreed. "I don't know Ares. I love Drake. I want to keep loving Drake and I need to be strong enough to help him, so you need to get these poisons out of me. Then we need to get out of the chair we're tied into and go save my boyfriend."

Oracle leaned against the doorway and studied Finbarr. "You really want Drake rather than Ares?"

"Of course I do!"

"Most would love the god not the man."

"Why? Why would they love a raving sociopath? Ares is nuts. Drake is a complex being with a heart and soul and I have to get him back. Help me!" Fin almost dropped to his knees in an effort to impress his Delphic companion.

Oracle shrugged. "Just thought it was worth checking. You can return now, Finbarr. The drugs have purged most of their toxicity because of our conversation."

"I can't get out of the chair."

A nonchalant shrug from Oracle came with, "I can't do everything for you."

The Greek olive grove vanished and Finbarr returned to the dining room of the Vargas family with a sickening lurch. The door to the room opened and John Vargas walked in with his perfect wife on his arm.

Electra and Ajax stopped their foreplay. Neither parent reacted.

"Good, you're awake. This will be much more fun if he sees you paying attention," John Vargas said looking at Fin.

"This is a mistake. You don't want to do this. You have no idea what he'll do to get me back. Please, let me go and you can keep living —"

A crash from outside startled everyone in the room.

A flicker of worry crossed Vargas' face. "He's here."

"That was fast," muttered the mother.

"I shall go outside and meet him." Vargas fixed the cuffs of his expensive shirt, making certain the correct amount showed under the sleeves of his even more expensive suit. The diamonds in his cufflinks flashed in the light.

"You go out there, he'll kill you," Fin warned and hoped in equal measure.

Vargas shook his head. "No, he won't because you'll be in here with my wife and children. A life for a life. I'm not interested in eating your soul, Finbarr. It has little to recommend it when I can feed on that of a god. Can you imagine what he will taste like, Finbarr? Ambrosia indeed." The man's blue eyes sparkled like his diamonds. A snake excited at the sight of prey. Deeply unnerving.

The wife came and stood beside Finbarr, her perfume overwhelming but still unable to hide the stink of her rotten existence. He gagged. How had he never noticed it with Ajax? Was it all part of the illusions these creatures created?

Fin twisted in his chair, trying to see where Vargas was going. He headed towards the double doors that led to the garden terrace, but just before he reached them all the glass in the room exploded inwards and doors blew off their hinges.

Shards flew around Fin and he hunkered down behind the heavy protection of the high back of the chair. Electra screamed. Ajax bellowed a curse when a chunk of wood pierced his cheek but Vargas appeared untouched by the tumult.

The moment the last shard tinkled to the ground, Fin twisted in the chair and watched Ares, in full battle armour, breach the room.

"Holy shit," he breathed.

The god stood at close to seven feet tall, even without the helmet and its tall crest. Massive corded muscles covered in dark burnished skin and littered with scars replaced the swarthy lean frame of Drake York. The shadow Fin had seen in the grove that first mysterious night was nothing compared to the full glory.

Vargas stepped back some considerable distance. Ares turned his head to take in the room and the weight of the dark gaze fell on Fin, coming from behind the face guard of the helmet to settle on his shoulders. A warm comfort in a scary room.

"Let him go," Ares said, his voice darker, older and more like rough sandstone than smooth marble.

"You agreed to surrender, a simple exchange." Vargas held his hands out. "His soul for yours."

"Do you know what dining on the soul of a god will do to you?" Ares asked.

Vargas nodded, his colour high and the desire written all over his face and body. "Oh yes, oh I think I know exactly how it will make me and my beloved feel. We will become powerful beyond all our dreams and you will be there, always, to take from. I have bonds able to hold you, Ares and you will submit willingly. I have been trying to trap a god for centuries and thanks to my wayward son I have one."

Ares cocked his head to one side. "You would bind me and keep me as fodder?"

"Yes. I will keep you. My goodness, you are beautiful – isn't he, my dear?" Vargas looked over his shoulder at his wife.

Fin glanced up at her – she almost drooled. "I can taste him from here."

Rather than fight the ropes, Fin decided to change tactic. He pushed deeper into the restraints binding his right hand and managed to touch the table top. His skin burned at the effort. With everyone's focus on the Greek god he kept pushing forwards, wriggling his slim arm through the rough bonds and over the shiny surface towards the steak knife someone had thoughtfully laid when they made the table.

His fingers curled around the handle he pulled back, the knots beginning to give just a little. The knife, well made and well balanced, turned in his hand and Fin pointed it back up his arm. He started to saw at the rope.

Saskia & Cerberus

"WHERE THE HELL IS HE?" Saskia asked Dr Moran, bending close to be heard over the music and drinking songs.

They were in the Student Union bar and it heaved with beer and revelry, the floor sticky. Saskia and Dr Moran had left the protest site half an hour before, expecting to find Fin and Drake either at Fin's halls of residence or Drake's apartment. They had stopped at the bar on the way just to check they weren't joining the party.

Dr Moran chewed the inside of her mouth. "I have a bad feeling about this."

"What kind of feeling?"

Rather than answer, Dr Moran grabbed Saskia's wrist and pulled her outside. "I can't think in there, it's too loud for me and too many smells." She took a deep breath of the night air and nodded.

Saskia tapped her foot. "Well?"

"Oh, yes, bad feeling. I caught a faint scent in the air. I believe it might be Ajax or his sister, they smell alike. I can't tell which in this form, it's too limited." Dr Moran shuddered.

"Okay, where?"

"Outside Fin's building."

The first tendrils of real worry snaked through Saskia's limbs. "Can you give me a timeline?"

"Recent. It's a still night so even like this I can smell them, maybe thirty minutes, possibly a little longer. Then I can smell Drake in the area but his scent shifts fast."

Saskia strode off up the path to the third-year halls and Dr Moran followed her. "Smell more."

"Excuse me?"

"We don't have time for me fucking about with a saucepan to scry for them – smell more – find out where they are."

Dr Moran looked like she wanted to argue but realised the pointlessness of it and shrugged. She closed her eyes and drew in a breath over her tongue and through her nose. A snag of something surprised her. Broken plastic. A bitter odour and unnatural, obvious in the wild of the night. Tracking the scent, she knelt and picked up several bits of what was once an expensive mobile phone.

"Shit," Saskia muttered when Dr Moran held up the pieces. "That's Drake's."

"Yes it is but it doesn't smell right. It smells older, darker, it reminds me of something else..." Dr Moran's eyes glazed as Saskia watched her search her memories. "Oh, oh dear. Oh, this isn't going to go well for anyone."

"What is it?" Saskia wanted to strangle the older woman.

"I think Ares is back – really back – I think Drake's lost control and the only thing I can think of to make that happen is for Finbarr to have been attacked again. Only this time it's worse."

"I don't think I can help with more serious, Dr Moran. Mixing potions and love spells, conjuring images in water, seeing auras and the sprites of nature was one thing but since Drake York rolled into town things have become a lot darker and more serious," she said.

Dr Moran looked up at Saskia, eyes predator sharp. "You have to, for Fin's sake if not Drake's. Fin trusts you and so does Drake. They will need you and I need your help, Saskia. I'm just a hound and if I go in there as a human woman – they will kill me – if I go in there in my true form I lose many of the ties that keep me safe and sane in this world. I will feed into

Ares and he into me. We will need you and Finbarr to act as our balance or…"

"Or?" Saskia asked.

Dr Moran could see she didn't really want the answer but, like watching a car crash, Saskia couldn't look away.

"Or this town will know war the likes of which will engulf all of Annwn and then the wider world. Ares won't be satisfied with the Aegis Corporation. He'll take everything and turn it into bloodshed and sorrow."

"You mean people will be compelled to fight?"

Dr Moran rose at last and brushed the mud off her hands. "Yes. It'll start with husbands and wives. Siblings and lovers. Then villages and towns. Next cities, until entire countries rip themselves apart in civil war before attacking their neighbours. Ares on the rampage always kept Hades busy – and me. Many of the Greek myths make light of him, but don't forget, people joke about what they fear the most. War is no joke. Drake York coming into existence was the best thing that could happen to humanity, Saskia. We have to stop him going…"

"Nuclear?"

Dr Moran shrugged. "If you like."

Saskia squared her shoulders. "Where are they?"

"Follow me," Dr Moran said, tossing her car keys at Saskia before striding off into the night.

Saskia jogged to catch up and watched as the urbane lecturer shifted seamlessly into the huge hound. Cerberus put her nose to the ground and growled as she pointed in the direction Saskia knew she'd find Ajax's house.

"Come on then, get in," Saskia said opening the car door and letting the hound climb into the backseat of the small runabout Dr Moran owned.

Cerberus watched the young woman correct the driving position and the mirror, waves of fear coming off her firm skin, turning her usually sweet scent a little rancid. She started the car, wound down the windows and drove off. Cerberus stuck her head out of the rear passenger window and behaved like a huge dog from a cartoon.

"I feel like I'm in an episode of Scooby Doo," Saskia muttered watching Cerberus in her mirror while navigating the narrow lane towards the house.

They arrived at the front gates of the building and Saskia opened the back door for Cerberus to leave the car. The huge hound jumped out and put her nose to the ground. Saskia followed and they found a large hole in the wall. Cerberus growled low in her chest.

The rumble seemed to affect the child of the soil. Saskia smelt weaker, Cerberus didn't like it. She hunted with men and women of power. Just the thought of the battle ahead made saliva drip from her powerful jaws. Saskia stood back, the grass turning black where the drips hit the ground.

"Just don't bite me," Saskia muttered clambering through the hole in the wall. "Aconite poisoning isn't something I need to dealing with."

Cerberus snuffed and grinned.

Saskia began muttering under her breath, "I'm here with a hound of death and an enraged Greek god. That's why I can't think of how to bloody well help anyone. I can't even remember a simple bloody incantation to start a candle flame never mind taking on four soul eaters. This is insane. I should be back in the bar getting pissed."

Cerberus padded over the manicured grass. It had little or no sense of growth, not like the wild grasses in the fields and meadows. The night animals were silent, and she knew they were the closest thing to cavalry, which meant if anything went wrong they were on their own.

Saskia stopped at the edge of the spill of light from the room with the smashed doors and stared. "Fuck..." A figure, tall and broad, stood in the room. "Ares..."

Cerberus shouldered her way in and just stood for a moment, bathed in the power emanating from her old companion. How small they had all become in the modern world. She even smelt Saskia's wonder.

Having waited long enough to join her Olympian brother, Cerberus bounded up the final flagstone steps and stalked into the room behind Ares.

Saskia opted to remain outside, on the edge of the light, looking for Finbarr.

Chapter 21

ARES STOOD IN THE ROOM and snarled, "If you bind me, keep me, you will bring down the wrath of my kind upon you. Are you ready to face the gods of Olympus? I give this as fair warning, soul eater."

Vargas laughed. "Gods of Olympus? I think we can handle them. If they are all as weak as you are, as easy to capture, then I shall be feeding for centuries on nothing *but* gods."

"You're a fool, but it matters not to me. Release Finbarr. Give your word he will be permitted to leave this place and you will not allow your children to touch him or the sorcerer and I will give you what you want."

Ares stepped forwards. A strange tingle began between his shoulder blades and he reached out for the sensation. He smiled in the darkness of his battle helmet. "Although, we might be balancing the odds a little more in our favour."

A snarling, drooling creature of death walked to his side and leaned her massive body against his thigh. Her nose wrinkled up and the long white fangs shone in the light.

"I would like you to meet Cerberus. The great hound of Hades himself. She counts me as a friend. I would suggest you reconsider your threats. Or I shall make you a promise. Nothing can survive her bite and I will feed you to her one piece at a time." He looked at each of the four soul eaters in turn to make it clear he meant all of them. The stink of fear filled the room. He caught the flash of silver against Fin's wrist and realised his lover was determined not to remain the damsel in distress. This pleased Ares a great deal.

Vargas licked his lips, nerves clear and his eyes focused on Cerberus and her teeth.

A movement snagged Ares' awareness. The girl moved with preternatural speed.

"Drake…" Fin's voice pulled Ares' full attention away from Vargas.

Panic filled the young man's face.

The panic hit Ares foursquare in the chest. He stepped forwards, hand outstretched. "No! No, please, stop." His eyes focused on the fine needle already embedded in Finbarr's slim neck and the hand holding the plunger.

"I'll stop when you're on your knees in father's bonds," said Electra, her smile treacle sweet.

The world came down to two choices; lose Fin because he couldn't move fast enough to save him from whatever poison existed in that syringe or capitulate and hand himself over to the enemy.

Ares reached up and removed his great helmet. Dark hair tumbled free and Fin's eyes widened as he took in all the differences between the god and his true lover Drake York. Ares, a creature born for and because of violence, found it hard to reconcile the sense of sadness and grief pulling his heart into pieces as he gazed at the young man who had captured his essence and held it safe in a fragile, mortal, heart.

He knew the right thing to do, the correct path to take, but Ares also knew the pain and grief his sacrifice would give Fin. That pure heart would ache, needle sharp, for a while at the loss but in time it would recover and Fin would love again. Ares had no choice. He had to hurt Fin to save him.

"Have no fear for me, or of me, Finbarr. All that matters to me in this life is your safety and wellbeing." He dropped to his knees in supplication and turned to look at Vargas. "Allow the others to leave and I shall remain to do your bidding. I will not be responsible for another death among the children of the soil."

Vargas snorted with disdain. "Nobility, the crushing stupidity of those who think themselves above the rest of us. You are pathetic." Vargas strode to the other side of the large room and a heavy wooden cabinet.

The moment the doors opened Ares felt it, a wash of power so dark and alien to his world it made his body quiver in fear. Cerberus whined and snapped her mouth shut. She took a step back from Ares.

Ares did the only thing he could. "Go to Finbarr, my faithful friend. Keep him safe." Ares didn't turn to the hound. He kept his eyes on Vargas, who smiled with unfettered joy as he brought a large chest out of the cabinet and placed it on the table.

Vargas opened the heavy wooden lid, the iron bands black with age. A wave of darkness rushed out. Ares heard Fin gasp, the swirling black ink-like substance rolled over the table top, thick and oily. It morphed into a snake's head, shining black skin undulating as it shifted form, coalescing and dissolving in turn, trying to fix its essence as it scented its environment.

"I had a good friend of mine make these, with the promise they would come in handy one day. I had no idea your daughter was capable of foresight…"

Ares dragged his eyes away from the black substance sliding towards him, dripping off the table and reforming on the floor. He tried to concentrate on the soul eater, but the black substance stole his composure in a way a thousand armed Spartans could not. "You know of Annihilation?"

Vargas smiled. "I know of a great many things. I don't need an Oracle," he waved a dismissive hand in Fin's direction, "I have access to the one being in this vast universe able to travel through the quantum realm thanks to her creators – your precious children of the soil. She was born from smashing atoms into their fundamental elements and as you can see she can use that to create all manner of fun things."

Ares' massive chest rose and fell in rapid time as the black quicksilver touched his leg. It burned with ice and fire. He gritted his teeth refusing to give into the pain.

"Fin leaves before this thing takes me," he gasped.

Vargas waved a hand at his daughter. Electra, clearly disappointed, removed the needle. "Shame, I was looking forwards to taking this boy to bed with Ajax."

"Father you did promise him to me," Ajax whined and moved to grab Fin.

Vargas couldn't take his eyes off Annihilation's gift. "You will feed on the god, son. Trust me, playing with that toy will seem insignificant in no time."

Ares' kept his eyes on Finbarr. "Go, stay strong. Find a way to save the grove. That's all that matters, Finbarr. Take Cerberus and leave. Please."

Electra now cut Fin loose. His eyes though were only on his lover. "How can I leave you like this?"

The sliding crawl of Annihilation's gift to Vargas hurt, it tore into Ares' mind and pulled at the substance of his being. "You must, Finbarr. A god's word is his bond. You have to leave. Please. Go. Before it takes me..." He began to pant from the pain and felt his massive shoulders bow under the pressure. "Please, leave. I have to know you are safe..."

Cerberus moved past Ares, keeping a long way from the black substance crawling up Ares' waist and dragging itself over his heavy muscled belly. She approached the soul eaters clustered around Finbarr and snapped at them. They all moved away from the young man.

Fin took several steps towards Ares. "We can't leave him," he said to the huge hound.

Cerberus whined and crowded him, forcing him backwards. Fin tried to push against the huge chest his eyes darting between the hound and Ares.

"Go, Fin. Run. If the Fates, in their wisdom, deem it right, we shall meet again." Ares' watched tears stain the cheeks of his now lost love and as Cerberus dragged Fin away, he felt the darkness of his daughter's gift close over his thick wrists and form a solid at last.

He looked down. A pair of heavy bonds with no end and no beginning collared his thick wrists. They were a perfect pitch black, not a blemish nor a carving of occult symbols necessary. At last he realised what could hold him, what Annihilation had done, she'd created these from nothingness. They were a void in time and space. The only thing in this universe of material substance able to hold a god for an eternity – *nothing.*

FINBARR'S HEART ACHED AND HIS mind screamed at him to do something – anything to save Ares from the soul eaters. Cerberus kept a firm hold on his hand now, her teeth closed over the fine bones of his wrist. She didn't hurt him but if Fin pulled away, she'd tear his skin and her aconite laced saliva would make Ares' sacrifice worthless. Ares' rose-gold eyes tracked his movements as he left the room. When the door swung shut Fin watched Ares bow his head as the stinking fingers of the soul eaters took their fill from his flesh.

A sob wrenched through Fin but Cerberus continued to drag him away. He considered grabbing something to beat her so she'd let go but realised the only chance he had of saving Ares and removing the bonds holding him was finding a way to make Cerberus help.

Rather than wail like a broken child now, Fin decided to take decisive action. "Come on, we have to leave."

She opened her mouth with total obedience but Fin noticed she kept between him and the door. They made it to the outside, rushing through the kitchen and out into the night. A roar of such agony tore the night's peace to shreds. Fin gasped at the mirror of the pain caused in his guts.

"Oh, fuck, Ares," he moaned, hitting the grass with his knees and bending over the agony caused by nothing more than empathy.

"Fin?" called Saskia, rushing towards him from the shadows. "What the hell happened in there? Where's Ares? Who the hell is screaming like that?" She sounded so young.

"They have him," Fin cried out, voice as broken as his heart. He clutched at her arms and sobbed. "They have him and they are feeding from him and I can't do anything."

"We need to get the hell out of here," Dr Moran said, walking towards them in the clothes she'd worn to the protest that day. "We need to get out and come up with a plan because I can't save Ares alone and I'm going to need help."

"Who can help him?" Fin cried out. "You should have done something before they took those bloody – whatever they were – out of that chest."

"That was nothing – the absence of everything harnessed by Annihilation. I knew she hated her father but this…" Dr Moran flinched as another mighty wail shook the walls of the old house. "Come on, we can't help him here. We have to be cleverer than that. How the hell did she know he'd come here?"

She looked at Fin and it wasn't friendly. He took a step away. "What?"

"It's you," Dr Moran pointed at him. "She knew he'd come here because of you and that damned Oracle. Shit."

"How? I didn't know Oracle —"

Dr Moran waved his protests away. "It doesn't matter. Come on, we need to go." She hurried over the grass.

Saskia slipped her hand into Fin's, much to his surprise. He glanced at her. "I'm sorry I didn't come into the room. I just…" She looked at the ground. "I was scared, Fin. So scared." He saw tear stains on her cheeks and a pang of regret hit him.

He dragged her into his body and hugged her tight. "Me too, Sassy. Not your fault."

They followed Dr Moran back to the car. Another great cry of agony died away on the rising wind as they drove back to the town. Fin curled up on the backseat and covered his ears, drawing his knees up to his chest as he tried to block out the sound of Ares' suffering.

By some silent form of consent they returned to Drake's apartment. Fin let them in using the spare key Drake left in the garden.

"What do we do?" he asked. Fin's body ached from the night's events and his heart beat with a rhythmic misery. He tried to make tea but his hands shook so badly Saskia took over and opted for the brandy Drake kept for cooking.

Dr Moran sat on one of the stools around the kitchen's island, her hands clenched on the cool surface. She rubbed her thumb over the knuckles with endless restlessness. "We need outside help but who to trust? Some of them would love to see Ares knocked on his arse for a few centuries —"

"Centuries?" Fin almost shouted. "I'm not leaving him up there a single fucking night with those... those things." The tension inside him made his bones ache.

A knock at the front door drew all their attention. "I'll get it," Fin snapped, unable to stay still. He listened to Saskia apologise to Dr Moran which just infuriated him further. Without considering the consequences he yanked open the front door. "What?"

A man stood there, tall, slim with fine corded muscles on his naked arms and hair the colour of palest gold. His eyes were crystals of brightest sapphire. "Hello, Finbarr. I'm Hermes and I'm here to help." He wore a white sleeveless t-shirt, tight jeans and pair of expensive trainers.

Chapter 22

FIN STEPPED BACK. THIS NIGHT couldn't be any weirder.

"Hermes?" he heard Dr Moran say behind him.

"Hello, Cerberus, it's really good to see you, old friend." Hermes walked into Drake's home, pushing past Finbarr with a bright white smile. He and Dr Moran embraced. "I've missed our runs."

Dr Moran looked close to tears. "Oh, Hermes, oh, it's so good to see you. I... How are you here? How did you know?"

He squeezed her arm and smiled with tender kindness before he said quietly, "Father sent me."

Fin watched the colour drain from Dr Moran's face. "Zeus knows I failed to protect Ares? He knows Ares is here?"

"Why don't we get inside properly and I can explain." He herded Dr Moran and Saskia into the other room.

Fin stood in the doorway. He wanted desperately for the day to stop. For time to ease up, maybe go backwards, so he would wake up in Drake's arms and not have to go through all this again. "What the hell is happening in my life?" He closed the front door and followed the others.

Hermes stood in the kitchen with a large brandy in his hand. He sniffed. "Hmm, he usually does better than this." One swallow emptied the glass and he handed it over to Saskia for a refill.

Dr Moran removed the glass from Hermes and the bottle from Saskia.

"Hermes, before you get drunk could you tell us what's going on? No more until we get Ares back." She waved the bottle in his face.

The blond man pulled a pout. "Fine. You used to be more fun."

"I used to be a lot younger," Dr Moran said. "Now, explain yourself."

Hermes stroked his long, fine fingers over the tight denim covering his thighs. His lips were full and red against his pale skin and his jaw delicate rather than rugged. "Fine. Zeus needed to flush out this little deal Annihilation had with the soul eaters. Ares doesn't exactly plan ahead when someone he cares about is threatened. It doesn't matter how different Mr Drake York," Hermes said this with irritating contempt, "thinks he is – he can't defeat his nature. Athena is the planner, Ares is just the gun. He's no good at being cunning and never has been. Zeus knew he could get Ares here before the Oracle moved on with this one's life," he made a vague wafting gesture at Fin, "that he'd fall madly in love like he always does and overreact. Like he always does."

Fin sat, his knees going weak. "I was used as bait by Zeus?"

"No, the Oracle was used as bait. You just happen to be carrying them at the moment. Of course, Mother needs him as well, which added to the lure." Hermes arched a golden eyebrow. "Mind you, with a package like you, I'm surprised Ares needed any extra inducements to fall in love."

"I don't think he loves me."

"Oh, he does. He loves you a great deal he just doesn't want to scare you."

"Get to the point, Hermes," Dr Moran snapped. "I have no wish for the sun to rise on Ares' captivity if we can prevent it. I don't think that would help any of us."

Hermes huffed at her but seemed to accept her point. "No, it wouldn't. Zeus needs those cuffs locked around Ares' wrists. While the god of war has been sulking because of the idiocy created by the children of the soil, Annihilation has been seeding trouble all over the world. She is more dangerous than any enemy we've faced and she's turning the new gods against each other so aggressively Zeus is actually scared. Not that he'll admit it. They are more powerful than we ever were." Hermes spoke with a distant dread, as if privy to information no one else could understand.

Fin decided he couldn't take on the worries of gods; he just needed to save one. Practical, not emotional – that's what he needed to be to save Drake.

Dr Moran sat on the arm of the chair Fin occupied. "You mean to tell me all this warfare is Annihilation's doing?"

"It's like the woman's footsteps are able to turn neighbour against neighbour. She's attacked a few of our kind over the last seventy odd years while Ares has been in hiding."

"He's not been in hiding, he's trying to understand how to be a different person," Fin protested.

The eyebrow rose again. "He's the personification of war, he can't change. He's a fundamental part of the human condition."

Saskia had been watching them all and now stood behind Fin's chair. She said, "He's changed. It doesn't matter what you say or think. I can see it. He wants to save the grove."

Hermes clicked his fingers. "Oh, yes, I almost forgot. We have to save that as well, it's rather central to the theme of things. So we need to completely destroy the soul eaters while rescuing Ares and keep the bonds holding him safe, while we save the core of Mother so she might be able to survive the destruction currently being bestowed on her bounty." Hermes gave a bright smile having delivered his message.

"Is that all?" Dr Moran pinched her eyes as if she had a headache coming.

Fin wanted to crawl into a corner and cry. All this was his fault. Drake losing himself to Ares and being captured was all down to his stupidity. The soul eaters would become more powerful. They would capture other gods and it sounded like Annihilation wanted to take on the monotheistic religions as well. At least that wasn't his fault, but making the soul eaters more powerful could only add fuel to the fires burning all over the world. The more power they had the more they could destroy.

"How do we kill them?" he asked Hermes.

"At last he asks a sensible question."

Fin's eyes narrowed. "Just answer the bloody thing then." He didn't like Hermes.

"They are going to perform a ceremony. They are going to cut Ares open and eat him. After the initial feast of course."

"Oh, God, I'm going to be sick," Saskia said, rushing from the room. Fin heard the bathroom door open and slam shut.

Fin pushed away all extraneous verbiage. He had one mission, the facts of that didn't change because Hermes liked to throw emotional hand grenades at him. "I'm guessing we need to get there before that happens and I thought they wanted to feed from him for years to come?"

"They do, they are also greedy and Zeus might be pushing them into a position where we stand a chance at reaching Ares." Hermes tapped his immaculate nails against the arm of the sofa.

"Why can't he just send a lightning bolt? Strike them all down?"

Hermes then spent a long time looking at his perfect nails. "Possibly because Zeus is a little busy with something else and sent me to help."

Dr Moran snorted. "Who is the old bastard fucking now?"

"I wouldn't like to say."

"Bet Hera is pleased."

"Hera is busy with her own problems. Listen —" Hermes sat forwards and became the definition of focused. It made his soft face harden and his eyes glitter. "I know you have no reason to trust me, any of you, but I have a way to get this done. You just have to trust me and have a little faith in me. That last part is quite important."

Fin wanted to throw a cushion at the messenger god. Have faith in that popinjay? That might be a miracle too far for this dark night. He reined back his temper and prepared himself to listen. "What do you want us to do?"

Dr Moran placed a hand on his shoulder. "Don't agree to anything until you've heard the plan, Fin. Promising Hermes anything can lead to problems down the road you cannot imagine now."

Hermes flopped back on the sofa as if struck a mortal blow to his heart. "Oh, Cerberus, you wound me."

"Shut up you fool. Ares left Finbarr under my protection. You know full well what that means. I work to keep the boy alive and on this side of the River Styx. That means you don't get to cart him off anywhere."

Hermes stuck his tongue out. "You really are quite boring these days."

"And you are just as juvenile as always. Talk."

"Fine, now your witch is back after her belly aching, I'll explain the plan."

Saskia sat on the other side of Fin, looking pale but determined. She balanced on the other thick armrest. He felt odd and safe sandwiched between these two women. They were so much stronger than he had ever been and they gave him courage.

"I need to get to Ares. I have a – well – a device that can free him and return the bonds on his wrists to their liquid form. Like that they can be brought under control and caged. I just need a distraction. The soul eaters will be at their most ecstatic during the ritual, after they cut Ares open —"

"No, we aren't leaving it that late," Fin cried out. Even the thought of Ares suffering in such a way made Fin's body go weak and his mind start to babble incoherent panic.

Hermes shrugged. "We'll have to, there's only the four of us."

Dr Moran shook her head. "Fin's right. We aren't leaving it that late. There's no telling what damage could be done to Ares' mind if he goes through that kind of pain. Look at Prometheus."

"It's hardly the same thing. Besides, Prometheus is okay now – kind of."

Fin wanted to smack someone. "I don't care about Prometheus. I care about Ares and the man I love Drake York."

Hermes and Dr Moran shared a look that writhed with guilt. Fin's hands clenched. "What? What is it?"

"There might not be a Drake York left inside him, Finbarr. You need to understand that before you go all in."

"Drake won't leave Fin," Saskia stated.

Fin wished he believed her but he didn't think his luck would deliver him a happy ending. One thing he did know for certain, he never, ever wanted to hear the cries of pain he'd left behind in that cursed house again.

"Just tell me what I need to do to get him back."

Hermes said, "I need you to storm the place on my signal. Then I can slip in behind you and reach Ares. Once he's free and knows you're safe – that is a key part of the plan, don't get caught by the soul eaters – he'll take them down."

"Take them down?" Fin frowned.

"Kill them, Finbarr," Dr Moran said in a quiet voice.

Fin knew she understood what it would cost Ares to take a life, even one as twisted and dark as the soul eaters. She also knew about Fin and Ajax. Her concern for him might be touching but he didn't need it or want it. He wanted to fight for himself and for Drake. He wanted to fight for the grove, for Mother, for all the places in the world torn and broken by greed, sucking the soul of the earth to the point Mother would die forever.

"I want them dead." Fin's hands formed fists and he ground them against his thighs. "I want them all gone from Annwn."

"Even Ajax?"

"Yes. You have no idea what he put me through. What he's capable of and that sister of his…" Fin shuddered. An unbidden image of Electra with her hands, elbow deep inside Ares made bile rise in Fin's throat. "We have to go, now. I don't want to risk leaving this any longer."

Dr Moran rubbed her eyes. "I'm too old for an all-nighter."

"Just think about it as hunting rabbits, you'll be fine," Hermes said, his grin tinged with satanic glee.

"I forgot how bloody annoying you can be."

Hermes rose from the sofa, all lithe grace and offered Dr Moran his hand to help her up. "I'm not annoying, I'm bubbly and fun. Everyone says so."

Chapter 23

THE PAIN SCREAMED THROUGH ARES. In a vague detached part of his mind he realised there weren't words in any of languages he'd known over the millennia to describe his agony. No metaphor or simile was clever enough. No cliché dark enough.

Dark... He longed for it. A child of the soil would have died by now but not he, not the god that stood in the centre of the firestorm created the moment the first atomic weapon exploded and gave birth to a daughter called Annihilation.

She was the reason he screamed in agony.

Whatever the thick bonds holding his wrists were made from they tore into his mind, igniting every nerve ending and firing every synapse. He endured to give Finbarr and the others the chance to escape.

By increments the pain began to diminish. The screams lessened and he panted through the torn and bloody vocal cords, trying to from words to beg for death despite knowing he wouldn't receive that mercy from these creatures. They wanted their prize.

He jerked away from the fingers carding through his sweat soaked hair. "Don't touch me," he croaked and his throat burned. He spat blood on the polished wooden floor.

"Now, now, the pain will ease as the bonds grow used to their duty as jailer for a god. You should be thanking me, it could be worse. Your daughter offered us a coffin made of the stuff." Vargas stroked Ares again and the first tendrils of the soul eater's 'gift' searched for the core of his being.

Ares fought the sensation of the slithering lightning burning through his being trying to find the soul Vargas needed desperately to reach and taste. He pushed back hard but the bonds on his wrist flared and he couldn't fight the the combined pain of the soul eater's hunger and Annihilation's dark gift. The agony scattered his resources and wrenched his barriers into barbed cobwebs. Ares wept as he felt the creature sink dark claws into his soul and suck. He had no way to fight, he could only surrender. The penetration in the centre of his body defiled him. There would be centuries of this torment ahead.

"Father, let us taste."

The god of war managed to turn his head and saw the daughter, Electra. Her eyes were bright, her mouth open, she panted with the lust burning in those barren blue eyes. Ares flicked a glance at her brother, Ajax. The illusion of the cold and handsome young man slipped enough to show the dark and savage joy at Ares' destruction, his humiliation.

He sauntered over and ran a finger over Ares' sharp jaw. "Fin chose the wrong side. He'll come back to me and I'll feed from him forever. I'll even let you watch as I impale his pretty body with my cock."

"You will never have Fin," Ares gasped before another scream clawed itself from the bottom of his soul.

Vargas groaned. "Feed, wife, children."

The well of agony as the four of them plunged through the spirit gifted to him on the day of his creation began to waver, pulse with a sickly yellow – infected and ugly from their feeding. A god's soul is not that of a child of the soil and he knew their corruption would turn him into something truly dark and more dangerous than even his daughter. The cuffs, tight around his wrists would control the monster inside for a time but the soul eaters were so hungry for him.

"We could devour him," Electra said, sounding as if she were on the verge of orgasm.

"We should keep him alive."

"He'll live, look at the old god Prometheus. He died every day to be reborn anew with each dawn…"

Ares tuned them out. They could not understand the true agony of Prometheus or the reasons why he endured his suffering for so long. The penance he paid…

Ares retreated into memories, shutting down the knowledge of the violations he suffered. He thought about Fin's smile and conjured memories of the beauty their love inspired in him. He thought of the places they'd visit together and the stories the man, Drake York, would share of his many centuries in the warmth, the heat, of Greece. The balm of the seas and their translucent quality, so alien to this dark land in the north. The taste of the rich olives and the feel of the oil as he rubbed it into Fin's soft golden skin. It would be truly golden under that sun. Dusted from the sun's kiss.

He remembered the soft winds, the smell of sun-baked earth, the rough feel of the almond tree's bark, their flowers so ephemeral in the early spring.

Even as the soul eaters dragged Ares through the house and out into the gardens he dreamed of times to come, times that would never be.

There would be no salvation, no olive groves, no hope.

They hauled him up onto a stone table, a vast slab of smooth granite.

"Quick, the chains," Vargas said.

"His wrists are cuffed, he can't do anything, he's weak, pathetic," Electra crowed before licking up Ares' neck and over his jaw. Another lick over Ares' mouth made him rouse again to his surroundings.

"An altar? How old fashioned," he murmured with a chuckle.

"You think this is funny?" asked the wife.

Ares realised he didn't even know her name and yet she'd be a part of his downfall.

While he studied the soul eaters he thought about his past. How many children of the soil had prayed to him for their safety during battle? How many had prayed to him for the collapse of an enemy? For victory? And he now lay in chains about to be fed on by monsters.

And each and every one of those prayers meant the death of someone else. Even if a soldier prayed he'd never have to look into the eyes of a man he'd have to kill, he walked in the shadow of death and violence. A shadow Ares created by standing in the light. War touched every corner of this world, man's violence created Ares and he fed it right back.

He deserved this. Every agony, every whip of pain striking his nerves, it all came down to one thing and one thing only – the consequence of his existence. The new god of this land believed in penance and Ares finally faced his.

Something around him shifted. Voices came from the darkness, beyond the torches but he couldn't understand them. The pain morphed everything, the world wavering.

"Ares! Ares!"

A rough pinch on the inside of his thigh made him turn his head. "Ouch."

"So, you're still aware then."

Recognition took several long seconds as Ares sorted through memories. "Hermes?"

A bright smile penetrated the fog surrounding him. "Hello, Ares. How are you?" The smile faded and doubt clouded the bright blue eyes. "Oh, well, stupid question really."

"Yes, Hermes, very stupid," Ares croaked. He hoped he managed a fond smile. He cared for the mercurial nature of his half-brother. Being a shepherd of souls to the afterlife they'd worked together many times and Hermes did all he could in his role as psychopomp to make the journey easier for the dead.

Hermes grinned at him and winked. "I'm going to save you but I need your agreement."

"Agreement?" Ares managed.

"Zeus is offering to free you, but you'll owe him. I have something that can remove this part of Annihilation – she's an odd creature —"

"Hermes, focus," Ares whispered.

"Oh yes, they won't be able to keep the soul eaters busy for long."

"They?" Ares asked. The sinking feeling in his guts had nothing to do with the black absence of life force holding his wrists and soul down on the sacrificial altar.

"Oh, Cerberus and the children of the soil you like so much. He's a cute one, that Finbarr. A good match for you I think —"

"Fin is here?"

"Fin is integral to the rescue, which I'm not getting on with fast enough. The deal, you get rid of Annihilation – or this bit of her – and protection for when Apollo comes looking for the Oracle again, in exchange for a favour to Zeus. Just one."

Ares would have laughed if he could draw in enough breath. "Are you mad? I can't owe Zeus some unnamed favour – not again."

"It's the only way I can help you. Ares, you have to agree or the soul eaters will kill Cerberus and the others. I can't see the old dog die and I'm fairly sure you won't survive Fin dying."

"If he dies I will go mad and it will end."

"If he dies Oracle dies with him."

"They will be reborn."

Hermes stayed quiet.

Ares tried to focus on him. "What aren't you telling me?"

"Just agree to Zeus' demands. Please, Ares. You don't have much time."

Ares stared into Hermes' bright eyes. He'd always been inclined to trust the smaller man but Hermes had his tricky moments. "Zeus... I can't owe him a favour. It will lead to more —"

"Drake!" a scream from Fin shattered the illusion of peace surrounding Ares.

"You can't see him die. It's nothing to do with the Oracle. You are in love with the boy, Ares. Do something. I'll do all I can to help with Zeus but please, please, we need to stop Annihilation. This is the first step. Without peace we can't save Mother." Hermes' desperation bled through and Ares would have cried out if he had the strength left. Cried out in sheer frustration. He'd spent so long trying to escape his nature, his creation, his family, his father.

He couldn't see Fin die because he was scared of his father. He couldn't see Fin die because he hated his core nature. Hermes was right. He loved the boy. The Oracle just happened to be inside him. The Oracle just happened to choose another soul Ares could love.

Tears of shame and self-pity leaked from his eyes.

"I agree," he murmured.

Hermes dropped his head to Ares' arm. "Thank you, brother."

The bright golden head bowed for a moment and Hermes held his hands out. A sucking pop ensued with the arrival of a small clay jar with a lid. The ochre colour on the outside had darkened over the millennia to a rich red. The carvings on the surface were still clear and readable. They were images of death, sickness, chaos, famine, and many other terrible things unleased that fateful day.

A wave of panic hit Ares. "That's Pandora's —"

"Yes, but try not to worry about it. There's been a few modifications and now it should hold Annihilation. With some luck and a fair wind."

"Should?"

"That's the theory. This is the first time Zeus has been able to try it."

"Why did he send you?"

"Because you trust me." Hermes didn't meet Ares eyes. "Now hold still and pray this works, brother."

With terrible caution, keeping the clay lid facing away from both of them, Hermes opened the jar. They both waited. Until Ares gasped. Then groaned.

"What is happening? It's… fighting the pull of the jar…" Ares ground out.

Hermes, more confident now, lifted the jar over Ares' wrists. "Sit up would you and hold your hands out. It'll make the job faster. Just don't look into the jar."

"I'm not going to look into the jar," Ares said, struggling to sit up against the waves of pain. Without the soul eaters feeding on him Ares found it easier to fight Annihilation's essence. He hung over the edge of the altar and lifted his hands. Hermes shoved the jar underneath and the black goo melted into the jar within moments.

"What the fuck?" Ares asked, pulling his wrists away. They were badly scarred with deep fern-like tendrils.

Hermes placed the lid on the jar and closed his eyes, muttering under his breath. The jar vanished. Hermes slumped against Ares' thighs.

"What just happened?" Ares asked. He stroked Hermes' head for a moment.

With large and glassy eyes Hermes looked up at him. "Zeus placed a little of his essence in the jar and Annihilation isn't strong enough to resist his call. She isn't all powerful, Ares, but he can't fight her fairly."

A scream savaged at the peace on the altar. "Saskia."

"Go," Hermes said.

"You'll stay?"

"Yes."

Ares, unrestrained and full of gleeful vengeance, turned and stood on the altar. He flexed his hands and the sword and shield returned to him, the mighty helmet and armour covered his face and body.

"Vargas!" he bellowed. "Come and meet your death."

He leapt from the altar with a roar and rushed through the avenue of torches. Cerberus stood protecting Fin and Saskia, chest heaving, poison dripping from her jaws, her flanks covered in wounds. Fin held a baseball bat, a good weapon for the uninitiated in the martial forms, and Saskia two long knives.

The soul eaters surrounded them in their human forms.

When Ares strode into their circle, all lithe animal grace and power, everything changed.

The four soul eaters panicked. Vargas, the main devourer of Ares' soul, screamed in rage and rushed at him with sword in hand. Ares gave one contemptuous flick with his weapon, the two blades struck a spark in the night, and the soul eater's sword broke. Vargas stood before the god of war unarmed.

"Look away, Fin," Ares growled.

He grabbed Vargas' throat, the man finally registering the terror of his situation. He began to babble and cry out for mercy, the human cloak he wore dripped off displaying the body underneath. The foul creature they'd glimpsed in Ajax's mirror only darker, more foul and twisted by age and evil.

Ares put his hand over the creature's skull, closed his grip making the monster scream, and simply, irrevocably, ripped his head off.

"Nothing survives beheading," he growled as he threw the twitching body away.

Ajax raced towards Finbarr screaming for salvation but Cerberus collided with his body and she bit into his shoulder. The young man bellowed in agony as aconite poured into the wound. A soul eater might survive such a bite so Ares took his head with the sword.

The women launched themselves at him.

"Fucking Harpies are more terrifying," he snapped. The blade snick-snack back and forth, the female soul eaters lay in the bloody grass and Ares took their heads as well.

With some reluctance he lifted his gaze from the now rotting corpses and met the eyes of his lover, the young Finbarr Wiseman.

Chapter 24

FIN DROPPED HIS MAKESHIFT WEAPON. He stood and stared at the huge figure of the god of war and swallowed hard. Every fibre in his body trembled from the attack Cerberus had led to distract the soul eaters while Hermes rushed to the prone body on the altar. When they'd arrived in the garden Ares already lay on the stone slab, seemingly unaware of the events surrounding him and no longer screaming in pain.

Vargas had stood over Ares with a knife large enough to disembowel a dragon, never mind a god. He was chanting some nonsense and just moments away from striking down into Ares' belly.

Fin had screamed, which drew their attention and the three of them attacked. They couldn't kill the soul eaters, not even Cerberus could do that, but they could divert them long enough to save Ares. The true killer.

When Ares ordered Fin to look away he knew why, Ares didn't want Fin to see what a god of war was capable of doing to his victims. Fin though, didn't look away. He needed to understand the darkest parts of Ares so he could understand the light inside Drake York – the man he loved. Emphasis on man.

He watched the mightiest warrior destroy their enemies as if they were made of rice paper. It sent a thrill through Fin knowing the mighty god would bow his knee to someone as insignificant as a young child of the soil.

On shaking legs Fin walked across the lawn, the night quiet and calm after the storm.

"Are you well?" Ares asked him.

Fin looked up. Ares stood at almost seven feet and represented the perfection of masculine strength and endurance. "Are you?"

Ares removed his helmet, the thick black hair covering his wide shoulders and trailing over his chest. "Yes and no. I am relieved to see you and the others unharmed but I am…"

Saskia arrived next to him and looked up. "Wow, you really are the most handsome man I've ever seen."

Ares managed to smile and Fin swore the colour in his cheeks heightened. "I am a god. Though not all of us are fair, I was blessed by my parents not cursed."

The small sorcerer placed a hand on Fin's shoulder. "You two should go for a walk. You need some quiet time. Bring Drake back, Fin."

Fin nodded. He turned and started to move away from the battleground. Ares followed.

"Tell me you're unhurt, Fin."

"I'm okay. A bit knocked about maybe and more exhausted than I've ever been in my life, but I'm okay. I'm bloody glad to see you."

Ares lifted his gaze to the east. "The sun will rise soon. It has been a long night. I am pleased to see you as well."

They'd arrived at the front of the house and Fin leaned against the large Porsche SUV in the sweeping drive. "I left you in so much pain." Tears pressed against his eyes and he couldn't look at Ares.

"You had no choice, Fin. I needed you safe. I can't believe you came back."

Fin looked up. "I can't believe you didn't think I would. Have you so little faith in me?"

"I am not Drake York, they didn't want Drake York. They wanted Ares and I know you don't. I can feel it. You find me attractive because I am what I am, but you do not love Ares. You love Drake York. I did not plan on you saving me, though I am always in your debt and I am very grateful." Ares moved gravel around with his booted toe while he spoke.

Fin studied the strange creature in front of him. Ares was not Drake that much was obvious. He exuded a rawness Drake didn't, a rough and almost animalistic energy. Older, darker, more potent. An almost elemental vibrancy hovered about him. It drew Fin in, as it had Saskia, but he didn't want it to dominate his thoughts because it didn't feel real to Fin.

"Can you be Drake York again? Are you strong enough to stay? What happens now? Hermes... He, well, he said you wouldn't be the same. Allowing this —" Fin waved a hand at the god's new form, "– to happen snaps the bonds you've placed on yourself so you can blend with the children of the soil. Now those bonds have snapped, Drake York is gone. Is he right?"

"Probably. He usually is about these things."

"So I've lost you... Drake?" The tears fell one at a time down his cheeks but Fin couldn't stop them.

Ares stepped a little closer and lifted his large hand. He cupped Fin's jaw and with gentle strokes of his thumb removed the tears.

"You see the darkness inside me now, Fin. How can you love Drake York when I live inside him?"

Fin clutched Ares' thick wrist. His hand unable to close around it completely. "I didn't understand before."

"It would be very difficult for you to understand. But tonight you watched me ripped the heads off our enemies."

"You looked like you enjoyed it."

Ares smiled, a wistful expression on his hard face. "I did. They hurt me. They hurt you. They were evil and dangerous. I did enjoy it."

"I don't know how to live with that violence inside you." Fear of violence haunted Fin and the thought of Ares living just under the surface of Drake's skin made Fin itch with fear.

"Have you talked with Oracle about it?" Ares asked.

Fin shook his head. "Oracle is... They are, well, pretty useless to be honest."

Ares laughed. "You just dismissed an ancient being as useless. Though I have the feeling you're right. Oracle isn't really much use at advice or at understanding how the world works."

An idea began to form in Fin's mind. "I need to learn to trust this side of you. I mean I need to trust Ares."

"Yes."

"Can you teach me to fight?"

Fin watched surprise widen those rose-gold eyes.

"Yes. I've helped train the best warriors in the world including Achilles and Spartacus."

Fin chuckled. "Spartacus? Seriously?"

"I liked his courage. I gave him gifts as Mars to help him even though he didn't really want to believe in gods. Contrary pest. The Romans had pissed me off so the slave rebellion, although it wasn't my idea, seemed a good opportunity to teach them some humility."

The world according to a god of war.

Laughter seemed to be the only option to the surreal world Fin now lived in where he walked and talked with ancient gods. "Okay, Spartacus good guy."

"I never said he was good. I just said I admired him. You don't get to be the leader of a slave rebellion by being lovely."

"No, I don't suppose you do." Fin stared off into the distance trying to untangle his emotions and realities. "I want to learn to fight so I can understand this side of Drake – if you can bring him back – because from what I can gather, you are a creature made up of elements."

Ares thought about it for a moment. "Yes, though so are you."

"Mine are considerably more integrated than yours."

Ares thought about that for a bit as well. "Yes. I can agree to that, the children of the soil are more complex than us in that regard at least."

"Good. So if we allow this side of you to come out and play can I have Drake York back as well?" Fin asked.

"Is that what this is about?"

Fin nodded. "I guess so. I figured, if I can give you an outlet, a way to be your truest form, without you starting wars in the area, then you can exist as Drake York. We could even have others learn to fight so you receive some of their – adoration – I guess. It'll make you and Drake stronger, bind you together more, make him dominant and I have the feeling you'd like him to be the stronger version of you."

Ares shifted, making Fin start in surprise. He grabbed Fin's waist and lifted him onto the roof of the SUV. They were closer in height now. Fin stared into the bright golden eyes and the entire universe opened for him, just for a moment, before Ares closed the gateway. It drew Fin's heart and soul into the ancient god and he nestled somewhere inside Ares, safe and warm.

"That's cheating," Fin whispered.

"I know, but I need you inside me, Fin. Never has a child of the soil understood who I really am. Not the way you do. I want to agree to your terms."

"Idea, Ares. It's an idea, not a deal. A deal can be broken as can a promise or vow. I am giving us an idea to strive for, because I'm guessing we'll make mistakes along the way. Isn't that what we, gods and children of the soil, do? Make mistakes?"

Ares' face softened. "Yes, we do."

Fin reached out and stroked the rougher, heavier, more darkly handsome version of Drake. "Relax, Ares. Relax and remember Drake holding me, laughing with me. Let him back and we will find balance so you can live within him safely. He denies his true nature too harshly and it hurts him – you – so we need a different way."

"I still need to fight Annihilation."

"Then you will need Drake as well. He is better at navigating this modern world."

Ares nodded and the thrill of hope danced through Fin. "I can see your point and I think you might be right. Finbarr Wiseman indeed."

"So we get Drake back?"

"Yes. I liked being Drake when he wasn't being a maudlin shit over the mistakes I've made and if we could work on his fear issues about me being at the core of him, that would be wonderful."

"Then that's what we'll do," Fin said. He leaned in and planted a soft kiss on the end of Ares' nose.

"I think you'd rather kiss Drake."

"You're growing on me, big man." Fin wiggled his eyebrows and Ares laughed, lifting Fin off the car and placing him on the ground. He did it with such care Fin almost changed his mind and wondered if he could beg Ares to remain.

"You don't want that to happen, Fin. I am not the *man* you need," Ares said, and he took a deep breath and released it slowly. "The air smells good now. You smell good."

He reached around Fin's head and cupped it. Fin shivered, knowing how powerful those large hands were and the destruction they could wreak. Ares bowed over him a little and raised Fin's face.

"A kiss makes this easier for me," he whispered over Fin's parted lips.

Fin's entire body tingled and he felt his heart beat in every one of his fingers and toes. The god of war pressed his lips to Fin's in a gesture so tender Fin's heart broke a little. The rose-gold eyes slid shut and as did Fin's so he could feel every moment.

Ares shifted against him. The hands cupping his head grew smaller but no less powerful. The body pressing against him wiry, broad, but a snug fit against Fin's slim frame. Just big enough to make Fin feel safe and warm. He opened his eyes and smiled into the face he'd grown to love in such a short time.

"Hello, Fin," said Drake York.

"Welcome home."

"You saved my life."

Fin's smile made Drake laugh and hug him tight. They stood like that for a while, just wrapped up in each other as the sun made her daily entrance to the raucous sound of birds waking after a night of mystical mischief in the Annwn valley.

Chapter 25

DRAKE HELD ON TO FIN and just breathed. Fin clung in return and it gave Drake hope Fin would forgive him for being a monster. The memory of Ares hung around him. The damage the soul eaters did, never mind the cuffs sent by Annihilation, made him feel like Cerberus' chew toy. He snorted at the thought.

"What's wrong?" Fin asked, pulling back a little.

Drake smiled, looking into the beautiful and dear features of his lover. "I was just thinking I feel like Cerberus' chew toy."

Fin laughed.

"I heard that," Dr Moran called out from behind them. She and Saskia walked towards them. "The bodies are dissolving into the soil. It's leaving acid-like burns in the grass but I don't think there's much we can do about it. Good to see you, Drake."

He nodded. "Good to be back."

"What are we going to tell the authorities?" Saskia asked. "They are going to be missed the moment Vargas doesn't turn up for work and Ajax doesn't go to lectures."

"Our fingerprints will be everywhere," Fin said, tucked against Drake's body.

Hermes sauntered out of the house dusting his hands. "You don't need to worry. I've been over the place. It's clean. Maybe too clean but they'll think the family has been taken by professionals so it's not all bad. Throw them a curve ball and see where it lands. Hello, Drake."

"Hermes." Drake's acknowledgement sounded wary even to him and he knew the others had picked up on it the moment they looked at him.

"What's happened?" Fin asked.

"Nothing you need to worry about now," Drake said, kissing his head.

"How'd you clean the place so fast?" Saskia asked Hermes.

"Winged feet – messenger of the gods – shepherd of souls – I move fast when it's needed," Hermes said. "Though I could do with a lift back to town."

Dr Moran snorted. "Lazy bastard."

"Hey, at least I made good things happen tonight. I want a reward thank you very much."

"Such as?" Drake asked.

"Permission to remain in Annwn. I have the feeling it could be fun and I haven't spent time with you two for…"

"A long time," Dr Moran said.

Drake watched, amused, as Hermes gave Dr Moran a hug. "I'll take that as a yes."

"Just don't get any ideas about pulling me into any of your nonsense. I know you, Hermes."

They began bickering and walking to Dr Moran's small car.

"Freddie."

"What?"

"I want to be called Freddie if I'm staying."

"Why?"

"Mercury."

"Oh, for God's sake, Hermes."

Drake could hear her eye roll as they continued to bicker.

"Are they always like that?" Saskia asked him.

"Sadly for the rest of us – yes. They've been bickering since the day they first met and they love each other to death."

"Just as well really," Fin muttered, watching them.

"They've forgotten about us," Saskia said.

Drake said, "I need to walk." His arm tightened around Fin. "We need to walk. Sorry, Fin. I need to breathe."

Saskia cursed and raced off after the other two to get a lift.

"I guess the whole death theme between the three of you draws you together," Fin said. They watched Dr Moran slap 'Freddie's' hand as he tried to take the wheel off her while they were driving out of the gate.

"We are a little different to the others I suppose," Drake said. He turned and looked back at the building. "This place must be worth a fortune."

"What's going to happen to the mine? The bulldozers at the grove? All of the Aegis Corporation's industry?" Fin asked him.

Drake dragged his focus away from the building. "I don't know. The board of directors will probably take control but we'll have time to start legal proceedings against the demolition of the grove. I'll get in touch with some charities that have lawyers who know international law in this area and start the ball rolling. Then it should just keep rolling without my interference."

"Are you alright?" Fin asked again.

Drake smiled but it only made Fin frown harder. "No, not really. It's all been a bit much. I need the walk and I need some quiet."

"I can call a taxi if you want —"

"A walk with you and some quiet with you," Drake qualified.

Fin smiled up at him and the day became just a little warmer and better. They started down the drive and Drake remained mute for a long time unable to order his thoughts. He needed Fin beside him and they walked with their fingers laced which gave Drake the solid contact to the world he needed. Words were incapable of describing the turmoil he felt inside but he also knew he needed to try. Hiding from Fin would lead to their destruction, it never worked in the soft arms of love.

"The pain of Annihilation's cuffs was the most terrible thing I've ever experienced," Drake said. Fin leaned closer as he spoke too quietly. "I had no idea. She is... Not evil because she's nothing. She's total destruction."

"Like a black hole?" Fin suggested.

Drake shrugged. "I guess but I don't know. And having those things inside me…"

Fin bowed his head. "That I understand all too well."

"Sorry, of course you do. I just, Vargas was a true monster. I haven't had to deal with such blatant evil in a very long time. I feel…" Drake ran out of words.

"Soiled? Raped? Dirty? Violated?"

"Yeah. It's horrible."

"Yes, it is," Fin said, his voice a feather brushing against the wind.

Silence cocooned them as they walked down the lane. Autumn held sway over the valley, the trees yellow and brown, some bare in preparation for winter. The hedgerows were stark and the grass a sickly green or dull brown. No flowers were present and many of the fields were turned, the thick clay soil red and sticky, covered in crows as they feasted on worms and seeds. The clouds overhead gathered and rain would come again soon, but Drake knew they'd be back in his apartment by then.

"Move in with me," he said as they reached the outskirts of the town.

Fin stepped away, not releasing his hand but to look at him. "What?"

"It doesn't make sense, you paying for rooms on the campus. Move in with me. I'm sick of being alone. I love you, Fin. I know it's fast, I know Ajax did a number on you, I know I'm not exactly the most stable person in the world right now, but I just don't want to be alone. I don't want to wait because it's too soon. I know this is right. I'm a fucking god – I know."

Drake's chest heaved as he looked into Fin's startled face.

"You love me?"

"Yes, that was the entire point of what happened last night. My life for yours because I love you."

"You know how mad this sounds right?" Fin asked. "You've been a part of my life for like… I dunno, five minutes."

"Is that really how it feels?" Drake asked in return. His heart pounded so hard he heard it battering his ribcage. Fear might be an illusion but it didn't feel that way right now. Drake knew he asked too much but he couldn't stop himself.

Fin stepped closer and placed a hand on Drake's chest. "What's this really about?" The compassion in his voice undid Drake.

He heaved in a breath and the tears flowed. "I don't know how to deal with what happened to me. I've never been that vulnerable, that lost or alone or so fucking scared, Fin. I can't think. I'm so scared. What if she comes back for me? I don't think I can fight Annihilation and win. In fact I know I can't. I'm a shadow of my former self. I know that. Ares, despite what you saw him do to the soul eaters, is a shadow."

Fin studied his hand on Drake's chest. "Love is not something to use as a bandage because you're bleeding." He met Drake's gaze. "I love you as well, Drake York, but I will not live with you. Not yet. We will set rules. I spend weekends and one night a week with you, the rest of the time we are with our friends or our books. We'll rethink after Christmas."

"Fin."

"No… This is important to me, Drake. You're right. Ajax did some unforgiveable and unforgettable horrors to us both. We need time to heal. I'm going to talk to a student counsellor about it, the bits I can talk about anyway. We will talk about it as well. No ignoring it, no packing it in a box to fester."

"I can't feel like this. The inside of my skin aches." Drake's distress made him twitch and move his feet as if he needed to run.

Fin smiled, a sad and sympathetic creature. "I know. It will ache for a long time, no matter how many times you wash it away with water, booze or drugs. There will be no escape, Drake. This is how children of the soil feel when we're broken by events we cannot control. That's why we have friends. Saskia will help and she'll understand. There's Hermes —" Drake snorted at that suggestion and Fin grinned. "— well, maybe not him but you have people who will help."

"I've never been vulnerable."

"I know."

"I don't know how to do this."

"I know."

"I'm going to have to learn aren't I?" Drake said.

"Welcome to humanity, Ares."

Drake chuckled. "It sucks."

Fin laughed. "Yes it does but look at that." Fin pointed to a shaft of sunlight breaking through a cloud and hitting a rowan tree, the leaves changing from sickly yellow to gold. "That's what keeps us going. We'll work on the grove. We'll help Mother here and she'll grow stronger. We'll heal her and by doing that we'll heal ourselves and each other."

"When did you get so wise, Fin?"

"I'm the Oracle remember."

"They are responsible for that little pearl of wisdom?"

"Perhaps not, but I know it's true. It's how you saved me from Ajax and saved the valley. Through sacrifice and healing. Shedding skins to find out what makes us truly live and feel strong in our core. We can use that, turn the soul eaters' pain into a gift."

Drake tugged Fin into his body and hugged him tight. "You still love me though."

Fin nosed at Drake's throat. "I still love you."

"And you'll think about moving in?"

"After Christmas, maybe."

Drake sniffed, not mollified in the least but determined to try to give Fin the space he wanted. "You're coming home with me now, right?"

"Yes."

"Good because I want you inside me."

Fin looked up. "What?"

Drake traced his full bottom lip. "I want your cock inside me. I want to surrender to you in a way I haven't done in forever."

"Drake, I've never…"

"I know, beloved. I know. But we are equals and I want to be able to give that to you. If you want it?"

Fin's eyes widened. "Want it? How fast can we get to your place?"

Drake laughed. "Not as fast as I'd like that's for certain."

They began walking again but Fin set a faster pace making Drake move.

It didn't take them long to reach Drake's apartment and he already had his keys out so they tumbled through the door, kissing and laughing, the early morning rushing in behind them. Drake kicked the door shut with a bang while Fin struggled to unbuckle and undo his jeans.

"Damn it, buttons are complicated," Fin muttered.

Drake chuckled. "Leave it, I want to strip them off you." Hand in hand they walked to the bedroom. The need for peace came over Drake and he stopped.

"Hey you okay?" Fin asked, reaching up to push back Drake's hair.

"To be honest, I don't know." Drake's resources were spent.

A gentle and desperately kind smile warmed Fin's exhausted face. "Let me take care of you for a change."

Drake dropped his head on Fin's shoulder and sighed. "I'd really like that, I really like you."

Fin chuckled and ran his fingers through Drake's rats' nest of black hair. "I really like you too." The kisses over Drake's cheek and neck were soft. "Let's shower, get rid of those monsters and climb into bed."

"I meant it. I really need you to be in charge." Drake nosed Fin's exposed neck and felt the smaller man shudder in his embrace.

"It would be my honour to care for you, Drake York."

Chapter 26

FIN HELD DRAKE CLOSE THEN guided him to the edge of the bed, making it easier to strip him of clothes and shoes. They worked in silence, a comfortable quiet two people could share who knew they were meant to be together. Fin worked off Drake's boots, his socks, then undid his shirt one button at a time. He pushed it back off Drake's wide shoulders, stroking down the deltoid muscles.

"You are so beautiful," Fin murmured, placing kisses on Drake's collarbone.

Drake gazed at him as if the light of the world shone through Fin's heart. "You don't prefer the other version? The more powerful one?"

Fin dropped to his knees and worked on freeing Drake from his jeans. "No. When I said I wanted you back I really meant it. But I also want you to be more complete and denying your warrior nature it's going to help you. Maybe we can give fighting lessons to those who want to learn at the university."

Drake chuckled as Fin worked his jeans off. "Do you even know what 'fighting lessons' are?"

Fin grinned. "No, I have no idea what I'm talking about but I'm sure you'll be a very good teacher with lots of fun discipline."

"Disciplining students, I can do that."

Looking up Fin scowled. "I'm the only one you're disciplining if you're using that tone of voice, thank you very much." He tugged on a patch of Drake's leg hair making him yelp.

"*Ekdídōmi*," Drake cried out.

"Surrender indeed, you wicked tyrant." Fin pulled Drake up.

They walked into the small wet room with just enough space for two. Fin ran the water and pushed Drake back into the shower of faked raindrops from the large rose overhead. Drake tipped his head back, the black curls going straight, and groaned. Fin stepped close and licked up the taut throat, an offering he could not refuse. Drake grasped his hips and drew him even closer, until their cocks lined up.

Fin bit Drake's throat, holding it tight between his teeth, and he felt Drake's cock twitch in response.

"I do surrender to you, Finbarr," Drake growled, making his throat vibrate in Fin's mouth.

Fin licked the area he'd been biting, the water warming Drake's skin. "I love you," he whispered, burying his nose in Drake's chest, the wet hair soft. Drake wrapped his arms around Fin's shoulders and they stood under the water, pressed together as one. They allowed the flow to wash away the stains of the night and the painful emotions. In their place the water left the shining brightness of their commitment and love for each other.

Fin lay his ear over Drake's heart and heard the gentle thump resound through his body. He'd never felt so cherished. When the healing water revived Fin he turned his head enough to lick Drake's dark nipple. The larger man hissed in pleasure. Fin's lick turned to sucking and Drake groaned, cupping the back of Fin's head so he wouldn't move away.

Fin felt Drake's hands over his back and the sharp scent of the citrus and pine soap Drake liked. Those strong, confident hands explored his body while he abused Drake's sensitive flesh. He sucked marks into the swarthy skin and relished Drake's cries of pain and pleasure. When Fin dropped to his knees, the water cascading over Drake's shoulders, Fin pressed his nose into the soft scrotum and drew one hard ball into his mouth. The contrasts between water, air, soft, hard, steel and velvet, began to make Fin's head spin and he hummed in bliss as he felt the strong thighs tremble under his palms.

Forcing Drake's legs to part just a little more he licked between them drawing whimpers from the creature he worshipped. Fin's neglected cock ached in need but denying his pleasure became part of the game for Fin. He realised now he was free of Ajax for good, he wanted to own Drake and this act, the first they'd share after the event. It needed to be something special. Jerking off like an overexcited teenager wouldn't give due service to the enormity of what they were sharing.

"Oh, Fin... Gods, please, make him have mercy on me." Drake's cries were lost in the water but his fingers tangled in Fin's hair.

Fin blinked through the deluge as he looked up the long, lean body. "I'm going to make you come, Drake. Don't hold back. I want you deep as you come, then I'm going to fuck you."

Drake whimpered which made Fin feel as if he were made of a thousand stars shining in the night sky like Orion or Pegasus.

Fin took Drake's dark cock into his mouth, the shaft and thick head stretching his jaw and lips wide. Closing his eyes he started to work Drake deeper, licking and racking his teeth over the head when he needed to breathe clear of the water. Drake's hips rolled in steady waves and his words of encouragement prevented the floor of the shower hurting his knees. The larger man's legs were turning to a quivering mess and he leaned against the cold tiles.

Reading the signs, Fin moved faster over the cock and took the rest that he couldn't swallow in his fist. A porn star he wasn't, but he wanted Drake as deep as possible.

"Fuck, yes, baby, oh, Fin, I can't..." Drake's hips thrust hard, his fingers in Fin's hair tightening with painful intensity and the shaft throbbed in his tight grip.

Drake came hard, crying out his name and Fin whimpered, tears mixing with water as he swallowed. He wanted it all so he kept his mouth firmly locked around Drake.

Those strong fingers started to stroke and Fin drew off Drake's cock. Drake pulled him to his feet and they kissed long, deep, slow, Fin's hard cock trapped between them.

When Drake had enough he drew back and switched the water off. "I think we've indulged enough in wasted water."

"Wasn't a waste," Fin mumbled, sucking on Drake's neck again. "We needed this."

"Oh, Fin. I need more."

"I want you."

"Good, my arse is aching for you."

They left the shower and dried each other. Drake led Fin into the bedroom and lay him down on the soft blankets.

"How do you want to do this?" Drake asked, running a hand over Fin's chest and stomach making him shiver in delight.

Fin thought about it, had been thinking about this first time for a while. "I want to see you, could you ride me?"

Drake growled. "Gods, I'd love to ride that beautiful cock." He reached for it but Fin slapped his hand.

"No, don't touch, I'm too close. Give me the lube and I'll prep you while you kneel over me."

Fin laughed as he watched Drake move with a speed a little too fast for a child of the soil. Fin scooted up the bed so he'd be able to watch what he was doing and gave his balls a squeeze to keep them under control. Drake climbed over him with lube and a condom.

"I can't infect you, Fin, but for now it's best."

"After Ajax I want testing anyway." Fin's mood darkened for a moment but he pushed the thoughts away and opted to marvel at the beautiful man swinging his leg over Fin's lower belly.

Drake spread his thighs and lowered his head so he could nibble and lick at Fin's lower legs and feet. Fin gazed at Drake's solid backside, the light dusting of hair on the thighs and the dark entrance. He dripped lube over the crack and watched it trail over Drake's hole. With a finger he traced the tight pucker, watching the muscles move and listening to Drake's soft gasps. With care he pressed a finger to the hole and as Drake murmured 'yes', Fin breached his lover for the first time.

Fin's eyes widened in shock, the hot tight – so tight – muscles working to both prevent his intrusion but to somehow draw him into Drake's rocking body. Drake had his head resting on Fin's leg, the dark stubble sharp and unfamiliar against Fin's shin. Drake groaned with wanton abandon.

"More, love, make me take more," Drake purred.

Reaching for the hardening cock and heavy balls, Fin did as instructed. He worked more into Drake's forgiving body and the more he worked the more desperate the sounds from his lover. Fin began to force more of his fingers inside and when he reached a soft spot and brushed over the surface Drake cried out, his strong back arching as he pushed further onto Fin's fingers.

"You're a monster," Drake shouted.

Fin chuckled. "Time to fuck me, while I worship your tight arse, Godling."

Drake's dark eyes were black with lust and need. "I'll make you worship my cock later."

Fin raised his eyebrows. "I thought I did that in the shower."

Drake snorted. "No, I want you begging for a hard fuck before this day is out."

"I think we'll need to eat and sleep before we even attempt that one," Fin said. He hissed as Drake rolled the condom down his painful cock and covered him in lube.

Drake switched direction and without preamble gripped Fin's cock to hold it in place. "Gods, I've been waiting for this moment since I first saw you."

Fin couldn't reply. He watched Drake lower his body and felt the impossible pressure on the tip of his cock. Fin had only tried to penetrate Saskia a few times as her boyfriend, far more comfortable with giving her pleasure in other ways, and this was so different. So fucking right. So fucking perfect.

Tight, hot, slick. Strong, hard, dangerous. He was slowly impaling a man strong enough to snap his neck and Drake wanted him, wanted this. Fin gripped Drake's hips and just tried not to come. He wanted to thrust into his lover but he knew patience was the key – that and remembering to breathe.

Drake closed his eyes and a tender smile graced his beautiful firm mouth. "Oh, that's so good."

"Does it hurt?" Fin gasped.

"Not in a way I don't love." Drake rose up and pushed down, taking more.

Fin's entire body lit up like a firework and he panted, reaching for his balls to stop his orgasm being ripped out too soon. Drake worked, up and down Fin's shaft, rocking and rolling, taking his pleasure. The thick heavy cock full and needy once again.

"So, good, you are so fucking good, baby," Drake murmured and then murmured something in a language Fin didn't know.

When Drake's arse cheeks were resting on Fin's thighs and Drake rocked on his cock, Fin groaned and gazed up at the Greek god riding his cock with adoration and tears in his eyes. Drake stared back with heated desire and deepest love, his large hand splayed out over Fin's chest, the other on Fin's thigh as he began to fuck himself harder on Fin's body.

"I can't hold on forever, Drake," Fin cried out, writhing under the stronger body.

Drake leaned down and began kissing Fin hard. The angles gave Fin more control and he took rather than received. He fucked up into Drake's unresisting body while Drake's tongue invaded his mouth.

"Harder, baby, make me feel it for days," Drake said against his lips.

Fin growled and instinct led him to flip them over, pressing Drake into the mattress so he could go faster, harder, deeper. Drake cried out, reaching for his cock and fucking his fist until he cried out. The muscles around Fin's cock tightened impossibly, and Fin almost screamed as his long-denied orgasm surged through his heart, his soul, his spine, balls and cock.

His head hit Drake's chest before being lifted so Drake could pepper his face with kisses. Those strong legs wrapped around his back and held tight to keep Fin close and they shared their broken breaths for long moments.

"You were perfect, beautiful and all mine," Drake whispered his benediction over Fin's head.

"You were giving and patient," Fin mumbled before he eased out of Drake and used taxed muscles to sit back. They smiled at each other before Fin left the bed to clean up and fetch Drake a damp cloth, caring for him as Drake had done.

When he returned to the bedroom Drake lay propped up on one elbow watching, his dark eyes soft, his hair in a complete tangle and his lips puffy. Red marks littered his neck, chest and belly.

"Sorry about the love bites," Fin said.

"Don't be, I love being marked by you," Drake confessed. "Did you enjoy your first time as a top?"

Fin blushed, turning bashful and nodded. "Though I like being taken by you as well."

Fingers traced patterns on Fin's back as he cleaned Drake's taut belly. "Then we're going to be even better matched than I thought, because I adore being buried balls deep in you as well."

"So, is this it? Is this our life now? Me finishing my degree, you studying for your PhD, dinner with Saskia and Cerberus?"

"Don't forget Hermes. He's not going to let us ignore him."

Fin kissed Drake's nose. "How could I forget Freddie?"

Drake pushed Fin's hair back. "This is our life for now, Fin, but things always change. It's the one constant in this world. We work to protect the grove. We work to help Mother's message get out of this valley and into hearts and minds of all the children of the soil. We deal with threats and we help the children of the heavens who are as exhausted as I was when I arrived."

"You were exhausted?" Fin asked.

"I was fading from this world before I met you. Now I am..." Drake's gaze grew distant for a moment before refocusing on Fin's face. "I am not reborn, rather, I am strengthened because of you. Drake York is here to stay, Ares will always live inside me, but I think I can find balance by fighting for Mother in Annwn."

"It's certainly a unique place in the world," Fin said, climbing back into bed and snuggling close to Drake.

"Yes, love, it is. I can't wait to find out what happens next to be honest." Drake's voice began to drift as his body started to relax.

Fin smiled, resting his head on the solid chest and yawned. Safe, loved, warm and content, what more could a child of the soil ask for from his tamed ancient god?

Epilogue

Mid-Winter Solstice

Drake stood in the grove alone. He held a basket with wine, honey, bread, grain and a small jar containing a viscus red liquid. The dusk light on this midwinter eve penetrated the grove with vague tendrils of wandering sunlight. They were deepening to shafts of twilight and Drake sensed the moon rising above the hills despite not being able to see her among the branches of the winter kissed trees.

The damage to the land from the invasion done by Vargas and his crew would lessen in time and they hadn't managed to cut down one tree. With the police investigating Aegis Corporation, the Metropolitan Police no less, their fraud department and the IOPC – Independent Office for Police Conduct – were tearing into the local community looking for those who aided and abetted the Vargas family. They were also looking for the Vargas family. Not even a plane ticket could be found – they had vanished. Hermes did a great job at wiping all evidence of what happened that night.

In fact, Hermes was talking about opening a business in the town and Drake liked the idea. He'd always enjoyed Hermes' company and having a little of their dysfunctional family around might not be a bad thing. Providing Apollo didn't arrive, it should be fine.

He knelt in the freezing water and lowered the basket on a rock under the boughs of the mighty oak.

"You there, old man?" he called out.

The small, wizened man with large fawn brown eyes and tangled hair of deepest green wandered into view from the back of the old oak. He yawned and rubbed his eyes. The mistletoe now sat in his hair along with some holly in a misshapen crown. "You lived," he said in a voice made of tree bark and slow-moving sap.

Drake smiled. "I did, old one. You too for the moment."

The old man nodded. "I am. Though you waking me from the winter sleep doesn't help." His wrinkles collapsed in a deep frown.

"I apologise, but I do come bearing winter tidings of thanks and some gifts for your family." Drake held out the basket.

The grove lit up with motes of sparkling light that defied gravity and the breeze as they floated above his head. Small creatures with soft large eyes began to appear and Drake held still.

"You will stay then?" asked the old man.

"If you will permit us to remain, yes," Drake said.

"Others will be coming. The old kings have reunited on the hilltop, I feel the Wild Hunt returning to the land. Things are changing, Ares, god of war. Are you ready?"

"We are. It's time we returned to the world to fight for Mother, to guide the children of the soil to a better way, they have forgotten too much."

"They have. The Oracle?" the old man asked.

Drake's smile was instant. "Finbarr is well, strong, we are happy. I love him and wish to give thanks for him in my life. He is special to me in a way I have never known before."

"Then give thanks, Ares." The old man stood to his full height, a little over two foot and pushed back the tangle of green hair.

Drake lay out his gifts, spoke the world of his libation and muttered his prayers to Mother, to the grove, and to the soft spirits that made this woodland temple so special. He gave thanks for Fin and as his final act he unscrewed the jar. He closed his eyes and pulled on the core of his being, shedding the mantle of humanity and permitting Ares his release.

"You are a child of the heavens, Ares, never forget that. Your Finbarr will never tame the creature of wild power you can be," said the old man as Ares gazed down at him.

"I may be a wild power in this world, but for Finbarr Wiseman I would be nothing and his hand can gentle me. I allow it. Now, take my offering as a commitment to this land." Ares tipped the jar up and a flow of deepest red blood, his blood, fell and tangled with the water coming from Mother's heart deep inside the earth.

The old man was right, nothing could truly tame Ares but he loved Fin with every version of his being and nothing would change that, not in this world, or the next. Ares stepped out of the water and left the grove returning to the man, Drake York, on the journey. By the time he returned to the university Fin's lecture had finished, night had fallen and he collected his lover from the Union bar.

"Hello, love," he said, slipping his arms around Fin's waist from behind as he leaned against the bar next to Saskia.

"Hmm, I like being here with you," Fin murmured, turning in his arms. "Everything okay at the grove?"

Drake kissed his lover. "Everything is perfect. Christmas is going to be perfect. You are perfect and I love you."

Fin gazed up at him with warmth, contentment and joy radiating from his soul. "I love you as well."

The End

~ * ~ * ~ * ~

For more broken heroes and their dangerous adventures check out my other books.

Grove of the Gods:

Ares' Story

Arawn's Story (novella Jan 2021)

Hermes' Story (spring 2021)

Prometheous' Story (summer 2021)

Shadow Ops:

Fortune's Soldier

Fortune's Soldier Prequel (free short story)

Ultimate Sanction

Final Play

Lancing's Journey (free short novella)

Shadow Ops Box Set

The Knights of Camelot Series:

Lancelot and the King

Lancelot and the Sword

Lancelot and the Grail

Lancelot's Challenge

Lancelot's Burden

Lancelot's Curse

Betrayal of Lancelot

Passion of Lancelot

Revenge of Lancelot